Praise for
Cleaning Nabokov's House

"Required reading."

—*New York Post*

"How can a novel that begins with a woman losing custody of her children wind up so blisteringly funny? In Leslie Daniels's delight of a book, Barb Barrett's decision to divorce her husband lands her in a wacky plot line that leads to the discovery of a hodgepodge manuscript that she feels certain was penned by Vladimir Nabokov. She explains that the prose is so gorgeous, 'the reader is suspended in the perfect moment of now.' The same can easily be said of Daniels's gem-filled novel, a goofy little treasure on every page."

—Minneapolis *Star-Tribune*

"Love, attraction, literary values, cooking, cleaning, the making of good sentences, kissing well, raising children, and wardrobe malfunctions all come under scrutiny in this engaging story."

—Alan Cheuse, NPR

"The pleasures of the novel unfold in a series of tantalizing, laugh-out-loud twists. . . . I was swept along like a trout in a clear stream. Bravo."

—Janet Fitch, author of *White Oleander*

"Original and compelling, the sort of book that keeps a reader on her toes—wildly funny one minute and profoundly sober the next. The protagonist is delightful; the plot a marvelous weave of sex, food, money, and motherhood. Every page a joy."

—Karen Joy Fowler, author of
The Jane Austen Book Club

"One of the most engaging and caustic heroines in contemporary fiction. Go ahead, take a risk. You are going to love this woman—and this book."

—Dorothy Allison, author of
Bastard Out of Carolina

"Smart, funny, sad, determined . . . and it's compellingly entertaining to boot. A fresh, original voice speaks from this book. Read it and wake up to a brave new world."

—Sena Jeter Naslund, author of
Ahab's Wife and *Adam & Eve*

"A wonderfully original, charming, and funny novel about what to do when your world has turned upside down, and how to get through a long cold rural winter by opening a house of ill repute."

—Alison Lurie, author of *Foreign Affairs*

"Daniels accesses some new territory while still giving readers what they want in a light, semiliterary romantic comedy. . . . Authentic, often devastating depictions of a mother missing her children . . . raise this book above the rest."

—*The Boston Globe*

"A winning comic voice."

—*More*

"Daniels is warmly funny and audacious in this shrewd and saucy mix of family drama, gender discord, sexual healing, and high literature; a raucous yet sensitive tale of one quirky woman's struggle to overcome the lowest of low self-esteem to get motherhood and love right."

—*Booklist*

"Daniels's writing is slick and her characters richly detailed. . . . A pleasure to read."

—*Publishers Weekly*

"In Barbara, Leslie Daniels has created a character to root for."

—*Los Angeles Times*

"Daniels writes her story with refreshingly eccentric twists, holding readers' interest. Her characters live and breathe, and the humor, energy, wit, and edgy look at small-town mores make this a delightful read."

—*Library Journal*

"Barb is fine company—blunt, mordantly funny, with a winning combination of ruthlessness and warmth."

—*Kirkus Reviews*

"A laugh-out-loud pleasure of a read. . . . A totally original delight."

—*BookPage*

"Equal parts touching and ridiculous, and the result is delicious."

—*The Roanoke Times*

"Manages to be both literature's response to Louis C.K. and what readers should pick up after they've finished that Lorrie Moore short story."

—*Ithaca Times*

"A beguiling story of learning to grasp and hold on to happiness through the good offices of a darling new boyfriend and the ghost of Vladimir Nabokov. (Also a delicious curse on bossy first husbands everywhere.) An emotional spring tonic for everyone who longs for love."

—Carolyn See, author of
Making a Literary Life

Cleaning Nabokov's House

Leslie Daniels

A TOUCHSTONE BOOK

PUBLISHED BY SIMON & SCHUSTER

NEW YORK   LONDON   TORONTO   SYDNEY   NEW DELHI

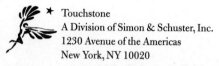

Touchstone
A Division of Simon & Schuster, Inc.
1230 Avenue of the Americas
New York, NY 10020

First Touchstone trade paperback edition March 2012

TOUCHSTONE and colophon are registered trademarks of Simon & Schuster, Inc.

For information about special discounts for bulk purchases, please contact Simon & Schuster Special Sales at 1-866-506-1949 or business@simonandschuster.com.

The Simon & Schuster Speakers Bureau can bring authors to your live event. For more information or to book an event contact the Simon & Schuster Speakers Bureau at 1-866-248-3049 or visit our website at www.simonspeakers.com.

Designed by Akasha Archer

Manufactured in the United States of America

10   9   8   7   6   5   4   3   2   1

The Library of Congress has cataloged the hardcover edition as follows:
Daniels, Leslie.
  Cleaning Nabokov's house : a novel / Leslie Daniels.
    p.   cm.
"A Touchstone book."
1. Self-realization in women—Fiction.   I. Title.
PS3604.A5345C54   2011
813'.6—dc22   2010043736

ISBN 978-1-4391-9502-4
ISBN 978-1-4391-9503-1 (pbk)
ISBN 978-1-4391-9504-8 (ebook)

For Mary Brett Daniels and Neal Daniels

ACKNOWLEDGMENTS

To my beloved clan: Mary Daniels (polar opposite of the mother in this novel), Valery Daniels, Andrew Knox, A.B.K., C.B.K., H.D.H., and C.J.D.H.,

To Tom Hartshorne, fine man, great father, and utterly different from the ex in the book (except for distinct eccentricity regarding the dishwasher),

To the dazzling Lucy Carson, a cocktail of charm and good sense. To marvelous Molly Schulman, To the talented Paul Cirone and the incomparable Molly Friedrich, possibly the best company on earth,

To Sulay Hernandez, extraordinary and valorous human being and editor,

To a stellar publishing team: Trish Todd, Stacy Creamer, Marcia Burch, Jessica Roth, David Falk, Meredith Kernan, Cherlynne Li, Martha Schwartz, Sally Kim, and Allegra Ben-Amotz,

To Maureen Klier, the Madame Curie of copyeditors (any mistakes are mine alone),

To Liz Karns for friendship and statistical support (again, I claim all errors),

To the Squaw Valley Writers Conference, a place of creativity and renewal for many, me included: Brett Hall Jones, Lisa Alvarez, Andrew Tonkavich, Louis B. Jones, Sands Hall, Michelle Latiolais, Rhoda Huffey, Michael Carlisle, and to the memory of Oakley Hall,

Acknowledgments

To the brilliant eyes, gorgeous heart, and incisive mind of Joy Johannessen,

To cherished friend and teacher Gill Dennis, who brings hope when he walks in the door,

To Ellen Hartman, true friend and true beacon,

To my exceptional writing colleagues: Liz Rambeau, Mary Lorson, Harriet Brittain, Lisa Barnhouse-Gal, Christianne McMillan, Diana Holquist, Rhian Ellis, Jill Allyn Rosser, Megan Shull, Neil Shepard, Greg Spatz, Masie Cochran, and John Jacobs,

I live in your light.

Cleaning
Nabokov's House

THE BLUE POT

I knew I could stay in this town when I found the blue enamel pot float-ing in the lake. The pot led me to the house, the house led me to the book, the book to the lawyer, the lawyer to the whorehouse, the whore-house to science, and from science I joined the world.

I found the blue pot on a Sunday afternoon right after my children left me to go back to their father. He and I had split apart and I was trying to become accustomed to living without my son and daughter without going crazy. Whenever they left me for him, sometimes crying, sometimes not, I felt I had to rush somewhere. But I had nowhere I needed to go and no money to spend once I got there. I would go with-out thinking, because thinking hurt. I would go hoping to get lost, but the town was so small I would simply end up near where I'd started.

On this particular Sunday in the fall, nearly a year ago, I kissed Sam and Darcy goodbye—no one crying—and tried not to hate the exper-son for taking them. Failed. Turned away to walk on the windy jogging path beside the lake where no one would see my face as it crumpled.

Towns install jogging paths as their median level of obesity reaches critical. My dear cousin the scientist told me this; there is a high cor-relation between towns with jogging paths and elevated kindergarten onset rates of type II diabetes.

I was thinking about my cousin, wondering whether he would have screwed up his life as badly as I had mine if he had lived to be my age, thirty-nine and seven twelfths. He bought himself a boat and fell off it a number of times. Being a brilliant scientist does not necessarily mean you know where in space your feet are. He spoke four languages and could explain neurotransmission. He loved French food—sorrel soup was his favorite. As I was remembering his appetite and his big raucous laugh at dinner parties, booming out of nowhere, a blue pot floated by me in the gray green water of the lake.

I clambered down the bank, thinking of the Monday headline in the *Onkwedo Clarion:* "Mother of Two Drowns, Apparent Suicide."

The pot smelled of motor oil, and I looked around for a boat to return it to, but there was none. I wrapped it in a plastic shopping bag that was blowing past and put it in the trunk of my crappy old car. I crammed it in with my books and a suitcase of clothes. They were the books and the clothes I needed most in my current state of houselessness.

I washed the smelly pot in the bathtub of my room at the Swiss Chalet Motor Inn. I scrubbed it with a little bottle of motel shampoo till it smelled like it had never met a boat. Then, on the hot plate I hid from the motel maids, I cooked some pasta in the blue pot, the kind of pasta that looks like torn lettuce leaves (lettucini?). I added a lump of butter from the farm across the road and a scraping of dry cheese.

I sat at the window, watching dusk gather and taillights disappear over the hill. The food was wonderful.

The blue pot reminded me of sitting around a dinner table with people talking, candles lighting their faces as they ate a meal some-one had made, maybe me. Although I never could follow a recipe, I did cook. My father would be at one end making his wry remarks, my cousin at the other end. We would be eating and laughing—I remembered this so clearly—everyone brought together for dinner. As I looked around that table in my mind's eye, there was my daughter's shiny black hair with her crazy zigzag part, my son with his sleepy sweetness and deep thoughts, and me. The meal gathered us, my wise father and my cousin too, before their mad stampede off to heaven.

I think of the blue pot as a gift from my cousin, one of those things dead people send you when they know you need help, a gift of peace. I would like to believe this is true.

CAMPING

On a gray spring Onkwedo morning earlier last year, when I was still married to the experson, I was loading breakfast dishes into the dishwasher while receiving instruction from him on how to do it properly.

I was good at a few marriage-related skills. I don't remember now what they were. Not the crucial ones—following his directions was not among them. The experson believed in order and control, which included control of me. But as the marriage bumped along, I was less and less able to do his bidding. My father's decline had made seeking order in the small things of life irrelevant to me, since the big things, life and death, were so obviously out of control. Making order out of dirty dishes, for example, seemed entirely beside the point of life.

At the dishwasher the experson said to me, "God is in the details," and I crammed his dirty coffee mug in any way at all and I walked out. You'd think that an argument about loading the dishwasher wouldn't be sufficient cause to leave someone, especially when children are involved, but that's what tipped me out the door.

Losing my children began at that moment. Before the coffee mug, there were just two married people at war with each other, but losing the children began right there. Losing my son and daughter was an awful set of events, inexorable, like "Found a Peanut," that song kids sing on car trips and you cannot stop them.

I walked away from my then husband, standing over me at the dishwasher telling me how to live. From the storage closet I hauled out our son's Boy Scout tent, sleeping bags, matches, and a flashlight and put them in the trunk of my car. I went back in the house twice without seeing the experson, once for Darcy's stuffed bear and the second time to pull off my wedding ring, which I left on top of my diaphragm case.

I drove to Onkwedo Bagels and bought supplies. I drove to the school and signed the kids out for "a family trip."

The campground was one we'd gone to with their father. It was just across the state line. We were the only campers there in the preseason. In the early darkness of the evening, we lay in Sam's Scout tent, the skylight unzipped so we could see the moon. Darcy asked me if bears were real.

Sam said, "Of course bears are real."

"Will they take my Stuffy?" she asked, tucking the toy bear behind her back.

"No, Stuffy is safe. We are all safe," I said. I gave her the flashlight to hold, and we slept.

The next day we climbed rocks and floated leaf boats in the stream. We saw no bears or even tracks of bears, only geese winging back north in wide Vs.

On the morning of the third day Darcy and I were sitting on a rock drinking slightly ashy cocoa and Sam was toasting a bagel on a stick over the campfire when three state troopers drove up in a car and an SUV. They asked my name, which they already seemed to know.

They asked for my driver's license, which was in my trunk. I went to get it. I turned around from the open trunk in time to see them put Darcy and Sam in the back of the SUV. My children's faces vanished behind the tinted windows as the tires spurted gravel. I ran after the SUV, screaming, "This is a mistake!"

The trooper who was left stuffed me in the backseat of the car, one hand on the top of my head, just like you see on TV. I was arrested for kidnapping, handcuffs and all.

The charges were later dropped when my lawyer made a deal.

The custody hearing was my first large helping of Onkwedo reality. It was also the last time I wore a dress. The D.A. was the experson's friend, the state troopers who drove the getaway car had gone to high school with him, the social worker mowed his lawn (she said it helped build her aerobic conditioning), and the family court judge had been his lab partner in chemistry.

It worked against me that everyone liked the experson. It worked against me that I was too angry, too sad, and too disbelieving that the custody hearing was happening at all to defend myself.

The legal process went south for me when the experson's lawyer asked me why I'd left. I had been strictly coached not to talk about the dishwasher, so I said, "Freedom."

My lawyer put his head in his hands.

The judge asked me where I went for freedom, and before I could answer, the experson's lawyer handed the judge a photo.

The judge asked me if it was true I had been living in my car.

I told him I was camping.

The judge called my lawyer and me up to his desk. He handed us the photo. It showed me peeing in the woods. It was not a vulgar picture, just a woman squatting in the woods. I didn't see the problem with it until the judge pointed out the sign posted behind me: Onkwedo Reservoir, Public Drinking Water Source.

I didn't remember seeing the sign. I suspected that the experson's lawyer had Photoshopped it in.

The judge asked me if I had anything to say. As he waited for my response, he pushed his glass of water toward the edge of his desk.

I looked around the courtroom at the faces. Nobody knew me. Nobody knew that I gave birth like a heroine. Nobody knew that I was missing my father. Nobody knew that only in my car did I feel like myself.

The judge's decision came a week later. He said that I was "unstable," both financially and emotionally. That I exhibited "bizarre and erratic behavior." And that my children would be better off with their father except for one weekend a month. Any alimony I might have gotten was wiped out by what I should have been contributing in child support. I hadn't planned on being broke, but the point is that I hadn't planned any of it.

You would think it was careless on my part to lose custody of my children over something as small as following directions. You would think that I was crazy or bad or stupid. That was what I thought too.

ONKWEDO

When the weather turned cool, I moved from the woods to the run-down Swiss Chalet Motor Inn, its name derived from a strip of ginger-bread tacked along the office roof.

Wherever I was, the custody decision droned in my head like tin-nitus: "Defendant is itinerant, financially and emotionally unstable . . . unable to produce character witnesses . . . exhibits bizarre and erratic behavior (see photo attached, Exhibit A) . . ." I'd memorized the whole thing. My brain kept going up against it, trying to topple it, to find a way around it, but it stood like a stone cliff.

I hadn't realized how much time mothering took up. Without my children I had acres of unfilled, unscheduled, lonely time. Cook a meal, sleep or not, take a walk or not—it didn't matter.

In my car were my books and a few clothes. I didn't miss the clothes I'd left behind. Those clothes represented attempts to make the experson think something about me: "Gosh, she's sexy," or "She's had two babies, but she's still got her figure." But he never thought those things about me at all. He simply didn't think about me. The feeling next to love is interest, and the experson had no interest in me. To him, I was like a big laundry pile heaped on the floor, not *his* laundry, but someone's.

I didn't miss picking out clothes every day. I wore the same pair of pants and rotated two shirts. I would wash one at night in the motel sink. It was simple.

At the Swiss Chalet Motor Inn I kept a pair each of my children's pajamas in ziplock baggies to hold their smell. I stored the bags under my pillow to help me sleep. The slight rustle of the plastic did not disturb me.

Life without Sam and Darcy at the motor inn gave me a lot of opportunities to think about failure, my failure. It was not the experson's fault that we'd flunked couplehood; control is not necessarily a bad thing. And I didn't blame the stylish couples counselor (stylish in an Onkwedo way, all big earrings and boots) we were seeing at the time. Couples counseling, now *there* is a career choice for embracing failure.

The experson had told me repeatedly that "failure to plan is planning to fail." Planning didn't come naturally to me. He was a thorough planner, who'd divided his life into chunks of well-ordered time. For the kickoff to his twenty-year plan, the experson chose me to be the mother of his children. He thought I was malleable, could be shaped into the right kind of partner if he could only get me away from the city to a wholesome place.

I know that he based his choice of me on the three key maternal traits he believed ensured survival of the young: big bottom (fertility, comfort), frugality (endurance), and the capacity to tolerate chaos, which he equated with child-rearing ability.

Two years ago, when the children were three and nine, he moved us from the city up to his hometown, the wholesome town of Onkwedo. It was the second stage of his twenty-year plan for our lives. The first had been two offspring, by a carefully selected mother; the next was his successful retirement at the age of forty. He'd designed a compression mold called a "bite" that is used in the production of car tires. For the duration of the marriage I understood his brilliant innovation, but with divorce my comprehension had disappeared.

I first met the experson in the spring in New York City. It was lunch hour and I was sitting on the back steps of the magazine office, letting the sun lighten my hair. I had just gotten a trainer haircut from the beauty school across the street. With the new haircut, I looked efficient and slick, no-nonsense. I looked unlike my regular self, which is probably what attracted him.

When he asked me what I did, I told him I worked in publishing. This wasn't untrue: I was a fact-and-statistics checker for *Psychology Now*—how many monkeys, what color M&M's they preferred, etc. My chief aptitude for the job was my ability to remember where in a book or an article a sentence or paragraph occurred. I was good at my job and I liked the work. The "facts" in psychology are squishy and porous, more like opinions or even guesses than hard scientific data. There is always an "on the other hand" in psychological facts. This never bothered me.

Because of the haircut, the experson probably thought I had a highly responsible executive job. I didn't intend to mislead him. In spite of his smooth voice and sweet smell, I didn't care enough what he thought of me to straighten him out. When he found out my real job title, it planted the seeds of his thinking that I was not a trustworthy person.

By then I was pregnant with Sam.

Friends' marriages with even less promise have worked out. Two classmates from Statistics 101 married the teaching assistants—went into their offices during midterms, broke down crying, got their tears kissed away, and soon thereafter got engaged. Both couples have children. You would think these statisticians would worry about watering down their gene pool, breeding with weepy D students, but they didn't.

I made it through statistics dry-eyed. Played Ping-Pong with my TA. Hit myself in the face with the paddle. Bled. Lost the game. He offered me a Band-Aid, which I took, but I didn't sleep with him. Why did I marry the experson and not my statistics TA? I recall that the statistician's sweat was acrid. Maybe love dwelled in my nose?

I know how stupidly random that sounds, but the actual doorway to the experience of pleasure—the oxytocin foyer—is the nose. I didn't have a better theory about me and love. And I *had* failed to plan. I just let things happen. In the motel room, I thought about this failure a lot. I didn't know if I had actually made a choice about love.

One of those squishy psychology facts is that women who have brothers pick better mates, and I had none. I loved my father and my cousin, both city men. I worked hard at understanding them. And I did understand, a little bit. If they were birds, you would say that I recognized their song. But it wasn't helpful in my overall understanding of men. Nothing about them lent itself to a rule that could be followed; each was a one-off.

Other than being men and being my family, my father and cousin had one thing in common: each could lift himself at will above the slog of day-to-day life and see the pattern. Sometimes I could do it too, pull up like a periscope above the crust of the earth and look around. It reminded me that the place where I stood was only one point on the overall map of the world.

I did that often in my first year in Onkwedo, reminding myself that the earth was huge and filled with many other people besides the ones I saw in this small town, the same wholesome people over and over again.

I should never have let the experson choose me. We didn't even speak the same language. Maybe I was like the women who come to America from France, not the Parisians, who know *quoi* is *quoi,* but the ones from the provinces who search out the biggest smuggest Owen Wilson look-alike they can find and marry him. In my mother's generation they went for the Gary Cooper type. You want to take these French women aside and explain to them, not *that* one, *pas cet homme-là!*

But I did end up married to the experson, with Sam, and then—following his plan—Darcy. And we did leave the city behind for Onkwedo.

Right after I left the city, my father left the world. He died in spring. April is the month when people's bodies say enough already, like trees whose sap won't rise again. After my father was gone, I was stunned by the specificity of my loneliness. I was lonely only for him; no other person could fill the void. Even if my city friends had come to see me—and they didn't—they could not have helped. I felt there was no one left on earth to make the loneliness go away. Grief and depression look exactly the same. It didn't matter which it was, I had lost my guiding star.

Living Upstate made it worse. Onkwedo reminded me of the bookshelves in the reception area of the *Psychology Now* office. Every title of interest had been taken from the shelves by someone and not returned. What remained were the blandest and most unwantable books. It was uncanny to pass my eye over row upon row of book spines and experience not a single flicker of interest. Here in Onkwedo it was the same, I thought, every sparky adolescent runs away, every troubled child is squashed firmly, every artist finds a way out. What remained were the people who belonged here, dulled and compliant and able to fit in.

That's how it seemed to me during that first long winter, gray upon gray. Even the clouds had clouds.

HOUSE

In my bed at the motor inn, after my dinner from the blue pot, I closed my eyes and let the pasta to do its calming work. I told myself that my children had each other. I recited this "fact" left over from my former job at the psychology magazine: sibling relationships are formative and predict future happiness. I told myself I could feel good that Sam had Darcy to look out for, that Darcy had a big brother, that they were a team.

Lying under the dank chenille bedspread with my eyes closed, I tried to periscope up, pulling my focus way high so I could check on my children.

I could see Sam, asleep in his bed, his body curled tightly around a pillow. Darcy too was sleeping, but she sought with her face, nuzzling, eyes closed, as if looking for something with her cheeks and lips. When I saw this, I got out of bed and sleep was gone for the night. I stood by the motel room window, looking out at the absolute blankness that was my current home, Onkwedo.

When morning came I drove to a backstreet behind the children's school and parked, waiting for kindergarten recess to start. Jazz was playing on the car radio, and the windows were rolled up. I wasn't exactly happy in my car; I had forgotten about being really happy. The moments of okayness, like this one, passed for happy. My clothes and books were still in the trunk, packed in boxes, reference books packed separately in case I needed them. I kept my cooking things there too, so I wouldn't get in trouble with the motor inn management.

I felt at home in my car, parked on the quiet street. But from the trunk, the blue pot called to me. It reminded me of the big stove in my parents' house, of all the people I'd cooked for, the ones I loved, hungry and gathered around a table. The pot called out for a big stove and a flame under it, a room with a table and people seated around it. I would be serving something from the blue pot, probably pasta.

My breath had steamed the windshield.

The parking spot gave me a view of the school playground, through two backyards. I could see my daughter through the naked trees of late October only when she climbed to the top of the slide. I saw her right before her descent, wearing a charcoal gray sweatshirt. The other girls wore pink or lavender jackets. The other girls had mothers dressing them in the mornings; matching mittens and hats, snowsuit sets. Even in the ugly gray hoodie she was heart-stoppingly beautiful. The air around her crackled and glowed, a corona of light. She looked entirely solitary.

Watching her made my chest hurt, I wanted to hold her so much. I had to satisfy myself with seeing her make her determined climb to the top of the slide, then disappear in a blur of gray. A pink blur followed her, then another pink, a lavender, then Darcy again.

Then the whistle for the end of recess must have blown, because the top of the slide stayed vacant. I wiped a clear circle in the fog on the car window to see better.

The houses on the street where I was parked were old and made of stone or wood. Some had been added to in such ill-conceived ways that they looked like cats wearing lipstick.

One was for sale. A woman came from the back door and walked to the corner of the yard. She was carrying a bowl. She lifted the lid of a screened-in cage and dumped some scraps. Compost, I thought.

I looked at the For Sale sign. I looked at the house. It had windows that covered one long side. It looked as if a young architect—fresh from Onkwedo's own Waindell University—had fallen in love with Frank Lloyd Wright, bought himself a pile of wood, borrowed a hammer, and set to work. The house was both beautiful and a shack at the same time, made with the young architect's good ideas about modern design. Like the Second Little Pig had been schooled at the Bauhaus.

The simple part of me began to count. I only do this when I am happy. When you are counting, time passes more slowly. Every child knows this.

One was compost. Two was the tall windows. Three was privacy, as if the house had its shoulder to the road, face turned away to the southwest. Seven through ten was the nose of the house pointing trimly upwind like a sailboat. I thought dully, *house*. I could have my own house. I could have rooms where the experson could not come and explain to me in his reasoned way how poorly I was doing at life.

What formed in my mind was not exactly a plan; it was just a picture in the dim fog of my sad head. Maybe it was a plan. Maybe that's what planning looked like. At the time it just felt like a retreat from pain.

I called the number on the sign and put in motion the many tedious steps that moved me forward—and it did feel like forward—into the house with its own roof, which I now must keep tight. The sale of my father's "good" car provided the down payment. I was still driving his other car, the one he'd given me when I'd gotten married. It had been his way of taking care of me, a gift of independence.

At the closing, the lawyer told me that someone famous had lived in the house—he couldn't remember who it was. It seemed an unlikely house for a famous person, but I thanked him and accepted the keys.

Later, when my books were alphabetized on the shelves and I was sitting on an overturned box in the middle of the largest, emptiest room, the doorbell rang and a Japanese person, holding a camera smaller than his thumb, explained the house to me. "It was lived in by Nabokov," he said, with practiced-sounding equal accenting of the syllables. "Vladimir Nabokov, the greatest writer of his times, for two years in the 1950s. He wrote a lot here, but he did not immortalize the house." We were standing in the foyer. I offered him tea, but he declined politely. He asked to take a photo for his website.

When he left, I went to look at the bookshelves. Most of the books had belonged to my cousin. After he died, in the fancy Boston hospital, with the nurses in street clothes and the doctors smarter than God, I had collected his books from his boat, stacks of swollen paperbacks, and taken them away with me. They'd been in boxes and were now alphabetized on the shelves of my new house.

On the N shelf, I found *Speak, Memory* by Vladimir Nabokov. It was his autobiography. I brought it into the built-in bed, the only piece of furniture in the large bedroom. It must have been where the Nabokovs had slept. I flipped through the book. There was a picture of his wife, Vera, taken for a passport. She was beautiful. The book was dedicated to her. The words were close together on the page, but "love" jumped out at me from different places. I closed the book and fell asleep.

MAIL

After I'd lived in the house for nearly a month, it still felt vacant. I had set up an "office" for myself in the basement: a table with paper, pens, envelopes, and stamps, plus an old beast of a computer, courtesy of my employer. My job was answering the mail for the Old Daitch Dairy. Following the wretched custody decision, the social worker had found this job for me. She said it would suit me because I liked to read. She probably thought I couldn't do anything else. She was pretty much right. I'd left the job at *Psychology Now* when Darcy was born and hadn't worked outside my home since then. My workplace confidence was nonexistent.

Every weekday I received a sack of Old Daitch Dairy mail. Mostly it was business solicitations, but there were also letters from customers, some of them angling for a free pint of ice cream. Once a woman wrote to suggest a new flavor: pancake batter. I quit working early that day.

The bills I put aside for Ginna, the bookkeeper. She worked from home too, and I would bring them to her once a week. Ginna was a mathophobe who sweated out her blouse every time she used the calculator. In spite of that, she said she'd never made a mistake. I guess it was the *idea* of making a mistake that bothered her. I wouldn't have thought the sweating would matter—the Old Daitch Dairy office is in a barn—but I guess she preferred working from home because it was easier on her wardrobe.

My new house had good closets, all nearly empty. Old Daitch Dairy paid me very little, and none of the money could go toward clothes. I owned one pair of pants that were fit to wear outside the house. I tried not to think about the state of my shoes.

The children each had a room, into which I put all my decorating efforts. I tried to make their rooms pretty and "homey" for when they came, with pictures on the walls, a quilt and an afghan from my grandmother covering each of their beds.

I had few furnishings. A couch had been left behind. It was a bit sprung in the seat, but ample. I was acutely aware that it wasn't stuff that made a home. My house needed people. It needed noise and play, conversation, even arguments. My new house was completely empty of love, of connectedness, of people up against each other.

This thought would drive me out of doors, out into the yard, which seemed less appallingly void than the space within the walls of the house. Or I would find a reason to go to the supermarket—a quart of milk—just to see and hear other people. I would eavesdrop on the women in the checkout line at Apex Market, wondering if we would ever be friends. It was a chatty kind of town. I would hear about what their kids would or wouldn't eat, and a lot about cleaning. Houses in Onkwedo were tidy and fussy looking, with little shrubs and two-toned shutters, color-accented front doors.

The women were often talking about "deep cleaning." I didn't know what that meant, but it sounded boring. Maybe we wouldn't be friends. I remembered from my old job that repressed people are always trying to rid their lives of filth. Hand washing and more hand washing paved the road right to obsession.

Maybe cleaning had replaced lovemaking up here. Maybe passion had gone extinct Upstate. I didn't know Onkwedo well, so this was an outsider's speculation, but the signs that no one here cared about sex surrounded me.

One morning, I was lying on the grass in the backyard of my new house. The mail had not come yet to start my workday. I lay there, thinking about love and waiting for the mailman. The earth felt slightly warmer than the air. I was thinking that when I lived in the city, there was no grass and people had more sex. We did. We ate less and had more sex than up here in Onkwedo. The perspective of hindsight was inaccurate, I knew. When you look back on your life, the hot nights of passion stand out and all the bowls of cream of wheat and vanilla ice cream do not.

Still, there had to be a location factor in lack of sex. It was cold Upstate, and people dressed badly and spent most of their time in cars. When people actually encountered one another, it was at the supermarket, which—aside from the mild frisson of the produce aisle—was the unsexiest place imaginable.

The clothes people wore up here said absolutely nothing about the bodies underneath: square shirts of bright meaningless color, big dumb pants in bulky, scratchy fabric with huge pockets to minimize the butt. There was no "look at my ass" up here in cow country. Even the pregnancies didn't seem like the result of passion but like a board game where the pawns had been moved into the end zone.

Lying on my back, looking up at the gray unicloud of sky, I was thinking that I didn't know where sex had gone or even if it still existed someplace. Young people didn't seem to be getting much. Gay people either, and it used to be you could count on them. If there was sex going on, it was in the city and certainly not here. Although in the city it might have shifted entirely into the commercial sector. Most pleasures now required transactions, contracts.

It shouldn't have bothered me. I should have had better things to think about, like the welfare of my children or even what was for breakfast, because that was something I could *do* something about. Yet I was thinking that here we all are on this green place for such a short time, and what if nobody makes love anymore? It was sad. It was as if there were no more music.

I stood up and brushed the grass off myself, went in the house, and turned on the radio. I found some jazz to keep me company while I waited for the arrival of the mail.

The mailman drove a white truck. His name was embroidered on his jacket in red thread: Bill. With the radio playing, I walked around the house opening and closing books, testing myself to see if I remembered what was on their pages. It was a kind of mental yoga. I used to be able to remember the pagination of every book I owned. I could read the favorite ones over in my mind without even opening the cover. After I nursed my children, that information disappeared. Sometimes I could still summon it up, like "Rich Rolled Sugar Cookies," page 872, *Joy of Cooking*. Perfect page recall is a dull talent, but it is not as dull as this one: I knew which container the leftovers would fit in best.

Over a trumpet solo, I could hear Bill's truck downshifting to climb the steep hill to my house. That gave me about seven minutes—three mailbox stops—until my workday started. With Dick Katz playing piano riffs on the radio, I changed into the Pants and a clean shirt, grabbed the mail sack, and went outside.

You would think there would be a correlation between having sex and owning nice clothes, but there is not. There is no correlation between sex and happiness either, or sex and fitness, or even youth. Sex is like the appreciation of jazz music; it can land on anyone at all.

My scientist cousin loved jazz. When we both lived in the city, my cousin would ring my doorbell well after midnight, waking me up to drag me out to jazz bars. He explained to me that you have to show up at the dive bars that never get rocking till after one a.m., and you have to stay till dawn, because when it happens—when the jazz fairy touches down—the music will last you the rest of your life.

For him that wasn't very long.

Maybe the sex fairy had quit?

I shouldn't have been thinking about that, but if I didn't, there was only death to think about: death, money, and food.

I was standing by the mailbox with my finished sack of outgoing mail when Bill drove up in his white U.S. Postal Service truck, its rear-view mirror framed in pink cat fur. Waiting outside for your mailman may have been breaking the rules of Onkwedo, I didn't know. It embarrassed me not to know the rules of the place where I lived—like the rule for smiling. People in Onkwedo smiled at me, whereas in the city no one smiled. When I first came here, I thought the smiles meant something, like that my pants were unzipped or they wanted to tell me how they had met Jesus Christ. But the smiles didn't mean anything. They weren't about me at all. They were your basic have-a-nice-day kind of smiley face.

Bill's smile was real. I met him out by the mailbox every weekday. I was probably one of the most regular customers on his route. Some days Bill was the only person I spoke to. He was the friendliest person I'd met here. Not the making-nice kind of friendly, but the real I-am-happy-to-see-you kind of friendly. When he spotted me, his face broke open like the sun through the clouds.

Today was no exception. "Hello there," he beamed. "You like to read?"

I thought he was making a joke because he was about to hand me a particularly big mail sack from Old Daitch Dairy. I often think people are joking, and most of the time in Onkwedo I am wrong.

My arms were braced for the mail sack, but instead Bill handed me a tote bag from the local sewing and needlecraft store. It was filled with books. "My wife thought you might like these."

"Thank you," I mumbled. I bent my head over the bag, pretending to read the titles, because I didn't want my mailman to know I was crying. "Thank you. I'll return them."

"No need," he said airily. "The garage is full of books—can't even fit the snowblower in. I tell Margie she reads too much, but she doesn't change." He said this last part like it was a good thing and slung a mail sack at my feet. The white truck roared off in a fog of diesel.

The books were mostly romances with pink and gold covers featuring half-naked men and aroused-looking women. There was also a purple book, *Visualize Your Business Success: See It and It Will Happen.* Maybe that was where passion lay in Onkwedo, all packed away inside steamy paperbacks. I couldn't decide whether to read them or burn them in the fireplace. Smoke from colored ink contains carcinogenic carbon chains, I remembered from my old job.

After I answered the mail and ate my roasted beet greens, I decided to reward myself with reading one of Bill's wife's books. It was still a long seventy-two hours till the children came to me. I could squander most of them on work, some on sleep, some on food. When the children were gone, I ate leftovers and the bitter, scary foods: kale, sardines, lima beans. When they were with me, we ate sweeter, more recognizable things: baked potatoes with butter, poached pears.

Dear Mrs. Coswell:
Thank you for your letter. We understand your concern about hormones in the milk. We do not give our cows preventative antibiotics. We do not have "free range" cows, as you suggest, because of the danger it would pose to motorists as well as to the cows

themselves, but our fields are ample, and within the fences the cows roam freely.

These practices are reflected in the wholesome and fresh taste of our ice cream. I believe it is particularly apparent in the vanilla. I am enclosing a coupon for a free cone, should you make it out to our stand during the summer.

Best wishes,

Old Daitch Dairy

In the spot by the window where Nabokov may have written whole books, I was writing to Upstate folks who had both the time and the need to communicate with their dairy products' source. If I were a more upbeat person, I would have thought of it as being part of the literary tradition of this house. But since I was not, it seemed like further evidence of the decline of civilization.

DARCY

Four whole weeks in my new house and it was finally my turn for the children, but I only got one of them, my daughter. Sam had hockey practice, which conflicted with my "visitation," that utterly wrong-sounding term. It enraged me to be cheated of him, and I wanted to fight it, but I didn't because I knew how Irene, the biased social worker, would interpret it for the judge. It would be me, the selfish mother, versus the son's health and fitness. Her view synchronized perfectly with the experson's. Instead I anonymously ordered another five pizzas to be delivered from Loro's to the experson's lawyer. It wasn't exactly passive-aggressive, it was more aggressive-aggressive. Extra cheese, all of them.

The only thing I liked about the social worker was that she was plain. Plain with a trim body. That kind of person was a good choice in a partner. For one thing, she would never lose her looks. I couldn't think of a second thing. Maybe she was a good driver. She commuted from Oneonta, where she cared for her wheelchair-bound father, three hours of driving a day to get to her work. She had a good job—two jobs if you counted the yard work. She had moved some of her things into the experson's house. I saw a robe and fuzzy purple slippers in his closet. And on the night table her book, *Training the Inner Child*. I saw this when I was snooping, pretending I needed pajamas for Darcy.

Irene was careful never to be in his car when he dropped off the children, but once I saw them going into the barbecue restaurant, all four of them. I was on my way back from the library. I didn't need to go to the library, but it was the only place in Onkwedo where I felt I might belong. Sometimes, after I read the newspaper cover-to-cover and looked at the new books, I would drive the main road loop like a teenager, wasting gas, wondering why I was here. That's what I was doing when I passed the parking lot of Stick to Your Ribs, recognized the experson's car, and saw him with his arm around Irene, the children following them into the restaurant.

I pulled over at the next light and vomited. I puked into the storm drain. It was about as tidy as public vomiting could be.

After I sluiced my mouth with water and ate a peppermint, I asked myself sternly, "Why shouldn't he be happy?" I answered myself like this: "Why shouldn't he be dead?"

I decided if she made my children call her mommy, I would do something bad. I'd read in the library's *Onkwedo Clarion* what they were serving for dinner that night in the Onkwedo Correctional Facility: *Chili, California Mix, Canned Pears.*

As usual, Irene wasn't in the car when the experson dropped Darcy off. I had arranged the house in readiness for my daughter: butter softening on the counter, piles of scrap paper and a pair of scissors, some new ribbon from the Dollar Store to dress her dolls. He rang the doorbell, and when I opened the door, he pushed Darcy inside like she was unwilling to come.

It was all I could do not to hug her, but I knew better. I gave her the three feet of space she required, like a maidservant gives the queen. I carried her jacket to its hook. I placed her sequin-covered purse beside her rubber boots. I inquired if she was ready to make cookies. Unlike her brother, Darcy refused to follow recipes. She liked to make "free-hand" cookies—cracking eggs, pouring vanilla, tasting dabs of sugar and butter. The cookies never came out the same way twice. Her favorite part was cracking the eggs. Darcy would break open every egg in the house. After she left, I would be eating omelets all week.

She didn't answer me. I switched gears from servile to efficient mommy. I bustled around, smoothing the ribbon, straightening the stack of paper. I stared at her covertly, my eyes drinking her in. Darcy, like all real beauties, has beautiful everything, even body parts that are intrinsically homely, like ankles. Her ankles are elegant as small sails scooped by the wind. The part on her head is beautiful: a white switchback trail separating sweeps of fine black hair. Her eyes were turned from mine, but when she glanced up, they startled me: icy blue with one wedge of brown, a slice of chocolate pie, a gift from her maternal grandfather. In some cultures the asymmetry would be the mark of a witch, an enchantress.

She saw the ribbon and pounced on it. "What's this for?" she asked, her voice scornful, as if all my offerings were cheap, pointless.

I reminded myself that she had to punish me for leaving her. "Decoration," I said. Darcy believes in decoration. She has the eye. My hands were yearning to touch her hair. I stuffed them in my back pockets. I watched her shoulders let down a little bit. She circled the paper, touched the scissors. I could see she was mad and she didn't know why. "Would you like some honey tea?" I offered. She wouldn't answer me. Honey tea was a spoonful of honey in hot water. She liked it with milk, my son with a squeeze of lemon.

Waiting for her to move toward me, I settled myself on the couch, back turned, breathing, ready.

She came up behind me and tugged my hair. "Do you want a ponytail?"

"Yes."

She left the room and I could hear her rummaging for a long time, running between the bathroom cabinets and various closets. She re-appeared with my business tote bag, crammed full. "This is a beauty store," she announced. "I am the . . ."—she thought a minute—"shampooler," she said with authority.

She began to comb my hair roughly, stopping to spray it with something that smelled weirdly familiar, but was not from the hair product family. Spray starch? Deodorant? I couldn't see the bottle. I hoped it was not a cleaning product. I held still as she twined ribbon through my sticky hair, braiding and twisting. She brought me a mirror. I could see that she had the right idea, to interfere with and alter every single hair, but the results were eccentric. I had the look of cornrows gone bad.

Holding the mirror, she stood close to me. I could smell her under all the spray, her little warm self. I didn't reach for her, but soon she was sitting on my lap. She weighed thirty-eight pounds. I could feel each precious one. "You look silly," she said. And then she looked me hard in the eyes. "Where *were* you?"

"I was here," I said. "I was getting ready for you to come back."

This satisfied her and she said, "It is time to make the cookies. Regular cookies," she specified, yanking one of my seven ponytails. "And decorate them." We moved into the kitchen, holding hands, preparing for her favorite taste: the raw marriage of butter and sugar. For the moment, my daughter and I were together, her small pink palm warm against mine. I let that touch fill every part of me.

BOOK

After Darcy left Monday morning on the school bus, I ate misshapen cookies for breakfast with a side of scrambled eggs. And then my luck changed. It changed while I was cleaning up our messes, alone and stuffed with cookies. This is how it always happens with luck.

I was gathering Darcy's lost purses. In the garage I found three of them. That wasn't the lucky part; she leaves her purses everywhere. Her purse collection included five mini-backpacks, one fanny pack, four shoulder bags, six clutches, five wallets, four change purses, and four handbags that fell outside any category. She carried one wherever she went, always crammed full. Each purse contained a mélange of her and my things. Any lipstick I had ever owned in the pink range had been purloined. She left me the muddy "naturals" and reds.

The purse collection had grown from Darcy's deeply feminine instinct to collect appealing and random objects and put them in any receptacle that snaps or zips. She'd done this since she could first crawl. My daughter fashioned herself as a femme fatale. During the cookie making she'd asked me how many times you are supposed to marry— "Six?" Greta Garbo started the same way. Little Gertlich crawled around gathering something shiny, something sticky, something soft as feathers, and something she had no right to take. It's the association of these objects and the mastery over them in their disparity that plants a girl on the path to sirenhood.

As I roamed through the rooms and yard collecting purses, I was wondering if Vladimir Nabokov ever cleaned this house. I was learning more about him from reading his autobiography, *Speak, Memory*. I found some things out about him on the internet too. His most famous book, *Lolita*, is the story of a grown man's obsessive lust for a young girl. Nabokov wrote it right around the time he was living here. It was the success of that book that enabled him to leave Upstate New York. A movie was made of *Lolita,* and the Nabokovs left off rented houses forever, to live in hotels.

Vladimir Nabokov had another interest besides writing: a deep scientific and aesthetic fascination with butterflies. He seemed like someone who wouldn't have been big on domestic life, the housey part of living. I wondered if he liked living in this house at all. It was a big step down from his family's mansion in St. Petersburg. To him it must have been a sabbatical squat, rented for a couple of years from an engineering professor who was off to Paris. To me it was the nicest place I'd ever owned. And I didn't own it yet, but every month from my Old Daitch Dairy salary I would pay down another two cinder blocks.

It probably doesn't matter where a writer writes, since he is living mostly inside his own head. Maybe his wife took care of everything, although Vera too was an aristocrat, as well as his muse and typist. I couldn't see him scrubbing anything or puttering in the garage. Maybe Vera even liked this house; the view from the kitchen sink was fine. Nabokov may have perched here in this house in Onkwedo, hating the chills and the grayness, mining his mind till fate and Hollywood sprang him loose.

I found one of Darcy's purses, a blue beaded handbag, in the back garden, adorning a fencepost. Her fuzzy black clutch hung almost invisibly in one of the prickly bushes growing in a dark, squat line. I loathed those bushes. If I had an ax and was thinking about Irene, the social worker, I could chop down the entire row.

In Darcy's bedroom, three handbags dangling heavily from my arm, I faced the bank of built-in 1950s "Modern" drawers that contained her purse collection. The collection was so large that to squeeze more of it in, I had to remove the cleverly fitted drawers. It was one of those boring jobs of which life is made, taking something entirely apart and putting it back together. I took the top drawers out and placed them on the scruffy carpet, trying to flatten the plump bags so they would fit. Darcy had insisted that her purse collection be kept in this house and in these drawers. Her father had complied, probably because Darcy was well beyond his capacity for control where purses were concerned.

The bottom drawer stuck, and I knelt down to wrestle it out. When I finally got it free, I peered inside the frame to see the impediment. There was a wedge of white behind the frame. I thought it might be my wedding clutch (why do brides need purses?), but when I reached in to pull it loose, instead of the grain of satin, my fingers met a smooth surface. I tugged at it.

It came free, and in my hand was a yellowed stack of cards, six inches by four and thick as a fist. I looked back in and behind another drawer saw several more stacks, each thick and yellowed. I pried them out. For no reason at all I sniffed them. They smelled exactly like green walnuts. If you have never smelled a green walnut, it's the smell that aftershave ought to have but does not.

The cards were covered with writing, mostly ink but with pencil corrections. I held them in my open hands. I could feel the modest weight of the cards with words written on them, the ink weighing nothing at all. I knelt among the purse piles and riffled through the stacks. Some cards were nearly blank, with only a word or two at the top. All were marked by deep parallel indentations from the pressure of the wooden drawer frame.

The handwriting was precise and regular. It was fairly easy to make out, though faded. I began to read, kneeling on the wall-to-wall indoor-outdoor carpeting, surrounded by purses. Sometimes the sentences flowed along, making whole scenes. There were parts that struck me as terribly funny. I would read a sentence and it would erupt within me, unbearably and weirdly hilarious, provoking the kind of laughter that makes you desperately lonely. There I was on the ugly rug that came with my unpaid-for house, reading some index card. I knew I was the only person on the planet reading that string of words, and it exploded in my brain. One minute I was laughing, and then I found myself crying, wiping my face on a pink handkerchief found in a random purse, a hankie I had been missing for six months.

When I looked up from the last card, it was dark outside. I un-kinked my knees, which had turned a deep lavender, my folded-under calves gone to sleep, and gazed around. There was no one to share the moment with—no friend, no lover, no husband, no child.

I made some hot milk and carried it to bed. I put the cards beside me on a pillow while I sipped.

The story was about Babe Ruth, sometimes referred to as "the Babe" or just "B.R." It was a love story, though twisted. It opened during Babe's early tour with an Upstate farm team. The setting was a thinly disguised version of here and it seemed completely current. There was the same horrendous taste in personal apparel, the same huge asses tucked forever into cars, the same vicious garden club, the same excessive and frightening niceness, the same silence that could be peace or utter isolation.

The nearly blank cards all clustered where a scene of playing ball would have occurred. The words at the top seemed to indicate the action of how Babe Ruth first pointed his bat to the stratosphere, then hit the ball clear out of the park.

The writer had made the Babe a sad clown of a big man, throwing money and love around like water balloons. The slugger was portrayed as tragic, handsome, and absurd, a great blues singer of sports, the Bessie Smith of batters. Whoever had written this—Nabokov?—wrote with total conviction, as if he knew exactly where he was in the world and why. The words were his coordinates.

I plumped my pillow and finished my hot milk. Could this really be Nabokov's work? If so, had he abandoned it, maybe forgotten it in his haste to leave? Or cast it off, unwanted and shame inducing, like a love child? If it was his work, then reading the found words was a stolen privilege, like watching through an open hotel room door while two famous actors fight and then have sex, wrong and irresistible.

Leaning against the same wall Nabokov must have leaned against to read, with the same pair of wall lamps lit, I held the cards carefully. Maybe he lay in this spot at night, on the side closer to the door, and wondered what he was doing in Upstate New York, so far from home. Maybe he turned on his hip to watch Vera sleep, taking comfort in her sweet, even exhalation. Maybe he missed the city, its complex order and brilliant chaos. Maybe the night silence was a big emptiness to him. Maybe he thought of his great love, not the one lying beside him, but the one he would invent on paper tomorrow.

TYPING

In the morning I went downstairs to my "office" and my Old Daitch Dairy computer, which took up half the table, the one in the basement, a level that in Realtor-speak is obfuscatingly called "the ground floor." In summer the ground floor was probably cool and pleasant, but since the weather had turned crisp, it was chilly and dank in a way that made me think of rheumatoid arthritis and chilblains.

I piled the cards beside me, well away from the bathtub of green tea I'd made to keep me going. Green tea is the drink of choice for bus drivers in Asia. It is a bitter drink, and good for getting where you need to go on time despite many stops and many bozos getting on and off with their lost tickets, incorrect change, and luggage that bumps other passengers.

I had to type a copy of the story for myself and not just so I could read it in bed with a cup of milk and not worry about spilling. I needed the words to go through my body so I'd understand them better, to see what I could find out about the writer, to see if I could tell if it *was* Nabokov. Maybe I would just know.

It felt beyond odd to be in possession of a possibly precious manuscript. Why would treasure be entrusted to me? I had already lost my treasure. Darcy wasn't under my roof, sleeping, sometimes even beside me, her hair a shadow on the pillow, her night breath hot. Sam was no longer nearby in his bed, solid and still.

When this thought came I shoved it aside, flexed my fingers, and began to type.

On the first card, in the very center, was written "*Babe Ruth,*" and beside it was an authoritative penciled note, "Alternately," and a numbered list.

2. *The Last Diamond.* This was crossed out.

3. *Yankee Go Home*

4. *Roots*—And beside that *Certainly not!*

Typing made me want coffee in the worst way, as if coffee were love and salvation and riches all rolled into one cup. I had given up coffee for economic reasons as well as psychological health. On coffee I would find myself cleaning the stove with Q-tips. Coffee made me think I could do anything—patch things up with the experson, for example. So I'd stopped drinking it, or even having it in the house. But now I wanted it back.

I could see Vera Nabokov scooting down the stairs with a freshly made espresso for her novelist husband, hard at work on his prose. I could smell the coffee and hear her near-silent steps on the crappy rug.

The actual day-to-day lives of all famous male novelists are probably bizarrely similar. They get up, hungover or not, eat breakfast, write for three hours, eat lunch, take a nap and a walk, write for the afternoon, eat dinner, drinking or not, read all evening, sleep. Here is the fascinating part: someone is in the kitchen making those meals appear. In Philip Roth's house, the actress Claire Bloom was in the kitchen. I imagined George Clooney poking his head into the basement, "What do you want in your omelet?"

I shook myself and kept going.

If this was written by Nabokov, what inspired him to write about baseball? What could have drawn him to Babe Ruth? It seemed to fall outside his strengths. Maybe his editor encouraged him to try something more plausibly commercial than the memoir. " 'Speak, *What*'? Try crime, sex, even sports," the editor may have advised. "Or what about a humor book?"

The characters were Babe, his sweethearts, and his fans, in a wild portrait of obsession, American style.

Baseball was a game I knew nothing about. My father wanted a girl child specifically so he would not have to teach her baseball. I'd never seen a whole game. No one had ever explained the rules to me. When I did watch baseball—or worse, played in one of those enforced camp or school events—it seemed like a sport where nothing happened for a long time, and then something would happen and people would cheer or shout derisively, sometimes at me. I never knew why and was embarrassed to ask. I'd given up long ago ever partaking in the enjoyment of baseball.

But this story on the index cards had captured the wildness of the ballplayer's fame: the young women chasing Babe Ruth, the way he made them lose control, lose all sense of decorum, young female baseball fans lobbing their knickers onto the dugout roof.

The images of the small ballpark landed perfectly, like the discarded hot dog bun trodden underfoot, pale and open like a moth. But when the Babe stepped up to the plate, there were nearly blank cards. One in the middle had a short list of baseball words: *squeeze play, suicide bunt*. That missing scene was a hole in the book, a frustrating gap. I found my attention straying to the cold draft on my neck, my stiff fingers, and a dire thirst for coffee.

One of the writer's main fascinations seemed to be with the idea of being a fan, the willingness to participate in a group identity. He portrayed that collective-identity aspect in a nearly freakish way, fans wearing the colors of the Yankee uniform, forsaking their individual selves in a carnival show of fan love, disappearing into the folly and joy of a crowd.

I was reminded of my own experience with sports, watching all the puzzling and dull moments, the moments when I wondered why I was spending my time this way, sitting on the stands, warm soda spilling from my cup, glad that the lives down there were not my own, alienated from the avid fans around me.

About halfway through the stacks of cards I compiled a list of the invented place-names. The writer seemed to have enjoyed the town names of Upstate New York, poking mild fun at the Native American sounds: Onkwedo and Otseekut. I wondered whether the writer was aware of the modern linguistic analysis showing that all the place-names in this area are traced to a common root, borrowed from the Seneca tribe that translates roughly to "Pink-face, go home."

I stopped typing only for toast. I didn't even meet Bill by the mailbox. It took me two days, but when I finished—after I had taken each word through my eyes and out my fingertips—I felt I had earned the right to have the book in my possession.

For the first time since moving to Onkwedo, I felt I might have something to share with the world. If the book was by Nabokov—even though it might not be his strongest work, or work that he wanted the world to see—I knew that I must help it find its readers.

Leslie Daniels

And even if it wasn't Nabokov's work, the story could bring together the people who liked to read about sports and the people who liked to read about love. The book could be a meeting place for the interests of men and of women. But that wasn't my concern. My job was clear: to bring the book to public attention, to get it into the right hands.

LAWYER

I needed someone who knew how the world of found literary treasure worked. From the internet I got the name of an entertainment lawyer. His office was in the city, of course, since there was no entertainment in Onkwedo (unless you counted reading about your neighbors' DWI convictions in the *Clarion*'s Crime Calendar). I picked the lawyer because his office was five blocks from my favorite croissant shop, Ceci-Cela. I called and made an appointment for the next afternoon.

It would be my first time back to the city since I had moved Upstate. I wasn't sure if my car could make the trip, so that left the bus. I got up at four a.m. and put on the Pants. My underwear assortment was now the dead letter office of panties. In the business tote I borrowed back from my daughter, I carried my one remaining pair of city shoes and "dinner" in a cottage cheese container: a decent pasta salad with good oil and minced chives. The tote also contained the typescript of *Babe Ruth* and a photocopy of the original title page card.

The bus, inaptly called the Short Line, rambled along, making stops for buying drinks and using restrooms. The driver came from a failed career as a wedding singer. He sang along to Motown on a latte-size radio which must have been against regulations. "I'm a Soul Man," he sang each note flat. He was so distinctly not a soul man.

When I arrived, the Port Authority bus terminal was exquisitely filthy. I walked out on the Eighth Avenue side and called to the bustling street, "Hi, honey, I'm home." No one looked at me, which counted as the first brand-new thing I loved about the city.

Going back to New York City once you have stopped living there is like visiting an old lover who has found someone new. Your old love is wearing trendy clothes that seem a little tight but still desperately in fashion. You miss him, and you feel like you know his vices better than she does. But it doesn't matter, because you are old news.

I leaned against the Port Authority building and changed into my squeaky shoes. People do that kind of public personal grooming all the time in New York City, and no one stares at them with disapproval. I gave the shoes a quick back-of-the-pants buff, and I was ready to meet the entertainment lawyer.

The Pants and I walked east toward his office, because after the bus ticket, I had the cash (three dollars and twenty-five cents) to buy one fabulous chocolate croissant from my favorite bakery and nothing more, certainly not taxi money. The color of the Pants was aubergine. It went well with nothing. The cut of the Pants was noncommittal. I told myself frequently that they would do, but I didn't believe myself. Every pair of pants I passed seemed to have more of an opinion than mine.

When I lived in the city, I was almost beautiful. (I *think* that was true.) I had the kind of looks that people would get interested in changing, a raw-material, fixer-upper type of beauty. But coming back from Upstate at nearly forty, wearing my dumb clothes, I felt like no one noticed me at all. Maybe the Pants were actual invisibility pants.

The lawyer's office was on a swanky block in the East Forties. The decor was fancy/neutral, with polished granite walls outside and series art inside: big beige painting, bigger beige painting, biggest of all beige painting (Cy Twombly meets the Three Billy Goats Gruff).

In the waiting room on the twenty-ninth floor, the lawyer's assistant appeared. His name was Max and he was wearing a big square blazer, inside of which he could have been any shape at all. Max ushered me into a conference room made entirely of velvet and steel and left me there. Except for the spotlights on the paintings, there was no light. The five-hour bus ride caught up with me, and my eyelids got very heavy. As I was drifting off, I must have reached up to stroke the velvety surface of a painting, because Max's voice startled me awake: "Don't touch, please." It sounded friendly, but as though Max often had to deal with art petters.

He waved me through an inner hallway to another door, and I followed him. Max might have been a robot, or simply the smoothest-walking person in loafers. Inside the door was a big desk with the entertainment lawyer behind it, talking on a headset.

I sat in a suede chair facing his desk. The entertainment lawyer had the only sexy comb-over I had ever seen. It was actually a comb-back, making his skull look like a set of drag racing strips. While he was talking, his right hand typed and his left did something entirely different. I think it was working on a separate case.

There were framed photos on the desk, and I edged over in my chair so I could see them. I was relieved to find out he was not one of those lawyers who has pictures of his wife in a bikini on his desk. He may still have been with the starter wife. In one photo she was wearing extreme skiing gear, holding her helmet under her arm. Two tall children stood beside her, each with a snowboard. They were fair and strong looking, like a master race.

He finally finished his call and looked up. I began talking fast. I knew that time was money, and the money was mine.

I told him how I found the index cards, and I started to tell him the plot. I got as far as "baseball love story," and he held up his hand for me to stop.

"There are two issues," he said extending a long finger. "One: Is it by Vladimir Nabokov? I can find that out. It won't cost you your first-born child." He did not smile. "The quality of the book is not important," he said breezily. "It could be shit." I flinched. "Let's say it was actually written by Nabokov." He held up a second finger (during all this his left hand continued to work on the other case). "Do you want to sell it to a collector as an artifact or to the public as a book?"

He waited as if he were counting dollars jumping into his bank account.

"Wouldn't it belong to his son, Dimitri Nabokov?" I asked.

"Technically it's trash. Discarded papers are trash. If there had been an attempt to retain the pages on the part of Nabokov, then it would be remaindered to his estate. But since he clearly discarded the pages, and there is no one who can refute that, I think we might be able to consider that the provenance is clear." He almost made sense. "Of course there might be a fight." The idea of a fight seemed to make him happy. He sounded like who he was: someone accustomed to picking a position and justifying it, winning.

"But would it get published? Would there be an actual book that people could read, or would it go into someone's private collection?" His left hand actually stopped working. "It's a great book," I said. "The love parts are amazing. The sports parts will interest a lot of, um, men," I said, my voice rising unintentionally. "Something for everyone," I added lamely.

"Then you will need a book agent," he said dismissively. "There is a good one in Onkwedo, right where you came from, Margie Jenkins. She mostly handles romances, but she knows publishing."

"Onkwedo?" I was incredulous. I couldn't believe he was sending me back Upstate. Worse, he thought I *came* from there.

I handed him the copy of the manuscript title page, which he put in his in-box without a glance. He told me that he might need the original but that he would "ascertain the veracity" and get back to me quickly.

Then he asked me where I bought my shoes. This was his way of telling me to get up out of his six-thousand-dollar chair and leave. He walked me to the elevator and gave me his card. His hand was wonderfully rough and dry, like a real person's.

As I walked toward my favorite bakery, I marveled at all the people surrounding me with places to go. I had forgotten that aspect of life in the city, everyone had a destination. I reveled in the movement, the dazzling fact of all those bodies in motion. Underneath the blare of car horns and the whoosh of buses, I could hear the polyrhythms of our feet: some gaits loose, some tight, staccato. In the middle of the block there was a measure when it all came into sync on the sidewalk. It was a hot, deeply funky beat. I felt it settle in my hip sockets like molten chocolate: I could have danced to the meter. Approaching the avenue from opposite directions, two midgets crossed, passing shoulder to low-down shoulder, no eye contact. It was perfectly staged. I could hear God in the wings saying, "Cue the midgets."

There is magic that keeps people in the city. Just as you decide to leave because your job got eliminated or your bike-riding friend got hit by a taxi or the newspaper man spat as he handed over your change, just when you set your sights on a green, quiet place with all the amenities of ordinary life, something magical happens: a two-bedroom apartment opens up in the West Village, a waiter gives you a free side of the chef's lime-cilantro sea scallop ceviche, you hear three teenagers in pink body stockings singing a cappella on the subway platform, better than the Marvelettes. And you know you can't leave.

But I did. And now I had returned like I was the jilted one, trying to look good, trying to act right so I wouldn't stand out as no longer belonging.

The awning of the bakery appeared, yellow-and-blue-striped. I wondered if Pierre would be serving, or one of his chic *cousines* from Paris. But the plate glass window had no pastries in it. The wooden bench beside the door was gone. The overhanging sign was replaced by a brass plaque announcing a real estate office.

I stood there and stared at the condo layouts displayed in the window, each one more industrial Euro chic than the last. My tongue curled in protest.

In New York City, money is like a big eraser rubbing out the past.

I could have found another croissant shop, but I didn't want any croissant; I wanted one made by Pierre with everything he knew from his life in Paris, with the bitter chocolate inside the perfect flaky pastry.

Back at the bus station, I bought a couple of newspapers with the croissant money and joined the line for the Onkwedo bus. I stood behind a group of people in dark suits, waiting with their luggage. They had just arrived from Beijing and were heading to the Astrophysics Department at Waindell University. I read my newspapers, first the *Times* and then the *Post*. I tried to think about world events and crime, but my mind kept sliding to the way dark chocolate looks in the middle of a hot croissant.

By the time I got on the bus, the seats were full, except for the one behind the driver where you can't see anything but the back of his head. It was the soul man again. I stuffed tissue in my ears. Rooting around in my business tote, I found I had brought Nabokov's *Pale Fire*. The book came from my cousin's collection of paperbacks, swollen from the dampness aboard his sailboat. I could tell that *Pale Fire* had been his favorite. It was so old and worn that it wouldn't stay closed, flopping open to the end of Canto Three.

My cousin wasn't the kind of person to write in the margins. I didn't respect people who wrote in books, but I wished he had left some pencil marks on his favorite passages, or dotted the places that made him laugh. I would have liked to know if we laughed at the same things.

In *Pale Fire,* Nabokov wrote, "The heating system was a farce." I think he may have been referencing his tenancy in what was now my house: nothing between the indoor climate, ". . . and the arctic regions save a sleezy front door." I knew that same breezy front door.

The Old Daitch Dairy job had made me a fast reader. In the time it took most people to slit an envelope, I already knew whether the writer was going to get a free pint of ice cream or simply a customer appreciation note, but I couldn't barrel through *Pale Fire.* The words were as much like math as they were like language, each word acting upon the one before it, changing the meaning, changing the outcome. By the time we hit curvy Route 17, the bus swaying from side to side, I had nearly given up on my ability to understand it. I felt like the book was reading me.

Maybe none of his work, but certainly not *Pale Fire,* contained confirmation of who I was. It was all about who I was not. The words took me to the edge of some great, unknowing place as if I were staring at the night sky from the crust of the moon. I felt right up against what I didn't know. Not just the stupidity of my American education but the limitations of my thoughts going over simple recipes and grocery lists, again and again, like a cow slogging between the barn and the pasture, and along the other rutted path: hating the experson, wanting my children back so my life would start.

Nabokov wrote much of *Pale Fire* in verse. How impossible is that? It's impossible. He had a wife for all his life. Maybe he wasn't faithful, but he loved her all his life. They grew old together, with tenderness, without boredom. How impossible is that?

I looked around the bus at the couples sleeping on each other's shoulders. I found myself envying couples, not the young ones—plump and smug, trolling through the mall, with the hell of their lives ahead of them—but the gaunt old ones, helping each other in and out of cars, finding the right cantaloupe, the right turning place on the road, walking together in the mornings to keep up their strength. I yearned for their naked tenderness.

And then I told myself sternly that I couldn't stand the boredom of fifty years together.

I would never know if that was true.

I pulled out my dinner. I kicked off my squeaky shoes and spread a newspaper over the Pants, opened the Old Daitch Dairy tub, and made the wretched discovery that it really *was* cottage cheese and not my pasta salad. Had to open and close it twice to make sure. I left it closed.

The typed manuscript of *Babe Ruth* was heavy in my tote. I tried to match up the complexity of *Pale Fire* with the words on the cards I had found. For the first time it occurred to me that maybe the found manuscript was written by the owner of the house, the engineering professor who had rented it to the Nabokovs. Maybe ole Professor Slide Rule was a baseball fan, and the story had nothing to do with Vladimir Nabokov at all.

I looked out the bus window at the stars in the pitch-black night. Sometimes it's better not to read, eat, or even to think.

AGENT

In the morning, back in Onkwedo, I looked up Margie Jenkins in the phone book. There she was: "Jenkins, Bill & Margie," no anonymity at all. I waited till seventeen minutes past nine to call her. She answered the phone with a deep smoker's cough. "It's Margie with a hard *G*," she said. I told her about finding the index cards and she interrupted me. "I know all about it. He called me after you left his office. We've known each other since college." She coughed again. "What's the story about?"

"Baseball."

"Jesus H. Christ," Margie said, "*everybody* has to write a freaking baseball book."

"And it's a love story," I added hopefully. I told her about Liza, the very young girl who had "known fifteen summers" before the one where she knew the Babe. I also told her about the missing baseball scene.

"Send me a copy," she said. "I have to take one of my cats in to be put down, I need something decent to read." I asked her where she lived. "Just give it to Bill, he can bring it home." I must have been quiet for too long, because Margie explained patiently to me: "Bill is my husband. Bill is your mailman. Bill lives with me." Her voice, aside from the rasp, had the warmest and most openhearted sound I had heard in a long time.

"Thank you," I said, but she had hung up.

I put the typed copy of the manuscript in an envelope and left it in the mailbox for Bill. Margie's voice made me long to be around people. The only place in my life that resembled a community gathering place was Apex Friendly Market. Sometimes, even if I didn't need anything, I would go there to see the Onkwedons and join the everydayness of their lives. We all ate. Some of us still cooked. And we all wandered through Apex trying to find sustenance among the brightly colored plastic and cardboard packages.

Apex did not have great food. The only good thing about the place was the Wednesday specials, helpful for staying within my thirty-dollar no-kids weekly food budget. Oh, and one of the cashiers. If I had a type—and I don't—he might be it: slightly wild looking, like he had just come in from a glade, silky hair, damp sheen on his skin. He looked like he smelled fascinating. There was something ready about him, like if someone said to him, come to the waterfall right now, he would close the cash drawer, take off his red apron and his red pin-on name tag, and leave.

Though probably not with me.

He was a very slow checkout person. I only stood in his line when I wanted to look at him or read the magazines. At *Psychology Now,* I once fact-checked an article on a study showing that the only consistent gender difference in employment efficiency is evident in tasks involving both repetitive decision making and people, like ringing up groceries while having to speak to customers. In a job like that, women perform at a rate that is 175 percent faster than their male counterparts. The reason for this, the article speculated, is that for males such tasks involve switching modalities from object to person, while for females the modality remains the same. If you could get inside it, the male brain would look like this: thing, *shift,* person, *shift,* thing, *shift,* person. The female brain would look like this: thingandpersonandthingandperson. The article suggested that you think of the male brain as a set of railroad tracks and the female brain as a canal or drainage ditch.

I was standing in the slow lane reading the relationship advice in the women's magazines. No matter what pattern of dysfunction or miscommunication was described in a couple, it resonated with what the experson and I had experienced together. It comforted me to know we were such a garden variety of bad couplehood.

I looked at the other shoppers around me. None of them seemed to have thought at all about their clothes that day. I suspected that no one had even looked in a full-length mirror. It was the usual "This still almost fits me" kind of outfit. Apex didn't even stock *Vogue* magazine, not that it would have helped me, considering the contents of my wardrobe. I had worn my clothes the day before. And the day before that.

When at last it was my turn to check out, I could see that the wild cashier was having a bad day. He had his head down and was slamming grocery items into plastic bags. He didn't offer the choice of paper or plastic, a choice I like.

I couldn't think of anything appropriate to say, so I just shoved my groceries along, helping the conveyor belt. I wanted to say, Quit your job and let's go to the waterfall, but I didn't think he would accept this invitation from someone who was buying cabbage, onions, and storebrand rubber gloves. I never got to see his thick eyelashes or his delicately drawn lips. He didn't look up at me at all.

Back at home, I looked through a pile of cookbooks Sam had assembled, and tried to make one of food writer Mark Bittman's twentyseven cabbage soup recipes, the one that calls for a surprising amount of water and caraway seeds. I skipped the caraway seeds because I didn't have any and I couldn't face going back to Apex Friendly Market.

The soup didn't come out well. Mark Bittman promised that it would taste better the next day, but I doubted it. He promised that the soup would remind people of their grandmother's kitchen on a Sunday afternoon, but I didn't come from that kind of grandmother. Both of my grandmothers grew up in homes that employed cooks. They each arrived at marriage knowing how to play the piano—one very well—and not much else, maybe how to make toast. Their marriages lasted until death, however, which tells you that playing the piano is underrated as a marital skill.

For once, I was grateful that the children were not with me to eat the soup. I knew exactly what they would say. My son would be too polite to show his disgust at the table, but Darcy would not be.

I finished the wretched bowl of soup and returned to my real work, the Old Daitch Dairy mail. I tried to treat myself as both employee and manager. I told myself that I was dedicated to my work: matching each letter with the exact right tone in my response. Young Mr. Daitch would never know how much I shone in his service. His only concern with me was how many stamps I used. He was afraid that I pinched stamps, or squandered them, decorating envelopes with extra ones. But I didn't.

One letter delivered that day was written on plum-colored lined paper, in carefully connected cursive script.

Dear Daitch Company,
It has come to my attention that you have discontinued the licorice chunk. Would you please let me know if it will be reinstated in the

near future, or if there is a way for me to special order it? If there is a way to special order it, would there be a minimum quantity that I would need to buy, and if so, how much would that be?

Thank you very much and I look forward to your reply.

Sincerely,

I'd have noticed that people who write to dairy companies are all sincere unless they are "Yours truly" or "Best wishes" or Triple Fudge from Onklervill, who signed off "Love, Onklervill."

I didn't know the dairy ever made licorice chunk—how disgusting. I'd have to check with young Mr. Daitch on that. At the start of my job, he'd given me a list of discontinued flavors. He wanted me to mark off the ones that were requested frequently. The only flavor that seemed consistently missed was cherry vanilla. They made cherry vanilla ice cream only in July, their Independence Day featured flavor.

The reason they didn't make cherry vanilla anymore was that his mother, old Mrs. Daitch, used to pick the cherries and pit them by hand. When Mrs. Daitch died, the flavor was retired, either out of respect for her or because they couldn't find anyone else who would pick and pit for free.

I tried to be efficient and simply move through the four stacks of letters to Old Daitch Dairy that awaited me, but I liked thinking about the people associated with my work, both the Daitch family and the people who wrote the letters. I was always left with more questions than answers. Stop dreaming, I told myself, and finish your work. Paper recycling was the following day, and I wanted to finish all the week's mail in time to recycle the envelopes. It wasn't necessary, but it gave some rhythm to my workweek.

Before going to bed each night, I drove by the experson's house to see if the lights were on in the children's bedrooms. Once I saw my son bouncing on the top of his bunk bed. I drove over a small piece of the experson's lawn because I was watching. If he had put them to bed on time, his lawn wouldn't have a deep gash from my tire.

NEST

One last letter before I was done. It was my weekend for the children and I could hardly concentrate.

Dear Old Daitch Dairy:

Thank you for all the ice cream! Every Sunday night my wife and I have a "Sundae Supper." I think you should make more flavors with chocolate and she agrees. Here is a sundae recipe I invented. My wife says it's better than sex.

Chocolate Surprise:

(What followed was a revolting series of toppings and oozy junk that didn't belong together, the worst culinary miscegenation since the gastronomy expert Mark Bittman gave up fluffernutter as an ingredient in his midnight snacks.)

I look forward to hearing back from you!

Sincerely,

Matthew O'Reilly

Ovid, NY

For him I used a form letter.

> *Dear Faithful Customer:*
>
> *Thank you for your letter. We regret that the volume of correspondence does not allow us to answer each letter personally.*
>
> *We hope you continue to enjoy our fine products. Please join us at the Old Daitch Dairy Scoop, open every summer on Route 323 just east of Onkwedo.*
>
> *Sincere wishes for your good health,*
> *Old Daitch Dairy*

I sent that to Mr. Matthew O'Reilly. In a separate envelope, a plain one addressed to his wife, Mrs. O'Reilly, I put my cousin's well-thumbed paperback of *The Kama Sutra*. It used up the last of the postage stamps.

I was dragging the paper recycling to the road when the experson drove up in his sports car. He rolled down the window. I could see the children crammed in the back, but he wasn't about to let them out till he was ready. "Hi, Barb." The experson looked good. He looked better since I left him. Not better *to* me; better *than* me. It was unfair.

He pointed to the back of my car, parked next to his in the driveway, and filled to the roof with empties. "Are you drinking all that beer?"

I felt even stupider and lumpier than I usually did around the experson. "I collect the bottles and take them to the redemption center." I said this like it was some kind of altruism, some kind of community service I did in my spare time.

But he knew me too well. "Barb, you cannot pay down a mortgage in nickels. You'll have to find a better way to make money." He was right, of course. He knew how little I took home from the Old Daitch Dairy. The most reliable feature of the experson was his rightness. He always thought of me as a lazy person. He may have been right about that too.

I reminded myself that once upon a time we loved each other, although I couldn't remember why. I told myself to smile at him. I did this. I smiled at him because he had my children and I wanted them back. I tried to remember his name, but hatred was clouding my name recall system and I couldn't.

Finally he let the children out of the car. As he drove away, I waved to his sleek car fender, the smile stuck on my face like the half-price sticker on a loaf of day-old bread.

Sam and Darcy were with me at last. We went inside. I helped them make a nest from all the bed pillows and the yellow duvet. We lay in it. Darcy was peeping. "Have a worm," Sam said, feeding her strands of cold spaghetti. I tried to get up to make us a proper dinner, but they wouldn't let me go. "Tell us about when you were little," Sam said. I told them about my father digging me a sand cave at the beach, and how he made the roof from driftwood. They listened, Sam's leg draped over mine, Darcy holding my arm. I told them about the house he made for me from a refrigerator carton. He cut arched windows into it and painted it red. One August I left home and lived in the backyard inside that box. I told them about all the houses my father made for me; doll houses and play houses and, later, the apartments he painted and built bookshelves for. "He wanted me to know how to make a home," I said. "Like a bird teaches its babies to build a nest."

We sat in the pillows and thought about their grandfather.

"What happens to your clothes after you die?" Darcy asked me.

"Sometimes people's clothes are given to their friends or their family, sometimes just donated to the Salvation Army," I said.

"I don't want yours," Darcy said, "but maybe someone else will."

"Don't talk about it," Sam insisted.

It was dusk. I made the fastest cream of tomato soup I knew. We ate that and went to bed. Darcy slept beside me, holding on to a fistful of my hair. I extricated myself and went to check on Sam. He was nearly asleep, but as I leaned over him, he inhaled deeply.

"That's your smell," he said, his eyes closed.

BREAKFAST

I awoke before the children and made a pot of black tea and carried it down to the computer. There was an email from my mother. My mother and I did our best communicating by email. We had a tacit agreement about the hierarchy of communication. Email was better than phone. Phone was distinctly better than seeing each other. If we must see each other, it was better to be in public with other people around. Email was ideal. It wasn't that I disliked her, rather that I distrusted her highly flexible relationship with the truth.

My mother didn't like bad things to happen to anyone, particularly herself. To be fair, she didn't like bad things to happen to me either, so she pretended they didn't. Her warding off of bad things involved vigorous revisions of reality. When I was a child, she told me two years in a row that "Grandma is in Florida and can't come for Christmas." The third year, I pinned her down and discovered that Grandma was dead.

Since the ghastly custody decision, whenever anyone asked after me, she informed them that the experson and I were "taking some time off."

I read her cautiously worded email. She wanted to know if we had any plans for Darcy "in the next few months." She again mentioned her growing fondness for the doctor who had attended my father at the end of his life. In a dumb sweep of caffeine-activated brain functioning, I got it. My mother was planning to marry the doctor and wanted Darcy to be the flower girl.

We all move along, don't we? I thought uncharitably. She seemed to be experiencing my father's death as the temporary absence of a husband.

After I used up every bad word I could think of for the medical profession, it dawned on me that I would have to wear a dress. The Pants would never cut it at her wedding.

I emailed my mother back.

> *Is there a role in your upcoming nuptials for Sam?*
> *Yr. Daughter*
> *P.S. He has gotten larger.*

(My mother thinks that I am psychic, but I found it easier with her to simply cut the preliminaries.)

> *P.P.S. I do not own a dress.*

Well, it would be better than going to the experson and the social worker's wedding, if they were to get married. Then I remembered how unlikely it was that I would be invited. I turned off the computer and, for good measure, pulled out its plug. I went upstairs to start breakfast.

For the children I made soft-boiled eggs and toast. The toaster came with the house. It dated back to Vera and Vladimir's time, and was as round as an Airstream trailer, with a frowsy cloth cord cover.

For myself I attempted a "health crepe." It was a bad idea, and I realized it only at the instant of plunging the blender wand into the single blobby egg and mound of wheat germ. The wheat germ tornadoed

around, landing on the toaster and my bare feet. I
inspiration was for that breakfast—something w
pour syrup on?

I would like to be one of those people who has her own iden
breakfast. Breakfast for me began the dumbly improvisational nature of
my days: Monday, who am I? Poached egg. Tuesday, who am I? Gra-
nola. And so on.

Vladimir probably awoke every morning to Vera's good coffee and
a roll with preserves, then moved with grace and speed into his well-
planned writing day.

Over breakfast I told the children about their grandmother's remar-
riage intentions. I had to explain the idea of a flower girl to Darcy in
great detail. She disappeared into her room, and I was left with Sam
as I collected dishes and sipped a second cup of tea. I fought the feeling of the weekend gathering speed toward the time when they would
leave me.

Sam had moved his pile of cookbooks to the table and was looking
through them. "Do you do everything they say?" he asked me, turning
the pages of *The Naked Chef*.

"I read the recipes, but then I do what I want." I try always to tell
my children the truth.

"I wouldn't want to eat food from someone who wasn't wearing
clothes," Sam said, and I agreed. "Anyway, he might burn himself."
Sam, like his father, was a practical person.

"We could make a cookbook, Barb," Sam said. He hadn't called me
Mom since the experson and I separated. "It would need a catchy title
like *Joy of Cooking*, but not exactly that."

Outside the window, Darcy trudged past. Under her winter jacket
she wore a long black dress. She'd drawn eyebrows heavily across her
forehead with my mascara. At her chest she clasped a small bunch of

gs that she was breaking and tossing vigorously into the snow in front of her.

"What is she doing?" Sam asked me.

"I think she's practicing for Grandma's wedding," I said. "She's going to be the flower girl."

"Do I have to be anything in the wedding? I don't want to carry the rings." Sam's voice sounded fearful.

"Grandma may need some help deciding about the food. Would you like to give her some advice about what hors d'oeuvres to serve?"

"No thank you. Well, maybe," he amended. "Baked Brie en croûte is my favorite." He pronounced it like kraut.

"Mine too," I said. "You could put that in our cookbook."

Darcy made another loop around the house, following her tracks through the muddy snow across our view. She had a fresh bunch of sticks that she was distributing. Sam and I watched her from the window, but she didn't look up at us. "She looks cute," Sam said, "but not in a wedding kind of way."

He returned to the cookbook pile. "My cookbook might have a lot of mistakes," he said. "Real chefs make something ten different ways to see what's best. When I cook with you, we throw things together. Some of our recipes don't come out and we still eat them." He was right, of course. I didn't know he had noticed. He continued, "Most of our dishes wouldn't ever be served in a restaurant."

"Restaurants aren't the only place good food is found," I said. "Sometimes the best thing is to make some food and eat it together and go on with your life."

Sam thought about this. "We could call it *Ate It Anyway*," he suggested.

Darcy trudged past a third time. The zigzag part dividing her black sweeps of hair gleamed white like a lightning bolt. She had run out of sticks and was throwing handfuls of stones on the path. Her expression under the big mascaraed eyebrows was grim.

I put my hand on Sam's soft shoulder. "*Ate It Anyway* sounds just right," I said. He didn't shrug me off. We stood like that waiting for Darcy to make another pass.

Too soon their father came. The experson was meticulously punctual, arriving at the dot of three to collect them. I walked them to his car and stood beside it, waving to them through the back window and smiling as best I could.

As they drove off, my heart felt pulled almost outside my body. My relationship with their father passed in front of me, and I tried to reconstruct it in a positive way, making myself nicer, thinner, better able to follow directions. Then, as though my memory had been sucking in its gut, the real me came whooshing back.

I turned to the house, stepping over a trail of Darcy's sticks and stones to reach the front door. Inside I picked up after the children, noting Sam's systematic piles and Darcy's distinctive chaos. I longed to picture their faces, but it hurt too much, so I didn't.

CREAM

I couldn't bear being in the house alone for a moment longer. I drove to the Old Daitch Dairy to get more postage stamps and to lobby for the discontinued flavor I had received the most letters about, cherry vanilla.

The farm was on a windy field overlooking the lake. The road divided the barn from the house, both of which stood too close to the newly widened blacktop.

It was a raw time of year. Inside, the barn was sweet with cow breath. It was beautifully kept, floors swept and gutters sluiced. There was even baseboard heating.

Beside the office entrance hung a round painting that I suspected young Mr. Daitch had done on LSD decades ago. It was an Amish kind of mandala, painted with a two-haired brush. From far away it looked like a colorful swirl, but as I walked past it, I could see that it was made up of a thousand ants marching in a spiral right into hell.

Though he was reclusive and tried to avoid me, young Mr. Daitch worked seven days a week, and he was there in the office, sitting on a high wooden stool at his desk. He was a thin man with an inner stillness that was almost creepy. It made me want to startle him into a wasted movement, just to see if it was possible.

I greeted him a little too loudly and watched his head swivel deliberately toward me.

Mr. Daitch puzzled me, as did most men. In school I never really liked playing with boys, until later, when they started chasing me. Even then, they remained strange to me. I found it was better not to look at Mr. Daitch when I talked to him. That way, his behavior didn't rattle me.

I looked down at the desk legs, each collared in a tin can filled with turpentine. I'd learned at our first meeting that this was young Mr. Daitch's protection against ants. He told me during my job interview that ants are a big problem throughout upper New York state. I took his word for it, although I'd never seen any ants inside the barn.

He unlocked a drawer and extracted a sheet of postage stamps. "I suppose you came for these." He passed me an accounting form to sign and mail to Ginna. The stamp for that envelope was already noted on the form as "interoffice," a grandiose term for going from a barn to a kitchen table.

I thanked him and said my piece: "There seems to be a strong desire for cherry vanilla to come back into circulation."

Mr. Daitch sighed.

I waited.

He was taking me in. I could feel his eyes on my shoes, my pants, my self-inflicted haircut ("fringe trim," I lied to myself), my rain slicker covering the fact that I was wearing two ratty T-shirts.

I waited some more while his eyes went past me to a cow framed in the open barn door, her square, wet nose pointing toward the lake. "We have extra cream, if you want it," Mr. Daitch said, apropos of nothing.

I reminded myself that some men needed to be treated like woodland creatures. I stood very still and looked at a spot on the wall near him, but not close enough that he would be concerned about the pupils of our eyes meeting. I held my hands open and slightly in front of me where he could see them.

"Cream," I said. "Are you sure you can spare it?" It was an inane question and Mr. Daitch didn't reply. Instead, he climbed down from his stool, fast and sideways like a spider after a fly. He disappeared into the refrigeration room and returned with a wide-mouth gallon jar, filled nearly to the lid with cream, which he set on his desk after lifting it to inspect the bottom solemnly for ants.

I thanked him, wondering if we would return to the cherry vanilla discussion. Before I could think of a way, Mr. Daitch spoke. "People don't know the taste of cream anymore." His voice sounded sad. "In my grandfather's time, we used to make plain iced *cream,* no vanilla even, just a little sugar. Now they want everything too sweet, and they want it to last forever. Stabilizers, guar gum," he snorted derisively. "People can't taste anymore."

My boss was his own man. I was not sure what his point was, but it was clear that it had very little to do with me. That was another thing I'd learned about men from the experson: just because you were there sharing a conversation didn't mean the conversation had anything to do with you.

I thanked him for the cream again and wondered if we were finished. I could have done the conventional thing and told him how much I enjoyed the work, and also how good I was at it. Neither of these was strictly true, and I would be flattering myself to think that answering dairy mail was a special skill. I went back to my main point, "Mr. Daitch"—I'd rehearsed this part—"your mother contributed one of the most popular flavors this county ever tasted. Not everybody likes cherry vanilla, but some people would drive down from as far as Onoontchewa to have your mother's cherry vanilla. Is there any way I can give them some hope that this flavor will be restored?"

It was the longest speech I had ever given young Mr. Daitch, and it left me breathless.

Mr. Daitch looked at the cream, then pointed his face to the small wooden window over his desk. His eyes reached past the line of bare cherry trees bordering the pasture. "When things go," he said, "they are gone."

He turned back to the papers on his desk. I thanked him a third time for the cream, pocketed the stamps, and with two hands lifted the heavy jar off his desk.

Back at home, I looked up butter making on the internet. The recipe instructed the butter maker to shake the cream for exactly forty-seven minutes, emphasizing that it must be done by hand: *Do not under any circumstances use the blender.* Then pour off the whey and add salt *to the cook's individual taste.* As though the cook would eat the umpteen pounds of butter all by herself. I went to sleep.

ONKWEDO ELEMENTARY

In the morning I set the timer for forty-seven minutes. I put on some zydeco music and shook the cream till my arms were exhausted. I tried tying it on a rope around my neck and bobbling it with my knees like a soccer ball. This worked pretty well except for the chafing on the back of my neck. Some globs of butter started to form, and by the twelfth song (I couldn't hear the timer over the music), the whole gallon had transformed.

I poured off the whey, to save for breakfast smoothies, should I ever feel the urge to start the day like that. I salted the butter lightly, tasting it before and after and during, and put it in the fridge in a bowl. I bet Vera Nabokov never made her own butter.

I started to make some bread in the bread machine for the children's afternoon snack—fresh bread and fresh butter sounded perfect—but I remembered that they would not be coming back to me, not getting off the bus hungry and needing me.

I stood in the middle of the kitchen, my empty arms hanging at my sides. The wall clock ticked loudly. It was before noon; the children were still at school.

In a blind rush, I put on my good-mommy scarf, something from the panties mausoleum, and the Pants of course, and headed out to Onkwedo Elementary School.

On the four block walk, I stopped into Elsie's Emporium for a newspaper. Elsie's window was draped in gray and green bunting, the Waindell University colors. Elsie told me to have a nice day, and I sang out, "You too," the way they do here.

Walking toward the school, I looked at the *Onkwedo Clarion*. Covering the front page was a photo of the Waindell crew team in their gray and green rowing shirts. You would think there was no real news in the world at all. The article invited readers to follow the monthlong series on the athletes, featuring "a new face in crew every single day."

At the school, while waiting for the receptionist to get off the phone, I opened to the sports section to see the day's rower. He was a handsome young man with a lot of cheekbone, Tim Somebody. He listed his condition as "great" and his hobbies as video games and sleeping. I tore out his profile and tucked it in my purse, more to look busy than anything else.

When the receptionist hung up, I told her that I was there to volunteer in the kindergarten. "Darcy's mother?" she said doubtfully. Maybe she had me on the potential kidnappers list. But she waved me toward Mrs. Contorini's room.

Mrs. Contorini was about to begin an activity concerning the letter *S*. The children were to rip black construction paper into the shape of a skunk and color it with white chalk. (In Onkwedo schools, scissors were now considered weapons.)

Darcy did not look happy to see me. "What are you *doing* here?" she snarled at me like I was blowing her cover.

"I came to help," I said.

"Help Corey." She pointed to a child with mucus dripping from his nose in two short columns, a snotty little Hitler. "He needs help."

I smiled at Mrs. Contorini, who gave me the warmest, fakest, most reflexive smile back. "Would you like to help Corey?"

"Sure." I didn't want to catch whatever he had, but I was willing to rip black paper with him while I spied on my daughter.

Darcy turned her little back on me. I offered Corey a box of tissues, which he stared at blankly. "It thtinks," he informed me, "the thkunk."

Corey was a kid interested in bad smells; I could see that about him. We ripped the tail and the paws and he chalked in the white stripe. All this without once using a tissue. When Mrs. Contorini rang the bell for cleanup, I helped gather the scraps of paper from the floor.

Darcy took her place at the end of the line without looking at me. She held her black lunchbox against her chest. The other girls stood with their partners. Corey was welcomed into a chuckling bunch of boys. Darcy stood alone, looking very beautiful, if odd, with a white feather paper-clipped to the back of her dark hair.

Mrs. Contorini made the children thank me for helping and marched them into the hallway.

I washed my hands three times, scrubbing up to the elbow. Without touching anything, I left the room in search of Sam.

His class was climbing the rope in the gym. I didn't know rope climbing was still sanctioned in elementary school, but here in Onkwedo there are pockets from the 1960s that are perfectly intact. Through the glass panels in the gym door I could see Sam holding the rope for another kid. I knew from his puckered forehead that Sam was not looking forward to his turn.

I watched the skinny monkey boys clamber up the rope. Even the girls could do it. I stepped back from the door so no one in the gym could see me watching.

Sam climbed the rope, now six, now twelve inches from the ground. His white arms in a skimpy-looking T-shirt tried valiantly to haul his soft backside away from the safe floor. The teacher stood close, in a kind way, both to encourage him and to protect him from the stares of his classmates, who were all frozen in different postures of watching my son fail to heave himself up the rope.

I couldn't bear it. I turned away, making my way blindly out the side door of the school.

I walked home without knowing it. Nothing looked familiar. I went inside my house and closed the door. I took my clothes off and got in the bathtub and cried. I don't know why I had to be naked to cry properly, but I did. Then I took a blanket to the couch and read *Babe Ruth* again.

I tried to read past the story to see what the person who wrote it cared about. It was a shape-shifting kind of book. The writer understood that even in the middle of the most ordinary of happy circumstances, shame and exposure lurked. I wasn't sure if the writer even believed in love, although there was a lot of love in the book. There were also long twisting paragraphs studded with horror—small shards of horror, like splinters of glass under fingernails.

I thought about Nabokov living here, looking out these same windows, wondering if it was going to rain on him when he walked to teach his class at Waindell. I wondered if Vera handed him the right coat for the weather, or drove with him in their big '46 Oldsmobile. I wondered if they ever went to a baseball game, and if they did, why?

None of these things were important, or even knowable, but the thoughts were a relief from my thoughts about the children and the impossible bleakness of living without them.

LUNCH

Margie called me midweek. "Solomon's dead, but I read your book."

"I'm sorry," I said.

"Well, he was old, thirteen. Bill found him when he was a wild barn kitten."

"Do you have other cats?" I asked her. I didn't really like pets, but I understood that this was something I shouldn't let people know about me. Besides, I was thrilled to be talking to an agent about the book. Only we weren't talking about the book.

"Seven." She coughed. "And allergies." She paused to breathe. "Tell me about yourself."

I told her everything: the kids living with the experson, the letter-writing job, my father. I even told her that I liked to cook.

There was a crash, which Margie explained as one of the cats knocking over her cherry Crystal Light.

"We should have lunch," she said.

"That would be nice," I said, hoping the thrill I felt didn't thrum in my voice. I'd heard that's how it was with agents: they took you to lunch. I wanted to go to a good restaurant in Onkwedo—maybe Bistro Moutarde, but really any restaurant—with an agent.

"How's one o'clock?" Margie didn't wait for an answer. "Come to my house. Bill can give you directions." She hung up.

I pulled clothes out of my closet and began trying to dress myself appropriately. I put on the goddam Pants, suede boots, and an orange turtleneck. I looked like a member of the road crew. I heard Bill's truck idling at my mailbox, and he tooted the horn till I came out. Bill told me how to get to their house on Lucy Lane. "It's not far," he said, "seven tenths of a mile."

I changed about six more times till I had on a version of the same thing, same pants of course. By then it was late, I was hungry and I left without looking in the mirror again. In my twenties I would have never done this. But at nearly forty, living in the fashion wasteland of Onkwedo, I thought, how good could I possibly look?

The house was a white ranch, like many of the houses in Onkwedo. Inside it had yellow walls and a sort of country-chintz decor, but I didn't notice this at the time because I was looking at my agent. She was tall and statuesque, as if someone had measured everything out before putting her together. Her clothing looked like it came from a magazine, everything going with everything. Each piece of her outfit was the same shade of taupe, but the textures were different, some fuzzy and touchable, some sleek.

"Come in." Margie took my jacket. "Well, aren't you a cute little thing?" she said. I was not used to thinking of myself as either cute or little, but next to Margie, maybe I was.

"Do you like grilled cheese?"

"Yes," I managed. I followed Margie into the kitchen. The house had cat ashtrays everywhere, maybe twenty-five all told. Many were displayed on shelves along the kitchen wall.

"Sit," she said. The tablecloth was linen with words cross-stitched on it, like a Scrabble game. I sat. Margie was making me a sandwich on her electric grill. I watched her carefully. I couldn't remember the last time someone made me a grilled cheese sandwich. She didn't ask me if I wanted mustard, just slathered it on, or squirted it really, since everything in her kitchen seemed to come from a squeeze bottle. She even squirted some ersatz butter onto the grill. "Zero calories," she informed me. I couldn't imagine what calorie-less butter would be made from—candle wax?

After she put our sandwiches and glasses of blue Crystal Light on the table, Margie sat down. It was the first time I could study her properly. Margie was beautiful. She had good facial muscles, maybe from smiling a lot or talking a lot or chewing gum. Everything on her face lifted up.

Grilled cheese sandwiches had apparently evolved since my mother's after-grade-school snack. These looked exactly right but contained new foods that weren't actually edible. The cheese was called Soyarella. Margie salted hers but barely took a bite.

"How do you like your new lawyer?" she asked me.

I was still choking down my first bite, so I nodded enthusiastically.

"He's the smartest person I ever met. We called him Summa in college, for summa cum laude. He earned all his own tuition money tutoring and got accepted at Waindell, only to find out his father had drunk it all away. He went to State."

I nodded some more, my teeth coated with Soyarella.

"The dad was a total lush, the only Jewish alcoholic I ever met."

I thought about that. I didn't know any Jewish alcoholics either, but they must be out there somewhere.

"Did he show you photos of his kids?" Margie sounded wistful. "Nice kids."

With my tongue I scoured the soy coating off my teeth. "I met his assistant, Max."

"He hires the same kind of kid he was: someone with all the smarts and none of the breaks."

I finished half of my sandwich, washing it down with the drink, which was the exact color of toilet bowl cleaner. I didn't know what the taste was supposed to be, possibly some kind of chewing gum. "He has an impressive office," I said.

"Great address," Margie said, "three doors up from the hottest cathouse in the city."

I smiled. I had absolutely no idea what she was talking about or why, but I really wanted her to like me.

One of her cats was scratching at the rug-covered post in the corner of the room in a way that made the hairs on my arm stand up. "Are you dating anyone?" Margie asked me.

I shook my head. I don't know why, but I gulped down the rest of my sandwich.

"There's someone out there for you," she said. "Someone wonderful. The universe is just getting him ready." She rattled the ice cubes in her glass. "Now let's talk about the book."

I held my breath while Margie talked. She thought that the love scenes were great and the setting was great. (She said nothing about it being Onkwedo by another name.) She thought the dialogue was great. "Whoever wrote this—and we really won't know till Sotheby's tells us—what an ear he had. Absolute fucking genius."

"What do you think could happen with the book?" I asked her.

"I never speculate about money," Margie said. "Doing that will make you crazy." She pushed her sandwich aside and lit up a cigarette. "The problem is that it's a love story *and* baseball, a wretched combination."

The cats and I watched a smoke ring rise.

"Would it have killed him to put more plot into it?" She stubbed her almost unsmoked cigarette out on her almost full plate. "Well, can't be helped."

Cats were circling her feet. One stood on the back of her chair, glaring at me, back arched and tail sticking straight up, like a witch's cat. I was grateful that they had left me alone so far, but I knew it was only a matter of time till they made a move on me.

We stood up. Or rather Margie did, so I did too. She looked me over. "When you go to the city again, to see old Summa or the Sotheby's people, I am going to lend you a sweater."

I didn't want to tell her how wool makes me itch. I wanted anything Margie wanted to give me. "Thanks. And thank you for lunch." I couldn't believe it was over already.

But it wasn't over. Margie led me through the trailer-like living room to a big square room with a skylight. She opened a wooden gate to let us in. There were bookshelves all around, window seats, wing chairs with reading lamps, and a large desk. "This is my office," she said. "Bill built this room with the proceeds from my first big hit."

"Which one was that?" I asked carefully, not sure if I was supposed to know already.

"It was huge. You probably saw it in paperback. It was a memoir, *Sleeping and Eating.*"

Outside were trees and birdfeeders. Twittering filtered through the closed windows. "I keep the cats out or they would go nuts trying to hunt the birds," Margie said.

I noticed there were no ashtrays either. "How can you work without smoking?" I asked before I realized how personal a question it was, but Margie didn't seem to mind.

"Smoking is only about food," she said. "And the cats, I love them, but I can't stand the way they smell."

The bookshelves lining the room were crammed. One wall of

spines was entirely pink, gold, and purple: the romances. The pillows on the window seats had words embroidered on them. *French Kiss* was stitched in red. I was afraid to read the others. I admired the skylight instead.

"Doesn't leak," Margie said proudly. "When Bill builds something, he does it right."

It sounded like a real marriage to me, full of understanding.

I decided it was time for me to leave. As I retrieved my jacket, I noticed a long thread dangling from the cuff. Margie noticed it too. "It matters how you look." She was studying my face to see if I was taking in this information. "Especially in New York City. It doesn't matter so much when you're twenty; there are fewer ways to go wrong."

I waited, listening.

"When you're older, it matters if you look prosperous, like you've done something with your time."

"About that sweater," I started to say.

She had clearly anticipated me, because she reached behind the closet door and handed me a dry cleaner's bag. The rustle of the plastic made the cats bristle. "Just be yourself; that's what they want to see."

"But why would they want to see me?" I asked.

"You found it," she said. "If they think it's real, they will need to believe in you as a plausible person to find a valuable manuscript. You are essentially selling yourself to them."

I don't know why it made me happy to be for sale, but as soon as I got out of sight of her house, I skipped the remaining six tenths of a mile home, the sweater in the plastic bag flapping over my shoulder like a poorly designed kite.

INSPECTION

Back at home I gave myself a pass on being a productive human being. Sometimes you can be a productive human being and sometimes you just have to read fiction, even romantic fiction.

Almost without leaving the couch, I sped through several of Margie's most successful romance novels. Each was about two people who absolutely should not be together living happily ever after. The pre-orgasmic heroines were younger, smaller, and poorer than the men who made love to them and made their lives complete. By those criteria, the experson and I should have been a raging success. They were redemption stories, the heroine moved from her "before" status to the "after" of sexual fulfillment and the one even more orgasmic step beyond it: commitment, a.k.a. marriage. It was propaganda, calling out with fervor to fallen women everywhere: Even though you have strayed from the fold, little sheep, you can still get to heaven on the back—or rather, the front—of a good man.

Something about reading those books makes you want to eat chocolate and dry-hump the couch cushions.

I resisted.

As if I'd conjured him, the experson called. He asked me to meet him for coffee at the Horizon Inn. In romance books, the couples share their deepest thoughts, but I'd found that it was better not to talk to the experson about anything. By the time he actually spoke to me, he had already had the conversation with me in his head, so what came out of his mouth was more a pronouncement than part of a discussion.

"When would you like to meet?" I asked politely.

"Tomorrow nine a.m." The phone clicked, signaling the end of our communication. Was there anyone in my life with appropriate telephone etiquette?

I had acres of time until I would learn what the experson needed to tell me, and I refused to think about him until I had to see his face. Instead, I continued to read romance novels.

I was still on the couch, in the midst of a steamy coupling scene, when the doorbell rang. A tall man wearing a brown McLean County jacket and holding a clipboard stood outside. Because of my romance reading, I first thought he might be a duke or a rock star in disguise.

"Good afternoon. This is an inspection visit from the family court," he said apologetically. He gracefully managed to avoid looking at my clothing, my usual *no one will see this* ragtag ensemble. "Are you Barbara Barrett?"

"Yes."

"Thank you." He made a note on his clipboard. I wondered if most of his visits were to people too hostile or stoned to sign their names. He handed me a document explaining that he was here on a court-mandated inspection, and that my cooperation was "strongly advised."

"I could go get some lunch and come back in an hour," he offered, careful not to look over my shoulder into the messy house, books piled everywhere. "Two hours. Here is their website with the FAQs." He pointed to the bottom of the page.

"Thanks." After he left, I checked the site and read up on vacuuming and asthma, secondhand smoke, the likelihood of grease fires in a dirty kitchen, and the inhalation of spray paint, also known as huffing.

I began cleaning and vacuuming as fast as I could. I hid all the nail polish remover and mineral spirits in the garage. I started to Q-tip-clean the stove but gave up and rushed to Apex (avoiding the wild boy checker's line) and bought multicolored kid-pack yogurts to fill the top shelf of the refrigerator along with a peck of apples on special. In the bathroom, I created individual toothbrushing stands with Flossing Is Your Friend signs. I took my daughter's pajamas out of my bedroom and put them under her pillow. I piled books into the size and shape of an ottoman and threw a blanket over them. It almost looked like a furnished house.

When the county employee came back, I noticed he was wearing beige suede gloves. He opened the door of the refrigerator. Several apples tumbled out. He looked surprised. "I bake pies," I said, scooping the apples off the floor and back into the fridge. It sounded defensive.

"I don't like pie," he said almost sadly. "Hot fruit. It's not my thing." He unfolded to his full six and a half feet, and I was reminded yet again of the unfair advantage of tall people.

"Look around," I said. "Ask me anything."

The inspector picked up the photo of the handsome rower I had torn from the sports pages of the *Onkwedo Clarion*. It had somehow landed in a prominent place on the kitchen table. He looked at me questioningly.

"I scrapbook," I said.

"My sister does that." He put the photo down. Under the three layers I was wearing so I wouldn't have to turn the furnace on, I could feel myself start to sweat.

The inspector walked dutifully through the house. He admired my son's stack of cookbooks. He picked up a photo of Sam in an antique silver frame. "He's a big-boned boy," he said. "Me too. I was like that. Loved to eat."

My daughter's room had a wall of magazine pages she'd carefully taped up. They were advertisements for perfume with the fragrance samples open and pungent. She called it her wall of smell.

"How old is she?" he asked.

"Five."

He stopped at the doorway of my bedroom and peered in. "Looks good," he said. We both knew he meant it looked lonely.

"Thank you," he said. "One more thing: Where is the TV?" He said it with the accent on the *T*.

"I am saving up for one." I pointed to a jar full of coins on the sideboard.

"Uh-hunh," he said, unconvinced, and made a mark on his clipboard.

"May I ask you a question?"

"Sure," he said without looking up.

"Who required this inspection?" I watched him shuffle his feet. I had never seen anyone actually do that, but he did, moving first one big foot and then the other.

"It's at the discretion of the custodial parent."

"Thank you," I said. "Would you like to see the dishwasher?"

"No, that's all right." He left looking grateful to be out again under the gray sky, his broad back moving toward a Lincoln Town Car that had seen better days.

"Have a nice evening," I called.

He waved a gloved hand at me without turning around.

TWO THINGS

Driving to the Horizon Inn, I remembered how specific the experson was in his location choices. No Onkwedons go to the Horizon Inn except for the weekend all-you-can-eat five-dollar breakfast buffet. It was the middle of the week. I suspected he chose the Horizon because he didn't want anyone he knew to see us together.

Inside, the restaurant was so dark it could have doubled as a mushroom-growing parlor. I sat where I could watch the door, at a maroon table in the nearly empty maroon and forest green room. I picked up the grubby spoon and wiped it on the hard green napkin. Maybe the experson and Irene wanted more couple time and he would like to off-load the children. I smiled at myself in the spoon.

Just then he breezed in and sat across from me, plopping the *Onkwedo Clarion* on the table between us. There was another bone-structure-blessed rower on the front page. "Coffee?" he asked me. I knew that when you were invited for coffee with the experson, it meant coffee, not coffee and a Danish, or coffee and a Danish and sex in a hotel room upstairs.

He got us two coffees from the serve-yourself bar because he couldn't wait another thirty seconds for the 280-pound waitress to come to the table. But she turned and waved. "Hi, John. How's it going?"

John, right. That was his name.

I'd put on mascara for this event and stashed a piece of chocolate from Sam's pre-Halloween candy in my green suede purse. I was trying to breathe without smelling the experson, John. I knew that if I smelled him, I might do whatever he wanted. John had a light but compelling scent.

He put my coffee in front of me and shoved the cream pitcher over. "What do you want?" I asked him. It wasn't a smooth opening, and he ignored it.

John started to tell me how well he was doing. Apparently his retirement was booming: one of his rubber inventions had been optioned by Subaru. Sam had lost an inch around his waist. Darcy . . . He got a little off track here, because he couldn't find anything measurable to report about Darcy.

I waited. I had the unlikely thought that he wanted me back.

I kept waiting. The coffee tasted hollow. I drank more of it.

"Are you doing OK?" he asked.

I couldn't imagine what he meant. Had I enough money? (No.) Was I making any friends? (No.) Was my car running? (Barely.) My children were gone—how could I possibly be doing OK?

As always with John, I felt the ground slipping under me. He had me backed into a corner and was about to score in some way that I couldn't yet see. I felt my blood heat up. All the smells of the room— stale waffles, eggshells, carpet shampoo, grease—stampeded through my nose.

"I'll be doing fine when my children are doing fine," I said, and took a big gulp of lousy coffee for courage. "And they're not. They miss me. They need me. And there is no substitute for time with me. Not *quality* time," I hissed into his smooth face, "big fat weeks of time."

He looked blank.

I babbled on. "My children need time with me. It has no particular value to the world, my time. But that's what I got from my father—time. I know how my father did ordinary things because we spent time together."

I slid my coffee cup aside. "He made cream cheese and chive sandwiches on pumpernickel bread."

The coffee had slopped on the table, and I tried to mop it up with the waxy napkin. "He polished our shoes."

John shoved his chair back to keep the coffee from dripping on his pants.

"He drove his car over embankments to escape traffic jams."

John's newspaper was soaked, the face of the Waindell crew member stained brown.

"He sang me to sleep at night."

John held his napkin as a shield over his lap.

"He opened the blinds to see the moon."

"Barb, it's over. That part is over. You're not a kid anymore." John lifted up the soggy newspaper, and the waitress took it smoothly from his hand. She wiped the table and poured us more coffee.

"We have cheese Danish," she said before moving on.

"My father wasn't afraid of anything, not even death."

John wagged his head. "Daddy's little girl."

My father didn't hate people, like I was doing, sitting there behind a full cup of bad coffee, hating John. My father simply let go of them. I felt hate fill a big balloon over my head, a forest green balloon. And I let it go, let it drift up to the greasy ceiling.

Half of me wanted to be anywhere but at the Onkwedo Horizon Inn. The other half wanted a Danish to wash down the second cup of wretched coffee. It was my usual feeling around John; the feeling that I would never get what I wanted, even if what I wanted was just a Danish.

"What is it?" I said. "Just tell me what it is."

"Two things." He sipped his coffee, holding his cuffs away from the still damp table. "I got a dog."

I nodded. A dog was not the point of the coffee meeting, I knew that much. There was something else coming.

"I know you hate dogs," John said.

Right as usual.

"I always wanted a dog and I got one. It will help Sam get some exercise. And it will keep Irene's father company."

"How?" I asked, but the hairs on my arm were already standing up.

"The children and I are moving into the Oneonta house with them next month. It's Thanksgiving recess, and the kids can start in their new schools right after that."

I stared at him. According to the custody agreement, John was obliged to give me two weeks' notice before any significant household change. It was the only point that my pathetic court-appointed lawyer won for me, and I think the judge awarded it out of pity. So there it was: we were meeting on the twenty-fifth day before they left. I didn't even have to consult a calendar. John would have made sure to follow the rules.

"The commute is too much for Irene. She's caring for her father in one place and her family in another."

"*My* family," I said. "They're *my* family."

Tears went straight down my cheeks in two lines. I pulled one of my dad's hankies from my purse. I'd given him hankies every Christmas, and after he died, my mother gave them all back. I blew my nose. "Oneonta is too far. My car won't make the trip. I'll see the children even less."

John was looking at the chocolate pumpkin lying on the table. It had flipped out of the purse when I'd pulled out the hankie. "Are you giving Sam candy?"

I unwrapped the chocolate and stuffed it in my mouth.

I didn't think grown-up life would be like this. I didn't think it would be all about being stuck in coffee shops with people who don't love you and don't have your best interests in mind, and having to hash it all out. But it turned out that adult life was nine tenths just that.

Chocolate and tears go fine together. It's the salt. Bitter plus sweet is an unbalanced taste; add salt and it's complete.

I looked at John. Since I could neither speak nor smack him in the face, I had no idea what to do. He was waiting for me to say something, I thought. Then I realized that he was only waiting for the check. I fished a five-dollar bill out and put it on the table. I stared into my cup. I had never wanted to pour bad coffee on anyone more in my whole almost-forty-year life. But I had missed my chance, spilled or drunk it away, and now my cup was empty.

John took his wallet out of his pocket and put it back.

I stood up, yanked my elasticless panties back down from where they'd climbed, and left the Horizon Inn.

In the parking lot, John's SUV was beside my car, dwarfing my old beater. I thought about keying his shiny paint job.

I didn't.

Inside his car a dog was barking. I didn't know if it was the give-me-some-chocolate bark or the get-away-from-the-car bark.

In my numb hand the car keys jangled. I fumbled my way into my car, finding the right key, which looked too big for the tiny slot. I squeezed it in and turned. The motor started.

I closed my eyes and waited until I knew what to do next.

John tapped on the window. I rolled it down. "Your tires are low," he said.

I nodded. Yes they were, soft and flabby. He knelt by his own tire, pressing it with his thumb.

I heard the dog again, a deep low woof. I hoped it would bite John's jugular.

I floored it, mashing my left foot on the brake. In my rearview mirror I could see two strips of rubber I'd left beside his car and his angry face. John had always hated my driving. In his SUV the dog's head popped up. It was the size of a bear's.

I don't know what happened next. The next fifteen or twenty minutes of my life have no memory attached to them. I was in some kind of a blackout or fugue state.

I awoke at the Good Times Department Store counter, having just purchased a seventy-dollar pair of jeans.

In my hand were my credit card and a postcard of Babe Ruth that I may have shoplifted from the bookstore. It was a close-up of the Babe's big rubbery face. He looked like he was thinking, "What the fuck is going to happen next?"

GOOD TIMES PANTS

At home, still numb, I put on the jeans. Miraculously, they fit. Or maybe it wasn't a miracle, maybe I had tried them on in the Good Times dressing room—I had no recollection. They made my butt look like it was only thirty-five, possibly even thirty-two.

I taped the Babe Ruth postcard to the wall beside my computer.

Outside, the sun was making a rare showing, and the tops of the pine trees were lit almost silver. I walked the perimeter of my property in my new jeans, the tags still attached and rattling from the pockets. I walked the irregular edge of the acre lot for nearly an hour, setting off my neighbor's territorial terrier at every lap. I thought about my dad and how he quietly and steadily worked, all of his long life, when he wasn't playing. There was a spareness to his actions, absolute focus. I could look at him at any moment and it would be clear to me that he was doing what he intended to do with that moment in his life: paint the porch, read about politics in the *New York Times,* eat a small bunch of his favorite Concord grapes.

Why am I here? I thought. Why am I *here?*

I had no answer.

I couldn't bear to go back inside the house. A house was for people, for family, for a couple, for mothers and their children. But mine was screamingly empty. I dashed in, gathered up the Old Daitch Dairy bills and a container of butter, and walked the six blocks to Ginna's house.

She answered the door looking disheveled and sweaty.

"I brought you the bills and some butter," I said. We stood in the mudroom, which had not a speck of mud in it, a good thing since it was wall-to-wall beige carpeting. In contrast to her sweat-stained shirt and frowsy drawstring pants, Ginna's house was immaculate.

"Nice pants," she said. "I guess they're new?"

I realized I'd forgotten to remove the tags, and I yanked them off.

"Can't return them now," she said.

There was a TV going somewhere inside. "Is your husband home?" I asked. Her husband was a sweet-faced man, large and soft-spoken.

"Mark?" she said, as if she might have another husband. "I have no idea what he's up to."

That didn't sound good, but I didn't know Ginna well enough to inquire further. "Young Mr. Daitch gave me cream, and I made some butter."

"How could you possibly do that?" she asked. Before I could respond she said, "Never mind, I hate to cook."

I handed her the pint of butter. "You should probably refrigerate it." I stood there feeling awkward, wondering if she meant to invite me in, and wondering whether I could stand being with anyone anyway. Suddenly her house felt even colder than outside. "I'll see you next week," I said.

"Would you like to have some tea?" she asked. But the moment had passed, and we both knew it.

"Thanks, I have to get home," I said, even though there was no reason at all for me to go back to the house.

"Take some dinner rolls, we have tons." Mark's job was driving the delivery truck for the bread distributor. "Like I said, I don't know when he's coming back, and he always eats out anyway."

"Don't you miss him?" I asked.

Ginna shrugged. "I'm used to it. Even when he's here, he's pretty quiet." She stuffed rolls into a bag.

"Where's your son?"

"At school," she said, sounding surprised. Of course I would know that children were at school during the day if I were a *real* mother.

"Thanks for the rolls."

She closed the door as I turned away, both of us relieved it was over.

AUTHENTIC

I was looking in the refrigerator, deciding on my breakfast identity and wondering how well stale dinner rolls went with homemade butter, when the lawyer from New York City called. Max the assistant put the call through.

"The work could be a genuine Vladimir Nabokov manuscript," he said without any preamble. He sounded excited. "An expert from Sotheby's gave it a preliminary rating of high possibility of authenticity. They'd like to meet with us in my office." He sounded pleased that the big auction house would be coming to him. "Sotheby's will need to see the complete original of course, before the meeting." He changed tone abruptly, yelling something about "the fucking Goldsmith affidavit." I realized he was on another call. Without missing a beat he returned to me. "Here's the interesting part: they asked if you would consider selling it before the official certification."

"Why?"

"From our point of view, should it be a genuine Nabokov manuscript, you would be avoiding any expensive lawsuits challenging your right to own it. They would assume full responsibility." He undoubtedly knew that I couldn't afford an expensive lawsuit, or even a

Cleaning Nabokov's House

bargain-basement lawsuit. "Should it turn out not to be authentic, it is essentially worthless, and we've missed the only opportunity for remuneration."

He probably knew many more words for money than I did. "But would they publish it?" I asked him.

"That would be an area beyond your concern. My point is that there might be some capital right now. If so, you should take it." I heard him give Max instructions about Goldsmith. "Of course you can take the gamble that it is real and that your ownership will go unchallenged, and that is where the big numbers could come in. Buy yourself some shoes. Hell, buy yourself a house!" He sounded jubilant about this prospect. He seemed to have forgotten that I had a house. "Hold on for Max."

While I waited for Max to come back on the line, I wondered how much money he meant. If he meant a house in the suburb where he lived, it would be a mountain of money. Money. I kept thinking about money, or trying to, suggesting meanings to myself. Money meant fixing the car. Money meant clothes shopping. Money meant eating Thai food in Thailand. Money meant what? What would it mean to my life? Without the children, what would I spend it on—beauty treatments? First editions of books I would never read because opening them would ruin their mint condition? Private lessons from a chef? A life coach? I couldn't imagine myself with money and no kids. What would be the point?

When Max got on the line I said, "I think it's real. I think Vladimir Nabokov wrote it and left it behind." He seemed to be listening. "I don't want the buyout. I want to go the whole way. I don't want to give up now."

Max made no comment. Instead, he instructed me on how to send the cards and the typescript safely and told me that they would need a month to read it. We made an appointment for me to come back to the city on the first business day after my children moved from Onkwedo.

Then he explained that I would be meeting with representatives from their media department when I came in, so they could evaluate my "TVQ." I vaguely knew what he meant—how you looked on television. Crap, crap, crap: clothes again. Presentation was my worst talent. After marriage.

LAST VISIT

The next month was agonizing. John gave me a "bonus" visit the day before the children left. The condition was that I had to drive to Sam's ice hockey game to collect them. I gave my car a big gulp of oil and tried to pump up the tires with Sam's bike pump. It didn't work.

The drive to the rink was long, and I pushed my noisy little rattle-trap hard. It used almost no gas, but I had to remember to stop frequently and feed it a quart of oil. I was trying hard not to be late for Sam's game.

John had put him on a vigorous physical fitness regimen and diet because he was concerned about Sam's weight. After I left, my plump little boy had blossomed into a tubby kid. I kept expecting Sam to grow taller and even out, but it had not happened. John's a take-action kind of person, and physical fitness was his new fixation. The last whole paragraph he spoke to me had to do with my son's weight. He said Sam was turning into "a fatty" and needed vigorous exercise. "Doesn't take after my side of the family," he smirked. He told me to stop feeding Sam carbohydrates. He described the ideal lunch I should pack for Sam on school days: a container of sliced turkey and either a pickle or carrot sticks. I was no longer speaking to him, not that he'd noticed.

Thinking about all this made me want to run him over, which caused me to accelerate madly. Nearly at the ice rink, I passed a policeman who was busy giving someone else a ticket. His square black-uniformed back glowered in my direction as I whizzed by. The car's shuddering urged me to slow down, and I did, to a nearly lawful seventy-five. I wondered what kind of a driver Nabokov was. He sometimes sat in his car to write. I knew that from photos, but I didn't know if he actually knew how to drive the car. And if he did drive, was he law-abiding, was he someone who stayed under the speed limit? I doubted it.

At the ice rink I was hoping to blend in with the other moms, maybe chat about our sons. I didn't recognize any of them. Over my head, they discussed the coach's offensive "blitz" strategy.

On the ice playing defense, Sam glided in circles, lifting first one skate and then the other. He looked almost like the other kids, because they all wear padding, but his blue jersey was stretched tighter and his skates looked too small to balance his bulk. He appeared to be listening to a Schubert waltz broadcast from the inside of his helmet, graceful and peaceful as Ferdinand the bull.

The mothers surrounding me knew every player's name. It was only when they began a vicious kind of cheering directed at the children wearing the same color jersey as Sam that I realized my mistake. I'd seated myself with the moms from the opposing team. I was in enemy territory.

A few rows down I saw Ginna, the bookkeeper. My colleague. I settled on the cold bench beside her, and we smiled at each other. Her son was playing goalie for Sam's team, and he had let in seven goals so far. "Use your knees, Ronald," Ginna called to him.

The opposing team zipped past Sam, who was doing a slow pirouette, and sent the puck past Ronald's knees into our net for a drubbing of eight to zero. At the end of the second period, our team skated dejectedly off the ice, Sam trailing Ronald.

Ginna turned to me and said in a snide tone that she was trying to pass off as nice, "Is this Sam's rookie season?"

I excused myself and went to the concession stand. I bought a doughnut, which was stale, the way evening doughnuts often are, and when I finished it, I brushed a curtain of glazed crumbs off my jacket. I need a friend here, I thought. I needed a mom to sit beside, not a sports fiend, but someone who was here only because her kid was on the ice, someone to whom winning was incidental, someone like me.

The game resumed and I returned to the rink, standing by myself at the edge of the bleachers. I could see John on the other side, shouting down to the ice, "Pay attention, Sam!" By his side was a woman who looked remarkably like the social worker. It was only my brain resisting the admission that it *was* the social worker. Irene. Tucked between them was Darcy with a fur hat and muff. They didn't see me.

Once you have failed at love, it is very hard not to believe that it's simply your own fault. That you could have done things differently, been more tolerant, kinder, tried harder, lost those five pounds. Well, maybe ten pounds.

My only comfort had been that I could imagine John thinking along the same line. But since he'd found himself a new partner fast and I could see they were in the throes of hunky-dory, I knew he'd never thought any such thing.

Suddenly I felt a whole year older than when I walked into the ice rink, maybe two years. Like time was moving faster here at the rink, bringing me closer to death. It might have been despair, or an acute sense of dislocation, or maybe the wretchedness of having to watch my son publicly fail at sports—sports being something that I seemed to be alone in caring nothing about.

To cheer myself, I thought about my agent and her happy marriage, her good work life, her beautiful office full of pillows with words on them. I reminded myself that I once had friends in the city, that I knew how to be a friend. Friendship was based on mutual interests. I tried to think of what interested me here in Onkwedo that could be shared: food, books, sex. Maybe I could join a cooking class. No, I was too rebellious a cook. A book group? Perhaps, but someone had to invite you in, and that seemed unlikely. Plus for book groups you must hostess well. I was about as good a hostess as I was a blacksmith. That left sex. Well, no, it didn't leave anything.

At long last the game was over. The final shot was by the opposing team's goalie. It bounced off of Sam's plump leg and past Ronald—the valet parking attendant of pucks—and into the net. The final score was in the double digits.

While Sam changed I hid in the ladies' room so I didn't have to see John. I made myself count my blessings. I was glad that Sam was coming home with me. I was glad that I had not been late for his game the way I often was. I was glad that I had baked a loaf of his favorite raisin bread (thank you, bread machine left over from my wedding day) and could feed him toast with butter to console him for his ice hockey defeat.

I washed my hands and dawdled, reading the names on the bathroom fixtures. They all came from the same city in Illinois. I wondered if it was a particularly sanitary place, that city in Illinois.

But I came out of the ladies' room too soon. Sam was still in the locker room changing out of his gear, and there was John flanked by Darcy and Irene. Darcy had her hands tucked into her muff. "We got a dog," she said, extracting one hand from the muff and patting its fur. "She eats five pounds of food every single day."

"Half Bull Mastiff, half Great Dane," John said. "Irene's boss breeds them."

Irene was smiling at me, one of her well-adjusted social worker you-too-could-love-yourself-enough-to-have-a-pet smiles.

Sam came out of the locker room pulling his hockey equipment in a duffel the size and shape of a body bag. I hauled it up onto my shoulder and smiled brightly back at Irene. "Does the breed have a name?"

"My boss is trying to register with the AKC for 'Bull Danes.' He already has a website."

I knew I should say something positive and encouraging, like "Isn't it swell that your boss is such a well-rounded social worker!" But I said, "Hope it's housebroken." John glared at me as if I was always trying to drag feces into polite conversation.

We all managed to say good night. I managed not to knock the happy couple's heads together like coconuts. And I left with the children, Sam and his body bag, Darcy in her fur ensemble.

Driving home, I could see my beautiful big soft boy in the rearview mirror. His skin was milky white. His hair was floppy and almost colorless. His nearly white eyelashes gave him a startled-bunny look. He seemed sad and very subdued. I watched him stretch his arms up and knead the padded ceiling of the car.

"I sucked," he said.

"Yes? I thought you were skating very well," I said carefully.

"Barb, you don't know anything."

He was right. I didn't know much about his world. I knew all of it when we lived together. If I had known what I would lose, I might still be taking lessons on how to load the dishwasher correctly.

Under the noise of the motor, I started to hum a lullaby. In the mirror I watched his big blond head loll back on the car seat. I heard his breath pour out of him in a sigh. When he was a baby, he used to make that exact big sigh before falling asleep.

Darcy had settled herself in the booster seat beside her brother and was whispering into one end of her muff. She stopped and held it up to her ear as if listening to a response.

At home I put a block of cheese on the table and made them buttered raisin toast, one piece after another. Sam kept his head down, eating, quiet and maybe sullen—I didn't pry. Darcy ate only the unmelted butter she could rescue from her toast. She seemed to be feeding the toast to an invisible companion beside her.

I peeled some tangerines. Sam ate a section silently. The phone rang and I let the machine answer it. We both stared at the speaker from which the experson's voice was coming into the kitchen. He wanted to talk to Sam about the game, go over a few plays. He wanted to know what I was serving for dinner. I reached for the volume and turned it down to a squeaky whisper. Sam looked up at me for the first time.

"Jelly with that toast?" I asked him.

"No thanks." Sam frowned at me. "Jelly is pure carbohydrate. Dad doesn't eat jelly."

I turned and started to load the dishwasher. I put the dishes in any way at all.

"Look at this," Sam called to me. He tossed a tangerine section high in the air and caught it in his mouth. He flung aloft another and another, positioning his mouth under the falling food with the skill of a zoo seal.

"Awesome," I said, glad to be able to encourage his interest in sports. "Where do you practice?"

"Cafeteria on Fridays. The lunchroom aides have a personal development workshop."

Darcy wanted to discuss the new dog. "She digs," Darcy said, "like this." She got down and started scrabbling at the floor. "And the dirt goes like this." From her upside-down, between-the-legs position, she flung the muff behind her.

"Dad gets mad," Sam said.

"Does it bother Irene?" I asked.

Both children looked at me blankly, unused to the idea that Irene might have an inner life.

I changed the subject. "Would you like dessert?" I put a bowl of frozen grapes on the table, thick-skinned gold grapes called Himrod, sweet and winey. "These are from harvesttime," I said, "from when the pumpkins were ripe."

"The cheese is ripe too," Darcy said, breaking a corner off the block of Old Daitch Dairy mild cheddar. "The mice are ecstatic."

Sam and I watched her nibble the lump with her front teeth, wiggling her nose up and down.

The morning came too fast, following a night where I slept not at all, padding between their rooms to look at their sleeping faces, listen to their breath.

At the sound of the doorbell, I watched Sam's shoulders draw up and his back hunch. I opened the door to their father.

"We have to check on Matilda," Darcy said to Sam. John had let her name the dog. "See if she's dug any more holes."

Sam shrugged into his jacket. I kissed the back of his head and sniffed, memorizing. His baby head scent had been slightly tropical, like freesia or a perfectly ripe mango. Darcy had been intoxicating, but not like a flower or fruit, more a sea breeze at night and something almost smoky. Sam still had the sweetness, but it was more like fresh hay.

"The moving van comes at nine a.m.," John said. "Both cars are packed. We'll be in Oneonta by sundown."

"Who takes the dog?" I asked.

John paused. "She's too immature for the kennel, they turned me down. Are you offering?"

The children looked at me.

"She digs very well," Darcy said.

"Could you handle an overnight?" John asked.

"Sure," I said, never having spent so much as ten minutes alone with a dog.

John said he'd bring her over in the morning with all her supplies and pick her up the following day.

"Great," I said.

I was aching to hold my little girl, but she stood stiffly beside her father. "She is a nice dog," Darcy said. "Her ears are silky and she smells nice, the doggy kind of nice."

"She likes to run after sticks," Sam said.

I watched them walk away from me down the brick path. Darcy was holding Sam's sleeve.

I went into Darcy's room and sat on the floor in the middle of all her little-girl things till the wall of smell drove me out.

DOG

At seven a.m. sharp the doorbell rang. I was still in my pajamas, decades-old brown flannels that my mother had sent me in college, presumably to keep me chaste.

John was outside with the enormous dog. The kids weren't with him, which meant they must be in Oneonta. I tried not to picture them with Irene, hunching over bowls of Cheerios and skim milk.

He dragged the huge creature inside my door and deposited a bag of dry dog food and a bowl the size of a foot bath. "She's not very bright," he said, as if I would find it comforting not to be out-thought by his pet. "Feed her only dry food, no table scraps. Walk her twice a day." He handed me a leash. "At least half a mile."

"Will she run away if I let her off the leash?" I asked.

"Don't find out."

I closed the door on his back, wishing he was on his way to Petaluma or Dubai or Hell. I couldn't remember the last time we had sex, or for that matter any time at all. It was the protective blank screen of blocked memory. Sometimes I loved my brain.

I wanted to go to the kitchen for breakfast, but the damned dog was sitting on my slipper, flattening my metatarsals. "Dog," I said firmly, "get off." She sighed and leaned against my leg, her weight nearly tearing a ligament in my ankle.

While I was immobilized, different breakfast identities floated through my head. Maybe I was a sliced-fruit-and-yogurt-with-a-sprinkle-of-oat-bran person.

Unlikely.

The dog finally shifted her bulk to a prone position, freeing my foot.

I made us each a piece of toast. I put on my parka and mittens and clipped on her leash. Using the toast as a lure, I coaxed her upright and took her outside with me to wait for Bill. The clouds were even lower than usual. I sat on the picnic table. The dog sniffed the ground near my feet for toast crumbs.

She was the largest dog I had ever seen up close, dappled black and white like a Holstein cow. I put my hand on top of her head, away from the slavering jowls. She closed her pink-rimmed doggy eyes. I thought about Darcy kissing her ugly face and Sam throwing a stick for her. I gingerly patted her spotted head.

This was what lonely people were supposed to do, I thought, get a pet.

I wasn't tempted. Still, the short fur was soft and warm, and the floppy ears with their raised veins had a satin appeal. The fact that my children loved this beast gave her a place in my life. The dog was a recipient of their love, a carrier.

Snowflakes had started to drift down from the low clouds when Bill's truck pulled up. Margie stepped out, holding my mail sack. She turned and waved to Bill, blowing him a kiss. "I'll walk home," she called.

"Hey, Margie, I'm glad to see you."

"I ride around with Bill sometimes. Against the rules but nobody

really cares." Margie was wearing high boots and a perfectly calibrated outfit, not too fancy or too plain. Under her shearling jacket
her shirt was tucked into her pants, a look that few women in America
attempted.

Margie slung the mail sack on the picnic table and perched beside
me, her long legs crossed at the ankles. She ignored the hundred-plus-
pound dog completely. She was a cat person. More snow fell. Margie
looked around my yard. "This is a good play area," she said, a note of
yearning in her voice. "Do your kids like it?"

I couldn't look at her. "Their father moved them to Oneonta today.
I won't have them back for two weeks."

"How can you stand that?"

"I can't."

"Why don't you fight for your kids? I don't get that about you. It's
one thing to leave a man, but how can you lose your kids?"

I didn't know how to answer her question. It was exactly what I
asked myself every single day, every morning and every evening of my
sorry life.

"What do you need to get them back? Money? How much?"

"I can't win against John. He has a plan for everything. Plus he
knows everybody in town. Everybody loves him. I lost in court, in front
of all of them. The judgment was against me. And nothing in my life
has changed. If I fought him now, I'd lose again."

"But you are their mother, for chrissakes."

I stared at the frozen grass. "I want them back desperately," I said to
Margie's boots.

She stood up. "So get them back. Make your own plan and stick to
it. Don't live on hope."

The last word landed on me like a rock. She was wrong. I had no
hope.

"Get a lawyer, get a shrink, hell, get a voodoo doll." Margie sounded upset. I didn't know if it was at me or at the circumstances. She walked off, calling over her shoulder, "They should be here with you catching snowflakes."

Watching her leave, I thought about how my father always knew what to do. I don't know how he did it, but he could always let go of the bad stuff. With four or five words he could make it fly away. My father was a Zen master at letting go. At the end he let go of the whole world. The world might still be on the same orbital path as when he was alive, or it might be plummeting, I couldn't tell.

I sat on the cold picnic table, missing him. The loss felt sharper even than right before sleep, or at the moment on waking in the morning when I had to tell myself again that he was gone.

Although I knew it was a bad idea, I decided to call my mother. I told Matilda to stay and brought the phone out to the frozen yard. Instead of saying hello, my mother asked suspiciously, "Who *is* this?"

I explained that it was her only child. Since I rarely called her, I tried to forgive her for not knowing me. Besides, she was in wedding hell.

I could hear the ping of the microwave bell and the sound of chewing. "Turkey hot dog," she mumbled. "No bun, unlimited carb-free ketchup." She was on her fourth week of the Atkins diet, she complained, and couldn't even look at a cracker.

"What size is your wedding dress, Mom?" My mother was a perfect four.

"It's a zero. I thought that was a good place to start, since marriage makes people fat."

"It didn't make you fat before," I pointed out.

"Well, that's because I had your father, and now he's gone." I heard a gulp that might have been a sob or the swallowing of a lump of meat.

She had served up this kind of dizzy logic my whole life. I knew better than to push behind it for real meaning.

I told her that John had moved the kids to Oneonta.

"Will they come to the wedding?"

Even knowing my mother's capacity to ignore reality, I was stunned. "Mother, my children have been moved two hours away from me. We aren't even in the same county anymore."

"I'm sorry, honey."

"I keep trying to think what my father would do," I said. "What would Dad do?"

"He would get them back. Your father was afraid of no one. He could talk to any man in the world. He could talk to *Osama* bin Laden," she said, as if there were another bin Laden who was a better conversationalist. "And he never wasted any time." The last was a reproach. It was also true. My mother believed I was extremely lazy. She'd criticized throughout my childhood while I sat still in one place by the window memorizing books. She didn't think I should make something better of myself, only that I should exert myself more, take a tap dance class.

"You're almost forty, Barb. Your father is gone. Your father was fearless, and he could fix any bad situation. He would work something out. He would never lose his family." She was right.

And unhelpful. I still didn't know what to do.

After I hung up I found I'd drawn a picture in the snow on the picnic table with a twig. Three stick figures—the tallest was me, Darcy in a triangle of a dress, Sam looking a little like a snowman. I'd drawn the sun overhead with rays, just like I used to do in grade school, and beneath our feet I'd scratched in the deck of a boat. The bottom of the boat appeared to be floating on a drift of snow.

I didn't need *Psychology Now* to point out the obvious about my subconscious. Here I was making an ark, for goodness' sake, instead of a plan. A damn boat adrift in the Arctic without a compass. It was pathetic and stupid, and for once, instead of being angry at John, I was absolutely furious with myself. How could I have let this happen? How could I even pretend to be my father's daughter?

Unless the ark was the Nabokov book. Maybe *Babe Ruth* was the way out: money, legitimacy even, a boat to float me out of this hideous custody mess, away from Onkwedo altogether.

THE BLUE DOOR

I couldn't bear another trip on the sluggish bus, so after John picked up his dog (I hid in the kitchen, pretending to be on the phone so I wouldn't do anything to him that could land me back in the clink), I got in my shoebox of a dying car and headed for New York City. I parked in Newark and took the train into Manhattan. That was the beauty of my car; I could leave it anywhere and no one would bother it. Its unwantability made it invisible.

After the drive alone in my automobile, the subway was a relief. Sitting on the hard seat of a train car hurtling across town, I was surrounded by people. Some were reading books, some thinking, some kissing each other, some sound asleep. Different bodies, faces, clothing choices—wonderful to be reminded that there was such variety among those of us here on the earth.

As usual all the people looked like they were going somewhere, and for once I was too. I'd spiffed up for the meeting, shined my squeaky shoes and tried to make my hair behave. Margie's sweater was too itchy to wear, but I imitated her look of all the same color in different textures: aubergine fuzzy, aubergine smooth, aubergine shiny, the pieces culled from the remains of my wardrobe. I couldn't decide if the effect was "artsy" or "demented professor." I had brought my own typed version of the manuscript. I was happy to have business here, real business, important business. I had found a treasure, and the experts who would appreciate it best, who knew its real value, were ready for me.

The lobby was teeming with well-oiled people, bustling into the workday fortified by their Ritalin and Xanax and double latte and meditation and prayer and hot yoga and tae bo and protein bars. They all wore black. I was given a guest name tag and sent to the thirty-second floor.

Max met me when I stepped off the elevator. He was wearing another very large blazer. He explained that his boss was in court but that he, Max, would be with me in the meeting with the Sotheby's and TVQ people.

The conference room smelled like lunch meat. Four people stood to greet me and planted themselves around the table again—a man with a forehead like a J boat and three women. I wondered which of them was from Sotheby's. Their smiles were uncannily warm, as if we were old friends.

"First we want you to know what we do," the shortest woman said. I figured her for a TVQ person. We watched a corporate DVD on a large flat screen mounted on the wall. It consisted of clips of television talk shows with different guests they had managed to place, all looking smooth and perfect. The music was loud. When it was over, someone said, "It's great, isn't it?" Another agreed before I had a chance to respond.

I didn't want them to know that I had never seen those shows and didn't know who those people were. And even if I did know who they were, I wouldn't rush out and buy a television set to watch them. The dumb loudness of the video mingled with the lunch meat smell and made me dizzy.

There was a pause during which they aligned themselves to face me. A tall woman said, "Tell us about finding the book." I began with Darcy's purse collection. I could see their minds wandering as they tried to remember if their children had such odd habits. Or if they had children or the nanny had taken them with her back to Tibet.

J Boat made a frame with his hands as if he was looking at me through a camera lens. "TV, yes?" he asked his colleagues.

The tallest woman, who was probably the Sotheby's representative, spoke slowly to me. "Can you tell us how you felt when you found it?"

I started to explain reading it that first day on my knees, the amazingness of Nabokov's writing. "Fabulous!" she interrupted. "What a fascinating story!" She reached down to her business tote and took out the stacks of index cards, wrapped in archival lignin-free tissue paper. "At best it might be an artifact for a library collection, perhaps under literary mysteries or unclaimed work. But we have established to our satisfaction that your cards were not written by the hand of Vladimir Nabokov." She said his name as if she were hocking something from the back of her throat.

J Boat took over. "We are all in agreement about that." He smiled around the table like this was a rare and good thing. "We are willing to issue an affidavit that the book was found in the house where he once lived." He beamed at me like he'd just baked a cake. "We are thinking of the finding of it as the real story. Perfect for reality TV: small-town woman pins her hopes on a star. Very relatable. Very human interest. It's kind of the anti-Lottery-winner story."

"But I'm not the story. The book itself is the story," I said.

"Think about it," he said. "You would definitely get your fifteen minutes." They all stood up. The tall Sotheby's woman handed me the stacks of cards in their tissue paper. I carefully put them inside my bag.

The short woman kissed me on the cheek, and the man shook my hand so warmly I could feel the heat move up to my chest.

"Marvelous meeting you," he said. "Max, show Ms. Barrett the way out of this maze." I wondered if Max was his real name or the firm had insisted on something monosyllabic.

As I followed Max through the corridors and two elevator rides back to the lobby, my fingers discovered a business card. J Boat must have palmed it to me. On thick, creamy linen stock was printed "Nancy Cohen, Image Consultant." That nailed it: I had flunked TVQ.

Max had said nothing in the meeting. We stood in the lobby beside a large corporate philodendron. "I read *Lolita* in college," he said now. "What a sick mind the man had. Way ahead of his time." He sounded full of admiration.

"What if they're wrong?" I planted the business card in the pot of woodchips surrounding the philodendron.

"The experts have the last word on this. If they don't say it's real, there's no way you can do a thing with it." He shrugged inside his big jacket. "I enjoyed reading *Babe Ruth*. Really sick. Even with the missing action scene." He turned to go.

"Max," I called just as he was slipping into the special elevator for assistants and mail carriers. He slid back to me like he was on a track. "There is a famous cathouse on this street. Do you know where it would be?"

Max didn't bat an eyelash. "Eight doors down, this side."

"Thanks. Can I ask you one more thing?"

"Sure."

"What is a cathouse?"

"Prostitution. The big business is at lunch. Nooners." He swiveled and glided away.

I was back out on the streets of the city that had no need of me.

They thought I was a fake, or trying to drum up some attention. How ridiculous was that? The last thing I wanted was attention.

And what about Nabokov? Now no one would know how much he put into this book and how wonderful it was.

My short-term solution was a chocolate croissant, and I found one at the corner store, probably made in a factory with dough conditioners to improve shelf life, a death leap down the pastry pyramid from the perfection of Pierre's at Ceci-Cela.

Now what? There was a bad croissant in my immediate future, but beyond that a lot of blank horizon. Get in my rattletrap car, and drive back Upstate, where I knew almost no one and few people liked me, with the possible exception of Margie? Go sit on Margie's floor and wail to her that I had lost my children, the manuscript was worthless, and my mortgage payment was coming up?

No.

It was nearly noon. I leaned against a building and peeled the plastic wrap off the croissant. I took a bite. It wasn't stale, but only because it had never been fresh. People were rushing past me on the sidewalk on their way to much better food. Across the street was a quiet-looking building of brown brick, eight doors down from the law firm.

There was no doorman, just a keypad on the outside. The windows were framed in blue steel and matched the front door, a handsome shade of robin's egg blue. It was tasteful and understated, especially for a whorehouse.

My leather business tote bit into my shoulder. John had bought it for me at Dooney & Burke when I was pregnant with Darcy. It cost four hundred dollars. He was trying to make me more businesslike. The bag was absurdly heavy, but it made me look like I was going somewhere important.

Munching my nasty "croissant au chocolat," I watched the blue door of the cathouse. The balance of delicate dough and slightly bitter chocolate center had been missed entirely; instead, it was a sweet mono-textured wad of goo. I ate it anyway.

While I lingered, a man came up to the door, carrying the same model of business tote as mine. It matched his shoes—"Honey Mustard" was the name of the color in the catalog. He looked happy. In my entire five hours in the city, he was the only person I'd seen who looked truly happy.

I thought he might be going in for a spanking. He had a way of walking, even though he was going forward, that said, "Presenting my ass."

Up where I lived, he could get a free spanking, I supposed, but in the city it was all about contracts and real estate. I watched him poke the buttons on the keypad. The blue steel door buzzed and the brown building swallowed him up, Honey Mustard loafers and all.

At twelve ten, the Sotheby's woman from the meeting paused in front of the blue door to adjust her patent leather pump. As she bent over, her bag swung forward and clocked her in the head. It too was the same Dooney & Burke business tote, hers in "Obsidian." The big pricey bags, heavy even when empty, peopled the whole block. They could rename East Forty-eighth Street Dooney & Burke Lane. She straightened up, one hand to her forehead, and motored on back to Sotheby's to ruin someone else's life. At the blue door, two more spiffy-looking patrons who were performing a kind of "After you, Alfonse." Neither looked willing to follow the other into the house of ill repute.

By one fifty-nine, I'd counted thirty-six men entering the building, mostly in suits or Burberry raincoats. Most of them had come out looking content, peaceful, ambling their way back to work or meetings with other important people. I suspected there was a rear door, because I saw no women arrive or depart.

I'd long ago finished the croissant, but I licked my fingers and ate the inferior pastry crumbs from the wrapper, almost chewing the plastic. Passion. Purpose.

TEMPLATE

Driving Upstate through the cold dark hills rolling away from New York City, I felt as if I was leaving life itself behind, leaving passion and purpose behind, leaving a real connection with a real Nabokov. My found treasure had turned into an inconsequential stack of cards.

I pulled up one of the cards in my mind's eye. Sometimes he wrote so fast that not a single *i* was dotted. He was going places. That was one of the elements of passion: urgency. He had no time for complacency, for boredom. Wasn't that a sure mark of genius?

I stopped to raise the hood, shivering in my city clothes, and poured in a quart of oil from the case I kept in the trunk. I thought of my cousin, so passionate. To him, boredom was to be avoided at all costs. When we were on a road trip together, no matter where we were headed, we would end up at the water. When my cousin got bored driving, he would make a left turn. It was not a conscious act, he simply went a different way. He had a knack for getting us lost but finding a place to take a swim. Sometimes it was off a rich person's dock, and my cousin would say, "Nobody owns the water."

He lived by passion. He would be in such a rush to get to the next place that he never bothered with socks, slipping into sandals or boat shoes, even in the snow, his light jacket flapping open. His mind was keeping him warm. He'd dated every blond friend I had. He liked them all. He didn't even mind the actress/actrocity one, he found her "refreshing."

I pulled into the driveway and sat looking at my front door. In the middle of another dead-quiet Onkwedo night, I didn't want to reenter the house empty of my children. I thought for a moment of the drafty garage, wondering if it was airtight enough for suicide by carbon monoxide poisoning. *Shut up,* I told my brain. *Make a plan.* Besides, I was almost out of gas.

Inside, I put down the Dooney & Burke business tote and kicked off my shoes. I poured myself some milk and heated it. I unwrapped the index cards and started to read them again. There was so much passion in *Babe Ruth,* in the characters who wanted something desperately, and in the words themselves. Not self-consciously so, just gut-wrenchingly beautiful or horrific or hilarious words, fierce in their individuality, as if they belonged only to that writer and the reader. Each sentence was a sprint away from boredom.

Why couldn't Nabokov have written the book? But why *would* he have? Maybe Vera and Vladimir were lonely in this house, having left Europe and all their writer and artist friends behind. Maybe that made him turn to Babe Ruth as a subject, as a way of thinking about America, or about fame. Lonely people think a lot about celebrities (another fact left over from *Psychology Now*), although I didn't; I thought about dead people.

If only he had left something to indicate he had written it here. But famous writers don't pen domestic histories of their lives: *Vera made me an egg, exactly the way I like it, and then I loaded the dishwasher, anything to avoid going back to the Babe.* Or her version: *Today I made grilled cheese sandwiches and Vladimir cleaned the bathrooms. I hid his latest work so he wouldn't destroy it. The baseball book is very frustrating to my husband.*

Screw the TVQ people and their asinine ideas about what interests humans. Screw Sotheby's and their disbelief. Why did they think they knew so much? I was furious with them for making this journey a dead end.

The middle of life has these cul-de-sac days. In your twenties you think, Surely I am going somewhere, and later—as in now—you think, Nope.

I went to bed. Lying there alone, I ran my hands over my body, wondering how a lover might feel me: bones here, stretch of skin, some discernible muscle or tendon, the squishy places. I lay there thinking how odd was aging. Just as a body got wise and more deeply knowing, it became irrelevant.

In the morning I called Margie. Max must have filled her in, because she was very kind to me. "It was a long shot, Barb."

I don't know why everybody knew that but me. "Are you still willing to try to sell *Babe Ruth* on its own merits, as a novel?"

Margie said she doubted it would make me any life-changing amount of money. We both knew what she meant by "life-changing."

"What about the missing scene?" I asked her.

"You're a writer. You could crank it out."

I didn't know how Margie got from my writing Thank you for your letter regarding the butterfat content of . . . to faking Nabokov, so I was silent.

"Do you like sports?"

That was another thing I tried not to tell people about myself. I liked people who liked sports. Just as I liked people who liked pets. But I never understood those people. It was better to keep quiet about these areas of darkness in myself, but I couldn't lie to Margie. "Not really," I said.

"I want you to meet Rudy. He's an old friend and a Waindell coach. He's got the crew team in amazing shape. Rudy can make anyone love sports. I'll tell him to call you. It's not a date, but it could turn into one. Wear something nice, for God's sake."

"Thanks," I said, but Margie had hung up, leaving me to think about meeting new people and dressing nicely. Instead I went back to thinking about the people I would miss forever.

At the end of his life, when he could stand my company, I sat by my cousin's bed in the fancy hospital and talked about whatever he wanted to talk about. He said he wished he'd had children, that he'd missed what was probably the best part of life. He asked me if I was going to marry John. When I told him I didn't know (I also didn't know that I was pregnant with Sam), my cousin said, "Too boring?" Dying people can say these things. What have they got to lose?

Then he told me to take all the socks his mother had knitted for him. They were piled on the windowsill in his hospital room, next to his books. The socks were gray and brown, made from the softest alpaca yarn. "Get them out of here," he said. "As if I need new clothes."

That was our goodbye.

A week later I got the call that he was dead. I drove out to his boat slip and sat on the deck under the clinking mast. The rocking didn't comfort me, but the gentle side-to-side roll was the best movement for sobbing. I used the spare key from under the hibachi to open the hatch, and I gathered the paperbacks. Some were in English, some in other languages. I locked the hatch and put the key back in the hiding place. I took the books and I told no one. I didn't have my cousin's fine mind or his sharp valuing of life, but maybe I would have more time than he did to read.

I shook my head to bring myself back to the present. Reading, yes. From the shelves I got down my cousin's copy of *Pale Fire.* Maybe I could make a kind of template of Nabokov's writing to help me, some guidelines. I knew I had to visualize the action in order to write the baseball scene, so I collected eight of my son's little plastic people and arranged them on the table. There weren't quite enough, so Barbie had to pitch. She was nude, as Barbie usually was around our house, and missing an arm. There must be left-handed pitchers, I thought. I started a list of questions to ask Rudy the sports expert if he ever called me.

I wondered if Margie had billed me as a date to Rudy. It had been a decade since I went on a date. I would have to put together an outfit, make conversation. But not yet, because the phone was stone silent.

Waiting for it to ring underscored my feeling of isolation. I told myself that isolation was good for writing. I read over the beginning of the manuscript and drank a quart of tea and ate four pieces of toast. In between I worked on making a template.

I couldn't make a template from *Pale Fire,* for Pete's sake—it's in verse. I tried *Ada.*

I came up with this: adjective, proper noun, and then a made-up word. A shift away from the POV, a verb that has at least one sexual meaning beyond its overt purpose in the sentence, something grotesque and something beautiful right up against each other. The ending image would be something that made you suck in your breath, a little tiny horror show.

It wasn't exactly helpful, and it didn't seem sporty at all. Reading Nabokov was like eating pâté straight, no crackers, with a chocolate truffle chaser. I tried another tactic: Pretend you are the smartest person in the world and you know all the words there are. Now tell yourself a joke. Make it a sports joke.

I switched Barbie's arm to the other side. The switch made her windup look even more exotic. I made the little plastic guys run the bases. In what I hoped might be a squeeze play, one of them stole home. I wrote two pages of terrible stuff using the sporty words from one of the cards. Margie had said the scene needed to be six pages of "oomph," but I had exhausted everything I knew about baseball, and I was out of toast.

I lay down on the floor and wondered if Nabokov ever got discouraged. I wondered if he ever ate all the toast in the house. I doubted it. There was a description in *Pale Fire* of watching a snowstorm from the windows of a "ramshackle house" they had rented. It must have been this house; I could see the snow from where I was lying.

I could almost feel him here, drawing nothing from the wooden walls, nothing from the big windows facing the hill, less than nothing from the toujours gray sky. I could imagine his frustration that life had thrust him into this simple house in this sleepy town where he had to work a grind job educating privileged young Americans.

The phone rang and I got up off the floor. It was Rudy calling. He sounded like he was at number fifteen on his to-do list, and it wasn't even noon. I agreed to get together for drinks in the evening and watch a televised game. "It's a historic baseball game," he said, but I was thinking about the drinks part. Beer is a manly drink, and I decided to have a Coke. Ordering a Coke would indicate that I was not high maintenance. That, of course, was a lie.

"Be ready when I get there," Rudy said, and hung up.

Shoot, now I had to deal with clothes. The Pants of course, and a pale green sweater set. Men of boomer age like the color green, I remembered from my old job.

I found a pink lipstick stashed in Darcy the pilferer's pinkest purse. I stole it back.

During the evening I would ask Rudy to explain to me the drama of baseball, the *point* of it if we got to that level of connection.

Nabby didn't have these resources.

If Rudy could make baseball dramatic to me and I could get it on the page, there might be hope that the found work would reach its readers.

Laying out the green sweater set, I felt that hope. It was an unfamiliar feeling, but a good one.

Before the date I had time to finish rereading the whole novel. It was beautiful. The sports hole was a problem, since it occurred at a crucial point, but Nabokov, or whoever it was, made words take flight in your mind. There must be a place for the book in the world. Here I was with an agent, Margie, who knew absolutely everyone and how to reach them (in part through her husband's work). Maybe all I needed was Rudy to help me bring drama to those men in uniform. He was picking me up at five thirty in his Miata. (Why had he needed to tell me the make of his car?) I had the implausible sense that it would all work out.

As I dressed, I told myself that with Rudy I must pay attention, take notes. I tucked the little plastic guys into my purse in case they were needed to illustrate ball game moves. Barbie stayed home.

HAPPY HOUR

At five thirty Rudy honked his car horn to summon me. He reached over and opened the passenger door for me to get in. I couldn't tell how tall he was or anything about his body. He seemed to be wearing black leather pants. I wanted to smell him, but I knew it would prejudice me. I told my nose sternly, Down, girl.

By the time we arrived at the bar, I had heard a lot about the Miata that I wouldn't retain.

The bartender at Hanrahan's happy hour greeted Rudy by name. We settled at a table close to the television. Rudy's skin was the warm color of having been in the sun all his life. His hair was grizzled. I tried not to stare, but I realized I hadn't seen an adult up close in a long time. He looked so . . . well, old.

The drinks came in pairs. That was what happy hour at Hanrahan's meant: two drinks for the price of one, and you got them both at the same time. It was intimidating: How many twin Cokes could I drink?

Rudy seemed very comfortable with himself in his leather pants. I could tell he didn't worry about having too many chips or margaritas (four and counting) or whether I thought he was interesting. Right before the game started, he asked me what I liked to do best.

"Read," I said.

I think he was hoping for something more active.

"Watch the game," he told me. He pointed at the large-screen television, as if I could miss it. I would rather have looked at his face. I could see from the intensity of his focus that the action on the screen meant something to him.

Rudy started to narrate what was going on, who the players were. "Baseball is like the movies," he explained. "One guy, with a past and a future, and everybody is watching him."

I scribbled down notes on cocktail napkins. For a moment I thought I got it.

"See, in life no one wins or loses, you just go along. But out there on the field, it gets settled. It's all clear." He looked at me. "You're not tracking the ball."

He was right. I was watching to see if the players talked to each other in the dugout. I was wondering if those were their real bodies, or if they wore padding under their uniforms that made their hips look so square. Rudy tapped the table emphatically, telling me exactly what to watch and why. I could hear his leather pants creak when he moved. I wrote words that might be relevant on the cocktail napkins.

There was a break in the baseball game in the seventh inning. Rudy asked me about my work. I told him that I was employed by the Old Daitch Dairy. It sounded respectable, I thought, like I had a place to go in the daytime. I waited for him to ask me something about my job, but apparently my turn was over.

Rudy leaned forward to talk to me. "I love my work," he said. I could tell that he believed in himself, even without the margaritas. "In winter I supervise the conditioning of the men's crew team. In spring we are outside again. We break the ice in February to row. Cold builds stamina."

Rudy told me his theory about work: Everyone who loves their job has two special fields that come together in that particular work. Rudy's two fields were inspiring people to do their best and making life a win or lose proposition.

Although he didn't ask, I'd also found a work area that involved two fields I was very comfortable with: dairy products and being polite to people I would never have to meet.

After the game, he drove me home. I couldn't tell if six margaritas impaired his driving, but he was concentrating hard. He eased his car down my driveway and stopped. It had been a long time since I'd kissed anyone. If he had kissed me, I think I would have kissed him back, if only as an experiment. I checked in with myself to see if I felt an attraction to Rudy. Instead of an erotic response to the nearness of his hairy arm, I had a strong picture of the cow whose life had been donated to make his noisy pants.

"We could do this again," he said. "You don't get baseball at all yet."

"We could," I said.

He reached across me to open my door. Then he stroked my elbow lightly, like I was an old auntie woman.

An hour later I could still feel Rudy's little thumbstroke on my elbow. It had promise, but it didn't go anywhere. It stayed on my arm like a ghost touch. I was reminded of the girl who'd shaken hands with President Kennedy in Dallas and *still* hasn't washed her hand. That must have affected the course of her life. She could never have been a nurse, for example. And it must have cut down on her dating life.

I missed touch, but I refused to let myself think about that.

I hung up the sweater set, pulled off the Pants, and put on an elephantine T-shirt. I tucked a blanket around me in my chair at the Daitch computer. From my crammed purse, I extracted the cocktail napkins along with the pink lipstick and the team of plastic people. Using Rudy's words as best as I could remember them, prompted by my smeary notes, I went back to my lousy start on the baseball scene.

Sitting in front of the blank screen made me want to either die or run out of the room, so I started scribbling on paper instead. I drew a picture of a bat. I knew that I had to care deeply about the scene or it wouldn't work. I tried to think about what it had meant to Babe Ruth to step up to the plate, believing in himself. Why had he even wanted to play baseball? Maybe it was because he was better at it than just about everyone? Was it because he could be a winner out there and bask in the crowd's love? Was it glorious fun?

I couldn't think of anything physical in my life that might be similar to his experience. I did enjoy nursing my babies, but it was hardly like winning the World Series. I drew a picture of a breast. I was tempted to call Rudy for more help. Rudy understood men and sports and winning. But I knew he would be dead asleep.

I reviewed the few non-Nabokov facts I knew about Babe Ruth from a biography I'd read standing up in the library. I knew he loved women and they loved him. He was feisty and a hard drinker. His father owned a bar. He was raised in a foundling home after he'd stolen money from his father. There he discovered his extraordinary baseball talent. Later he had a wife who could keep him in line. She had him drink beer instead of spirits. I drew a picture of a beer mug. She wrote him fifty-dollar checks instead of letting him control the money. She dressed him in nice suits. She traveled with the team, and when women called his hotel room, she answered the phone.

I wondered if Darcy would marry someone famous. I hoped not. She did not seem like the little woman type. I drew a picture of a bridal veil. I tried to banish all irrelevant thoughts.

I got out some blank index cards and tried writing words on them by hand, like Nabokov did. I shuffled them. The words made just as little sense as in the intended order. I wished Nabokov—or whoever—would come back and finish this thing he left behind. Why was it *my* job?

Filling in the blanks of such an extraordinary writer was probably beyond me. Maybe if I closely followed his existing work, but most of it had less action than I needed. *Pnin* seemed the most action-oriented. I flipped it open randomly and read some sentences. They were long and convoluted and absolutely impossible to ape. I needed something simpler. Then this one jumped out at me: *"Kind of muggy," said the hairy-armed attendant, as he started to wipe the windshield.*

That I could imitate: *"Kind of foggy," said the thick-armed batter, indicating the stratosphere with the bat tip as he straddled the plate.*

Phew. Not awful. "Bat tip" sounded queer, like a Batman accessory, but no matter. I found another: *He stepped briskly around the hood and lunged with his rag at the windshield from the other side.*

Right. *He ran briskly around the bases and lunged at home plate from the other side.*

I was on to something. I found another one, a big fat sentence that could pretty much accommodate anything, utterly useful. I was making progress. It was time to type. I arrayed the cards and the fake *Pnin* sentences across the desk, along with the cocktail napkins, Barbie, and the plastic people.

I knew I couldn't write the scene as one of winning and losing. I didn't really understand winning and losing, or not in the sports way, like Rudy and Babe Ruth did. So I wrote the scene to capture what I could remember about making love, like risk and surrender. I could barely remember the feelings of lovemaking, but I wrote it anyway. As a way of building in reader appeal, I used every word I possibly could that was titillating in a subliminal way. Here I relied on an article for *Psychology Now* that never got published. Certain words printed on the page are entirely erotic to women, it said. Some are obvious, like "pleasure" and "negligee," but some are not. For men "hard" of course, and any possible variation on terms for penis, but also many words that are counterintuitive, such as "pancake," "garage," and "acreage." I used all of those with every sex-type verb I could think of ("thrust," "slam," "slid," etc.), plus every single one of Rudy's words from the napkins. I banged out six pages.

I was done. The game was over. The Babe had won. Two of my major weaknesses had just met: sports and faking genius. There was a sheen of perspiration on my face and right across my chest, like orgasm sweat.

The scene was not a good one. I could already hear my agent's voice telling me it was lousy, but my agent's voice was a comforting thought. I could send it to Margie and move on with my life.

I printed out the bad baseball scene and put it in an envelope beside the front door. I took a shower and stood under the hot spray feeling every needle of water. I put on my softest clothes and tiptoed out to the mailbox in the darkness to leave the pages for Bill. I set the little metal flag on the box upright and stood for a moment enjoying the night.

The stars were out, and I thought about being on the sailboat with my cousin during an August meteor shower. "The Perseid," he told me. We lay on either side of the bow on our backs, looking up. I was making wishes on the falling stars (lose five pounds, get a good job, date someone both sweet-smelling *and* stable), and he was telling me how to make sorrel soup. First make a broth from a young chicken, cooked with onion skins for color. Strain it and blend it hot with handfuls of fresh-picked sorrel, leaving out most stems. Add cream. He said if you don't have cream, make the soup anyway. Be like a grown-up cow: eat the grass in front of you and let the babies drink the cream.

PAINT

In the morning, while I was trying on breakfast identities (who are the Shredded Wheat people?), John called. He was in the neighborhood and wondered if he could drop the dog off for an overnight. Who was I now, Doggie Daycare? He trusted me with his dog but not his kids. I said yes, only because I wanted to see what he was up to back in town already.

Too soon the doorbell rang. "Here," John said, handing me a retractable leash. "This is safer for you, since you must have a hard time getting her to obey you." He didn't mean to be a jerk. He thought of himself as a good guy. Other guys thought of him as a good guy. Irene thought he was a good guy, or a good catch anyway. The dog clearly thought he was God; she was leaning on his thigh, looking up at him with an adoration he didn't deserve.

I could see Irene behind the tinted windows of his sports car.

"I'll take her, but I want another day with Darcy and Sam."

"Barb, we have an agreement about that. It's a legal document."

"Fine. Keep your dog then." I held out the leash.

He dropped his head like he was trying to gather himself. "Why is it always impossible with you?" I knew I didn't have to answer that. "OK, an extra day this month."

I took the leash back. "Where are you going?" I asked, even though it was so not my business.

"Couples counseling," he said.

That pissed me off intensely. There he went, off to listen to Irene's feelings when he never wanted to listen to my feelings. I grabbed the dog's collar and dragged her into the house, even though she outweighed me by ten pounds. Or maybe it was the other way around.

I slammed the door. "I am feeling rage," I told Matilda once we were inside. She sat down on my foot. Her skin draped loosely, like she was designed to grow even bigger. She gave me what would be, if I believed in anthropomorphizing animals, a "What else is new?" look.

While I was immobilized, I remembered that there was nothing in the kitchen to match my day's breakfast identity of being a bagel-with-a-smear kind of person. Bagels dull rage, I remembered from an old cover story in *Psychology Now. Serotonin released by carb consumption alleviates both anxiety and anger but will not affect shame.*

I extricated my flat foot and put on yesterday's clothes (also tomorrow's clothes).

Unwilling to trust Matilda alone in the house, I loaded her in the front seat of the car and drove to the bakery. At the drive-through window I collected my breakfast. I parked in the parking lot of the hardware store next door and unwrapped my toasted sesame bagel.

Apparently in Upstate they don't use the term smear, because the cream cheese mounded on my bagel like a lardy mini Matterhorn. I looked around for what to do with it and found myself staring into the opaque brown eyes of Matilda. A string of drool landed on my knee.

I didn't know if cream cheese was bad for Bull Danes, but I scraped off the excess and offered it to her on the paper wrap. Matilda ate it in one gulp, paper and all. She seemed to want the bagel too, so I gave her half. I kept my coffee far away from her snout so she didn't get any ideas of sharing.

The parking lot was full of cars. In the window of the hardware store there was a pyramid of paint cans and a banner that read Designer Paints: All Colors Half Price.

Women were streaming into the store in pairs and singly. They were coming out at the same rate, looking purposeful, toting cans of paint.

While Matilda made cream cheese nose tracks on the inside of the windshield, I ventured inside the store.

There was a happy buzz around the color display. I drifted over and picked up a strip of sample paint chips, more to blend in with the other women than for any purpose. The Benjamin Moore blue-grays were very pretty, subtle and elegant. At the top of the strip, number 184, was the exact robin's egg blue of the cathouse door in the city.

I ordered a quart of exterior latex, number 184, and waited while the clerk mixed it for me. "Too cold to paint," he pointed out. That's how it was in Onkwedo; no one was eager to make a sale. There was a kind of "you keep your money, I'll keep my goods, and we'll all go home" attitude. It was a hard attitude to understand in commerce.

At home I masked off a square on the outside of the front door and painted a blue swath. It looked good, so I painted a matching one on the inside of the door.

I washed my paintbrush in the sink and fed Matilda some of her regular fare. Mixing water with dry dog food in her great tub cured me of any desire to eat for the rest of the day.

I lay on the couch. Matilda, having scarfed her food in four seconds, joined me. She stared out the window, watching squirrels scamper up and down the bare trees. There was nearly a plague of squirrels in Onkwedo, burying nuts and digging them up again, launching themselves under cars. Matilda's breath made a misty wreath on the pane. I rested one hand on her big shoulder—if dogs are considered to have shoulders—and looked out the window at nothing.

John had left me his town, not that I wanted it. With the children gone from Onkwedo, I had no reason to be here at all.

It was the exact moment in the day and in life when, if I had a television, I would be lying here watching the porn channel, or the porn/shopping channel, or the porn/shopping/cooking channel, and drinking my morning Irish coffee. Maybe I would sip something even more disgusting, like what the bartender drank during my two-day job waitressing at a jazz club (one day hired, next day fired): Scotch and milk.

I lay on the couch waiting for my agent to call or something to happen. I tried to conjure up a state of happiness. I moved my face muscles into the smile position. I tried to remember a joke. I thought about catching fruit in my mouth. I ran my tongue over my teeth. My mouth felt underutilized.

I turned my gaze to the blue patch on my door. It looked perfect, both welcoming and aloof. It said, Come in and you will leave enriched. It said, Come in now. It said, Come.

I thought about all the women nearby painting their bedrooms, the kitchen trim, the powder room. It seemed desperately unfair that, because of location, these women weren't having the exquisite pleasures of life, the passions. No chocolate croissants made by a Parisian for them, no frivolous and magnificent shoes, no dancing along sidewalks.

I spread my mind in a fine net over the city of Onkwedo, scanning for the activities of the women. Beside the painting and cleaning and snacking, in my mind's eye I saw a woman taking out the trash. In the county clerk's office a woman was doing sit-ups on the floor of her office, her feet hooked under her desk chair. Margie was on the phone with one of her lucrative romance writer clients.

No one in all of Onkwedo was having sex. No one except the

fertility-challenged couple next door. They were about to—their bodies having reached the optimal luteal phase temperatures—but it would have to be fast, as they both had to return to their jobs.

This vision of my sexually starved sister-residents should have made me feel compassion, but instead it seemed like a remarkable business opportunity. Why shouldn't someone open a cathouse here? Why shouldn't the cathouse serve the women of Onkwedo who were in dire need of pleasure, of passion? My mouth watered.

Yes, passion was something the town needed, and needed in the worst way. You could see the terrible dearth of passion in the overstocked carbo aisles of Apex Friendly Market. You could see it in the romance books flying off the library shelves, in the busy carpet clean-&-vac rentals, in the long lines of cars at the car wash. Passion is a messy, messy thing, and Onkwedo was smothering it, detailing it out of existence.

I began to feel the river of options—nothing specific. The city is a good place for ideas, an island in the river of potential, but the river of potential flows everywhere. I could feel the possibilities flowing around me, near, ready to be discovered.

There was a way to get on my feet again, get my children back, and I was going to find it.

High on coffee and latex fumes, I cut out some darling pictures of the Waindell all-star crew team from the *Onkwedo Clarion*. There was a Sid Somebody with golden curls, and a Janson looking like a model, both champions. It *is* a win-lose world, I thought, and then remembered that I knew nothing about winning *or* business, absolutely nothing. On my coffee high, this led to the realization that I didn't know anything at all. That struck me as the most profound thought of the day.

I decided to call my agent.

Margie told me she was exercising but to come over and we could talk while she sweated.

I dragged Matilda back outside, where she stopped next to the car. "We are walking," I said firmly.

At Margie's, I tied the dog to the mailbox, where she lay down and fell instantly asleep.

Margie was in her home gym, in the spare bedroom, wearing dove gray workout pants and leotard, gray ankle weights, and a gray headband. She was bench-pressing fifty pounds and looked almost as good working out as Princess Di had.

"Hunh," she grunted as she pushed the bar up on the last repetition of her set. She sat up and blotted her flushed face with a folded towel. "Talk to me," she said. "I'll talk back later."

I described the trip to the city and the wretched TVQ people. Margie was working on flys. I dodged the weights that kept sailing toward my face.

I tried to tell her about Ceci-Cela being closed, and about the ultimate chocolate croissant. "Don't talk about food," she panted.

I decided to do a little oblique research. "What do women in Onkwedo do all day?" I asked her. "Not the ones with jobs, but the other ones. What do they do once their kids are in school? Do they clean all the time?"

Margie grunted, which could have been either agreement or effort. She put the weights down. "Some do," she said. "The crazy ones clean."

"What about the others? Do they cook?"

"Nobody cooks anymore."

"Do they shop? There's nothing to buy here."

Margie was strapping on ankle weights. She grunted again. "They sure buy a lot of romances." Her voice was breathy as she counted out her reps, "Hobbies, volunteering, pedicures." Her muscles were straining with the effort.

That sounded dismal.

"Twenty-one, twenty-two . . ." She put the weights down.

I asked her if she'd read the scene I wrote. One of the perks of being married to a postal worker was that you got your mail early. "It's not *Nabokov*," she gasped out, "but it has a little pizzazz."

I thought agents were supposed to be up on the latest slang, but Margie's was from the 1950s.

She was dead silent as she finished what I could only figure was her gluteal set. She unfastened the ankle weights and squirted pink Crystal Light into her mouth from a squeeze bottle. "We'll need to put an author name on it. I was thinking something strong but slightly fake, like Lucas Shade."

That sounded fine to me. I looked at my friend Margie, gorgeous and sweaty in her workout clothes; she always knew what to do.

Margie unfolded a gray towel and wiped the sweat from her eyelids. "I'm going to send *Babe Ruth* to an editor or two, see what they think." She kept talking to me through the door of the shower room, "It might take a long time to get a response." Over the sound of the water she called out, "You should write something else. Try a romance."

"I can't," I said. "I'm too rusty."

She emerged with a towel wrapped around her and another making a turban on her head. She looked like a very tall advertisement for personal cleanliness. "Rudy thought you were a doll."

I was surprised. "I didn't think I was his type."

"Rudy knows his way around the women in this town. If you're a Waindell coach, you're a prince in this town. He knows what the women want; he's been busy not giving it to them for the last twenty years."

That figured. "You look great. How often do you do that?" I asked her.

"Six days a week, twice on Sunday."

I wish there were actual secrets to having a fabulous body, but there aren't.

Margie pulled the towel from her hair. "I'll take you to lunch Wednesday. That's the day I eat."

"Great," I said, hoping to sound casual, like lunch with my agent wasn't near the pinnacle of my aspirations.

Outside I untied Matilda and roused her from her coma.

I found myself skipping along. Skipping was the perfect speed to keep pace with Matilda's shambling trot, and it prevented her from pulling my arm from its socket. Why didn't people skip? It gave so much more pleasure than running. Darcy hadn't yet learned to skip; she did a step and hop which she called skipping, but it wasn't. And now how would I teach her? The thought of my little girl gone slowed my feet.

Matilda continued on, dragging me behind, her nose lifted to the smell of the frozen lake below us. We left the village area. Yards with fences gave way to woods, and the road changed abruptly from black-top to gravel. There was a sign announcing You Are Leaving Onkwedo. The woods verged on the edge of the lake, following its contour clear up to the Daitch farm and beyond.

I tried to keep pace with Matilda, thinking about what Margie had said about the Onkwedo women. Hobbies. Volunteering. Pedicures. Rudy to date! And not even a chocolate croissant to brighten the day. The dog tugged me toward a steep driveway, eager to get down to the water. The mailbox beside the driveway had been run over, probably by a snowplow. It looked like it had been lying there for a long time.

The driveway made hairpin turns, switching direction to accommodate the steepness of the grade. I worked to keep my footing on the loose stones. We stopped in a clearing, a wide area for parking. Through the leafless trees I could see the steep outline of a roof.

The dog and I scrambled down the slope and circled the building, an old lodge, maybe for hunting. I counted the dormer windows on the second floor. There must be six bedrooms upstairs. We stopped at the front steps, leading up to a wide, slightly sagging porch. The front door was covered with a piece of plywood. The lodge looked abandoned but not derelict.

Matilda leaned on me, pressing me down toward the lake below us, accessible only by a steep ladder-like set of steps. But I stood rooted, staring at the building. Even in its shabbiness, the sunshine reflecting up from the lake gave the place an expectant feeling, like it was bathed in footlights.

For Matilda we were still too far from the water. The dog pulled me down the steps to a pebble beach nestled between a cracked cement dock and an old-fashioned boathouse that appeared to float on the lake. We walked along the dock, stepping over big fissures with water lapping them. At the end, on either side, were two rusted iron rings and two sets of cleats to tie up boats.

Across the lake, the houses of Long Hill nestled into the hillside, spare and lonely. The sound of the water against the dock was a gentle clucking. Matilda sighed and lay down as if she had known her destination all along. I sat close beside her, needing warmth from her big body.

I gazed back up the steep bank of the lake at the lodge, which lay just outside the city limits of Onkwedo—repressed, starving-for-passion Onkwedo. Staring at the front door, I saw it de-boarded, cleaned, and painted. Robin's egg blue. In my mind the pale blue color on the door shimmered with possibility. I could imagine cars in the parking lot, the mom-mobiles and the smaller career-gal cars. *Seclusion,* I thought. *Lake view,* I thought. *Ample parking,* I thought. *Ideal location for the cathouse.*

I licked my lips. There are times when your destiny unfolds before you like a crisp sheet.

RUDY AGAIN

I put my hand on the telephone, trying to master the courage to call Rudy. I wondered if it would be better to talk to him about business over coffee or drinks. I nearly gave up right then. *These are the new rules,* I said sternly to myself. You have nothing left to lose. I straightened my back. I picked up the phone. I inhaled. I exhaled. I dialed.

Rudy answered like this: "Speak."

And I did.

I met Rudy at a college bar near the boathouse where the sculls were kept. This time I brought a notebook. The place was dimly lit and a large screen in the corner was playing pornographic cartoons. The students sat with their heads together in the darkness of the bar. They looked like they were discussing Camus. No one watched the screen at all. Betty Boop was doing something nasty up there, and I didn't want to decipher it. Betty Boop is horrendously cute. She's the morphing of baby and vamp designed to call forth the inner pedophile.

We ordered Scotches. I had already decided that whatever Rudy got, I would match him. "Blended," he specified, pointing to the Johnny Walker Red in the well. I was surprised to find out it was very good.

Rudy looked at me warily. "You're John's ex, hunh."

"Yes, we're divorced." I loved saying this.

"John and I were in school together. He used to win the science fair every year. How's he doing now?"

"Great. He's doing very well," I said.

"Has he still got that head of hair?"

"Yes."

"What a great head of hair," Rudy said wistfully. "Hi, Sherrie, get me another." Rudy looked appreciatively at the tall bartender.

"Is she your type?" I asked.

Rudy snorted. "Oh yes," he said. "She is exactly my type." He took a slug of his second Scotch.

I decided it was time to advance my agenda. I took a gulp of my drink and started talking. I explained that I was thinking of going into business. I watched his face tighten; he thought I was going to hit him up for money. I told him I didn't need capital; I needed advice. He relaxed a bit and sipped his drink. "I am in the planning phase," I said, the alcohol giving me courage. I described the cathouse idea, but obliquely, leaving out the sex part. I did talk about pleasure and relaxation, and said that women were the clients and men the workers.

Rudy listened attentively. He watched his drink rather than my face. This was what men did when they wanted to listen to your voice for lies or weakness. Either that or we were back to the male brain's object-to-person modality-shifting problem.

I used my tumbler to bump his along the bar. "Rudy," I said, "the women in this town are . . ." I searched for the right words. "In need of attention." I clinked his glass hard. "You know that as well as anyone."

He reached for his drink and held it is if it might fly away.

"What's the best way to get a business started in Onkwedo?"

"It's a hard place to break out, not a lot of money floating around."

The bartender cocked an eyebrow at me, and I shook my head. "It's really a company town. If your business isn't connected to Waindell in some way, it'll be very hard to get it off the ground."

"What kind of business does Waindell support?"

"Anything to do with research. Waindell is big on science."

I pulled out my notebook and put it on the bar.

"What's that for?" Rudy asked.

"Taking notes," I said. I picked up my pen and tapped it on the notebook. Rudy polished off his drink and got another from a male bartender without any visible sign between them. That kind of imperceptible communication is an example of the parallel universe men inhabit.

"I used to be a catch, you know," Rudy said.

I nodded.

"Dated three or four at a time." He was finishing his third Scotch fast. "I burned out." My pen was poised. Rudy groaned. "Cunnilingus," he said, "it's so boring." I craned my neck around to see if he was commenting on the pornographic cartoon, but apparently not.

For something to do, I wrote "cunnilingus" in my notebook. For something else to do, I sipped some more of my Scotch. The drink seemed to encourage parallel existence. Rudy was clearly in a different world. He reached down and hauled my purse up by the strap. "And when they show up with those big pocketbooks, I know I am in trouble." He seemed reassured to find my purse small. "They bring their own sex toys," Rudy complained. "Is that progress? I feel like the Hoover guy." Rudy was on his fourth Scotch.

Then, as if we were two guys in the middle of a Friday night drinking bout, Rudy told me a long joke about a woman having sex with her panty hose on. It was so dated I wanted to smack him into the twenty-first century. When he finished, I sat there and looked at him and waited.

"That's a joke," Rudy said.

I leaned close to him. He could look down my shirt if he wanted to, though we both probably thought (for different reasons), *Why bother?* And I said, "Rudy, it's a joke when the other person laughs."

"You're a funny one," he said.

"Why is that?" I had another sip of the fascinating Scotch.

"You're cute and all"—he wagged his head—"but it's like we're on the same team."

"Thanks, I guess." The Scotch tasted like the best thing that had ever happened to me.

"You're not gay, right?"

"No." I was starting to feel warm all over.

"You could wear some lipstick," Rudy said authoritatively.

"I am," I said.

"It doesn't matter. I like you."

"Thanks," I said. We both stared at the hot bartender. I caught a whiff of Rudy's neck. He smelled like a man, a grown-up. I reminded myself not to be such a smell slut.

Rudy was swirling the ice in the bottom of his tumbler, looking almost sad. "Do you ever wonder what it's all about?" he asked me.

"No," I said, which was the truth.

It was time for me to leave. I felt sober enough to drive home, and this was going no place, or no place I wanted to go. I stood up. From my small-enough purse I retrieved a twenty-dollar bill. I wished it were two tens so I wouldn't have to part with all of it. I left the money on the bar.

As I swallowed the last of my Scotch, Rudy said, "Hire young. More ambition, more chance of finding winners."

In his world, I may have kissed him goodnight. In my world, I sniffed what was left of his hair and slid out the door.

Driving home, I thought about what Rudy had told me: Onkwedo was a company town. With all the fields surrounding it, Onkwedo was like a plantation with Waindell as the master. If you got Waindell's stamp on a project, you probably had carte blanche. And the master loved science. Call something "research" and you could probably do anything you wanted.

This thought carried me most of the way home. As I turned into my street, it dawned on me that I had a friend, a guy friend, a relationship I'd never had in the city after my cousin was gone. And an agent too. I didn't have one of those in the city. As my first local friend, Margie was spectacular. Two friends and an agent. Onkwedo was becoming my town. I even had a dog part-time. This lifted my heart.

When I opened the front door, Matilda was sleeping on the mat. She may have been waiting for John to come back, but it didn't matter. I gave her a Scotchy kiss on her head.

BISTRO MOUTARDE

My mother had sent me an email at six in the morning:

Dear Barb,

I hope you are getting enough sleep? My mother thought that a good night's sleep solved everything. And for her it did.

Things are going very well for the event. She didn't write "wedding," in a rare moment of tact. *I have hired a harpist from the conservatory. We don't need a band, I think, but I hope there will be some dancing.* Hadn't she ever heard of DJs? Did she think we were all going to dance the Angel Stomp to harp music? *Our whole family will be there* (our "whole family" was me and the children) *and some very nice doctors.* The last three words were in boldface type. *I am only asking you to do one thing, and it is for your own good: Wear a dress! I am happy to take you shopping, you know this.*

Love,

Mom

P.S. What happened to the blue dress I sent you for the custody hearing? She was referring to the A-line wonder, in a color

I thought of as bad-luck blue, now turned into a rug and matching curtains in Barbie's cardboard condo.

P.P.S. Have you tried Sam on low carb?

Ignoring my mother, something I was excellent at doing, I began
dressing for lunch with my agent. For once I knew exactly what to wear:
new tight jeans (sans tags), funky but hip sweater (OK, *Margie's* funky
but hip sweater), Darcy's saddlebag purse with suede fringe, boots. I
looked in the mirror and decided I almost looked good, needing only
some remedial work on fingernails and eyebrows.

Just as I was sneezing into the mirror, tweezers in hand, eyebrows
sore and balding, I heard Bill's truck pull up. Mixed in with my ODD
mail was a letter bearing six stamps. The lettering of the address was
crude, and there was no name. When I opened it a clump of dark hair
fell out. Inside the envelope was a sheet of purple stationery. On it was
written, *I kt my har. DARCY.*

I wondered from where on Darcy's head the hair had been cut.
Most likely front and center, where she could see her work in the mir-
ror. I gathered the hair into my palm. It was easily three inches long.
Darcy must have cut it near the roots.

Sixteen more days till they came back. I had the dog till then. Apparently Matilda was too disruptive in the new house. It was pathetic
how much I was beginning to like Matilda's company. Especially since
she remained indifferent to me, offering herself for scratching or patting without enthusiasm, eager only for food.

Inside, the restaurant the decor said "bistro" with a heavy hand:
narrow dark bead board, oval mirrors, Piaf warbling mournfully, ab-
sinthe ads and Toulouse-Lautrec prints on the walls. In spite of that, it

smelled authentic, a meeting place of meat and hot grease. Margie was sitting in front of a plate of carpaccio—wafers of raw beef dotted with capers and drizzled with olive oil. I ordered a salad with chèvre and some word I didn't know, which turned out to be glacéed prunes, odd but tasty, and frisée, which tickled my throat going down. It was heavenly to eat something that I had not known since its midlife on an Apex Market shelf.

At the next table, two moms were discussing homeschooling. Two children were under their table doing what appeared to be a unit on campfires, with breadsticks and possibly matches. A baby was perched on one mother's shoulder, facing us. He—I think it was male—clutched a breadstick in his fist. He was one of those solemn and unblinking babies. He watched Margie, who was rolling slivers of raw meat around her fork and savagely, beautifully devouring them.

"Let me give you an update on the book," she said when she had tucked away enough flesh. A glacéed prune froze on my tongue. I felt my life poised to change. I had a vision of spacious bookstore windows lined with Nabokov's long-lost novel (written by "Lucas Shade," wink, wink). I saw a warehouse with pallets of shrink-wrapped, hardbound, shiny-jacketed books. I saw a modest acknowledgment to me on the final page, naming me as the book's finder.

Margie pushed her half-full plate away. She looked around for the cigarette she wasn't allowed to smoke. "The first editor who read the manuscript said that the crucial baseball scene was written with all the panache of a personal ad," she said. She quoted the editor's note: " 'This scene goes down like the *Titanic*.' " That was the editor's Smith College way of saying it sucked.

The frisée gagged me.

"You have to have a tough skin in this business," Margie said, piercing a morsel of meat without eating it. She balled up her napkin and tossed it on the table. "Hang in there. We still have several editors to hear back from."

I tried to swallow the packing material that was lodged behind my uvula.

The waiter hovered like he had just learned the Heimlich and was hoping to practice. Margie began telling me about the burgeoning market of baby boomer readers and women in PEF relationships (post-erectile functioning) freshly looking to romance novels. She told me that several publishers were launching lines promoted heavily through AARP and grandmothers' websites, with titles like *True Love at Last* and *Third Time Lucky*. Margie urged me to try writing a love scene for older readers. "It's just like sports," she said, kindly adding, "only you know more about it."

I wasn't sure she was right.

The baby made a cooing noise at Margie and caught her eye. We both cocked our heads at the dear little serious-faced person, doomed to a life of homeschooling and arson. He extended his upper lip toward Margie and made a careful and practiced raspberry. She answered him with a smile. Pointing his breadstick in the air like an eccentric orchestra conductor, he assembled all the muscles in his face and smiled back.

Conversation died around us as lunch eaters turned to watch the love match in progress.

I felt jealous of the baby getting so much of my agent's attention.

"I'll try it, Margie. I will."

Margie and the infant locked eyes. I took the opportunity to deposit the unchewable frisée wad in my napkin. The waiter had moved on to a more likely choker.

"When do you think we'll hear from those other editors?" I said, reminding her why we were there.

"A month, maybe two," Margie said without taking her gaze from the baby. Neither one of them blinked.

The waiter brought the dessert menus. It was a hard choice for me between crème brûlée and tarte tatin, but I was leaning toward the tart. Margie's menu clattered onto the faux-marble table. "I can't do this to my body," she said. "But you go ahead."

So I didn't. I put my menu down, flushed with longing for the sweet.

"Write that romance scene in the meantime," Margie said. "Take your mind off the baseball book. Waiting kills everything."

"Do you want to give me any tips on the romance writing?" My tongue was still on dessert.

Margie turned toward me. I could feel her focus in, like we were finally getting to the point of the lunch. "Write the scene where she first feels that the man is connected to her, where she knows he cares about her. Women readers—and *all* the readers are women—love commitment."

I sighed.

"You can do this, Barb." Margie signaled the waiter for the check. "And it's a lot less harebrained than you think." She pulled a large envelope from her purse and slid it across the table to me. "In here are book covers for the new boomer lines. Look at them for inspiration. They'll give you an idea of the target audience." She signed off on the lunch. "It's easy work. Just follow the rules and make it sexy."

Follow the rules, I thought. Right.

The frisée had left a freshly scoured sensation on the back of my throat. Still wanting dessert, I stopped at Bear Witness Ice Cream Parlor for a soothing scoop of coffee ice cream.

The Bear Witness cult was a type of dairy-based religion that promoted reverence for large mammals. The religion forbade the use of milking machines on cows. It wasn't exactly Amish, but it wasn't anything else either.

They had at least one dirty secret, the only one I knew, which was that they served Old Daitch Dairy ice cream and passed it off as their own from their "grass-fed dairy cows." Young Mr. Daitch had proudly revealed this duplicity to me. He didn't consider it lying, just clever marketing.

The high ceiling of Bear Witness was softly lit, out of respect for the peaceful consumption of ice cream. It had been someone's life work to restore the building, an old train station. They had left the ceiling of pressed tin, indented squares. Fans spun slowly, directing the heat downward, keeping the few sluggish winter flies in motion. Lamps hung suspended on long brass chains over the tables. The soft gray marble trim and floor were unreasonably beautiful. The ticket counter had been converted to milkshake, sundae, and cone service. Bear Witness was the only place in town that served real cream in little pitchers on the tables.

It seemed fitting that the Onkwedo train station was now an ice cream parlor. Here in Onkwedo no one was going anywhere. We weren't part of trade. Onkwedons just stayed in one place and consumed. We were the end of the line.

I was the lone customer. I sat at a corner table where I could watch the main road and the parking lot. Above the list of flavors, a man on a ladder was hammering something into the wall.

The server wore a brown sackcloth dress, or maybe it was woven of hemp, and her name tag said Penitence. After she scooped up my dessert, she went back to polishing metal sundae dishes, balancing them in careful pyramids of six.

If you pour a slow river of cream over your ice cream, it will harden into a delectable shell. Sam discovered this. He is the only person I know to have investigated pouring heavy cream on ice cream. I was practicing it at the corner table of Bear Witness Ice Cream Parlour, pouring slowly from the creamer onto the coffee ice cream, then cracking the shell with a dig of my spoon. The ice cream inside was soft and melty, but the cream hardened into the mouthfeel of chocolate, without sweetness to distract from the perfect texture.

I opened the envelope from Margie, and a stack of glossy paperback covers spilled out. They pictured silver-haired models walking hand in hand along beaches, or driving in open convertibles with their heads thrown back, smiling, a picnic basket visible in the backseat.

I wondered if Penitence ever read this kind of book. Without meaning to, I pictured her dress coming off. Underneath was her religious underwear. I couldn't imagine it exactly—no elastic, a couple of buttons, and a drawstring? Between bites of ice cream, I arranged the covers by preference, Penitence's preference, certainly nothing too frivolous. I knew Penitence was not the right age group for the book, but dressing like the Pilgrims, she was heading there fast.

Penitence would have to be courted by someone serious and worthy. Someone who appreciated the beauty of simpler cultures, of orderly lives. What kind of a man should he be? Someone capable and skilled, to make her feel safe, even as he made her desire smolder. Maybe a professor. (Professors had never made my desire smolder, but I'd watched more than one classmate give it up to the person behind the lectern.) Maybe he could have silver hair.

He would devote himself to her (what women want, Margie said), persist in getting her to remove her awkward garments. And his passion, his love, his attention would free her own animal spirit into the great modern world.

I stared at the man on the ladder and at the back of his jeans, thinking how unfair it was the way jeans fit men, the straight narrowness of their hips going into their thighs, the jeans becoming worn in just the right way along their leg muscles. Idly, I wondered why Penitence's husband (if the carpenter was her husband) wasn't wearing the sackcloth garb, and why men in the cult had the freedom to dress in worldly ways.

I went back to my task, spreading the covers out on the table around my ice cream dish, considering which image would stir Penitence. The red convertible car was too materialistic. She needed something that would appeal to her old-fashioned mind. One cover showed a couple standing in front of an ivy-covered wall that might have been the library of Waindell University. *Love at Last: Love to Last,* had been titled by someone who probably collected palindromes.

In the book with Penitence as the heroine, this is how it would happen: The hero would climb down the ladder, unfasten his leather tool belt, lay his level on the countertop, sheathe the drill. He would be intrigued by the hidden beauty of Penitence, perceived only by him, the prospect of the luscious body secreted under the wretched clothes.

As I thought that, the carpenter climbed down the ladder. He had what Margie called "a killer ass." He stood back to look at the display he had mounted on the wall. A series of wooden clubs that I knew to be dashers from old butter churns fanned out in a semicircle. The club ends were very headlike, smooth and worn, and the carved wooden rings around the necks looked like simple adornments. Seen that way, the butter dashers resembled African artifacts, like the long simple sculptures collected by Modigliani. The carpenter had made a beautiful display, serious and well balanced.

Penitence wrapped her rag around her fist and stood beside him.

This was where in the romance book his shoulder would brush her shoulder and his heat would penetrate the rough burlap and sultrify her smooth skin underneath. Sultrify?

Instead he appeared to be discussing the bill with Penitence. She gestured to the counter, offering him an ice cream cone, but he shook his head.

Unfeeling jerk, I thought.

He leaned the folded ladder on the wall beside my table and crouched over a large case on the floor that I hadn't noticed.

"I suppose you need me to move," I said, still huffy from his slighting poor plainly dressed Penitence.

"You're fine," he said cheerfully from under the table. He straightened up and began winding an extension cord in a figure eight around his palm and elbow.

"Will that be all?" Penitence asked me.

"Yes." I blushed like a teenage boy caught with his bad thoughts, imagining her drawstring sticking in the lumpy natural-fiber undergarment.

"Two dollars please." She picked up the empty creamer and looked in it.

I put three dollars on the table. She primly handed one bill back to me. "Tipping is not permitted."

The man laid a level on top of the table beside me and took a pencil from behind his ear. "What are those?" He pointed to the covers spread around me.

"Paperback book covers." I started shuffling them back into the envelope as casually as I could.

"Do you design them?"

"No." I fastened the brad.

"Good." He put his drill case next to the level.

"Why?" I tucked the envelope into my purse.

"They're ugly as hell." He stood beside my table, putting his stuff away. His tool belt was slung low on his hips. I tried not to look at it. Tape measure, check; hammer, check; screws in a shallow pocket. "Are you new here?" He addressed the top of my head.

"Yes. Pretty much. Two years."

"You like it?" He dumped the screws from his belt into a box.

"Sometimes."

"From the city?"

"Yes."

"You get out on the lake much?"

"No."

"That's the key. The lake and the woods are the reason to be here."

"OK." I began to wish he would go away. I instinctively looked at his hand for a wedding ring. He caught the glance and smiled at me, a very confident smile, then hoisted his ladder onto one shoulder, and carried it outside. Through the window I could see him fastening the ladder to the side of his pickup, and unlocking a big metal toolbox built into the back. On the side of the truck was printed Holder Woodworking.

I counted slowly to fifty and left.

As I walked up to my front door, I could hear Matilda's deep bark. Inside, she greeted me with a sniff and a lick. We were growing on each other.

I called young Mr. Daitch, who knew every landowner adjacent to his farm. He answered the phone on the first ring, sounding unsurprised that I was calling him to ask about the abandoned lodge. He told me it belonged to Granny Bryce and gave me her phone number at the assisted-living home. "She's spry as can be," he told me. "She only moved there for the food. She hates to cook."

I called Granny Bryce, whose voice mail informed me that she was in the dining hall. I left a message regarding my interest in the lodge.

Then I noodled around on the Waindell University website, trying to figure out how to make my next move. There was a link to research projects, and from there to "subject pool." If you were a legitimate researcher—and here my employment at *Psychology Now* helped—you could arrange to solicit subjects for your experiments through the research division. I reviewed the guidelines, which seemed reasonable, complete with a release form to download and print.

I wrote a four-sentence description of the project: *Research assistants needed for longitudinal study in human ecology. Privately funded investigation of adult human response/stimulus. Two afternoons per week, three to six month commitment. Physical stamina advantageous.* Ugh. It sounded terrible. I put some dollar signs at the beginning and end. I posted it in the research division and also on the Waindell crew website under "jobs/extracurricular activities/volunteering."

There wasn't anything to do now but cook. I put a chicken in the oven to roast, the two whole lemons recipe from old bossy pants Marcella Hazan's *Essentials of Classic Italian Cooking*.

Matilda parked herself in front of the glass oven door. Maybe she was waiting for the skin of the chicken to inflate, which Marcella Hazan promised would happen if you trussed the bird properly. It never had for me.

But this time the chicken puffed, golden and succulent. I poured the juice from the roasting pan over Matilda's kibble, and she ate it with delicate appreciation. I ate a breast, looking at the crew team's handsome faces cut from the newspaper, which I had pasted in a menu-like folder.

Two hours later, when I checked my email, there were a dozen responses from the two sites. Some had photos, and I could match the faces with the famous ones from the *Onkwedo Clarion*. There were Sidney Somebody, and Janson Something, each as handsome as Abercrombie & Fitch. It was a heady moment.

I wrote them all back, arranging an interview schedule for potential sex workers for the cathouse.

PENCIL SKIRT

I'd scheduled a full afternoon of interviews in Waindell's College Hall. Margie, without paying the slightest attention to why I would need it (she was in the middle of a book auction for the sequel to *Love at Last*), told me the classic job interview outfit: a tailored jacket, heels, and "a nice skirt." I found all three at the Salvation Army, where the clerk who unlocked the dressing room told me I'd chosen a pencil skirt. The dressing room smelled like mothballs, B.O., and death. A pencil skirt is designed to keep your knees together so tightly that only a pencil could fit between them. It made my butt look like two erasers, and not necessarily in a good way. I looked like the guidance counselor at a prep school. Not a hip prep school, a school like the one where Jean Harris was headmistress before she went to jail.

At home I tried the outfit on with tights of a patterned herringbone, left over from long ago, beautiful stockings that made the sharp plateau of my kneecap a decorative thing. When I'd worn them before, Darcy had refused to let go of my ankles till I promised her a pair. "Sstockingssss," she hissed to herself, all sibilant like she was speaking Parseltongue.

Waindell's College Hall was an imposing building. I had been assigned an interview room with vaulted ceilings and leather Chesterfield armchairs and couch. No one greeted me or checked me into room 104. There was a gas fire going behind a fake log. On the mantelpiece were brass plaques of varying sizes corresponding to alumni gifts. The Garantolas had given the furnishings, and Mr. & Mrs. John Mayfield were responsible for bequeathing the fake fireplace with the eternal flame. It was luxurious.

I'd brought a clipboard and a stack of the release forms. The interviews were scheduled half an hour apart, and I had nearly filled the four-hour allotment.

I was nervous about this day, and because of that I'd also brought snacks for the interviewees and for me. Stoned Wheat Thins and Brie. Since I arrived, I had eaten most of the cheese. A quarter pound of Brie sat like Sakrete in my gut. Someone *should* have moved my cheese. Sometimes I ate as though I was waiting for someone to come along and tell me to stop.

The names on the clipboard were from the crew team roster:

    Henry Bradford
    Tim Lakewell
    Scott Harrington
    Janson Waters
    Richard Dorsett
    Bradley Lambert
    Sidney Walker

It read like a dance card at a cotillion.

I was so nervous I wanted to vomit up my cheese. I reminded myself sternly that these men with the prep school names were younger than me. I was here on Earth first.

This calmed me a little.

I sniffed the leather of the couch. It smelled intelligent and expensive: a well-cured hide judiciously selected by a team of interior designers, architects, and decorators. I picked up the Waindell University telephone receiver and listened to the dial tone. Even that sounded rich.

It was still a little early. I counted all the curse words I knew. At number thirty-two (hell's bells), the door opened and Henry Bradford walked in. He smiled and held out a big hand for me to shake. The palm was thick and callused from rowing.

We sat with the low table between us, my knees crammed together in the tweed pencil skirt. The shoes were excellent for sitting down, and pointy like they had been sharpened. "Cheese?" I offered, sliding the scanty plate over to his side.

"Thanks." Henry Bradford picked up the remaining wedge, rind and all, and swallowed it.

"Where are you from?" I asked, before realizing he couldn't talk because his teeth were gummed together with dairy fat.

He made a mooing noise.

"Let me tell you about the project." I had calibrated this talk to sound scientific while still making clear that they would be expected to do anything and everything. My rehearsed speech went like this: "We are investigating human sexual response under clinical but emotionally plausible conditions, female human sexual response. The prevailing information about arousal patterns has been challenged by new data from both brain imaging and chemical measures of neurotransmission." I was particularly proud of that sentence.

Only I don't know what I actually said. It was possible that coherency stopped at "Where are you from?" and the rest was word salad.

Because Henry Whatever said calmly to me, "That doesn't sound scientific."

I said it was new work and experimental. I decided he was a little stumpy and maybe too hairy.

⸱ He finally swallowed the cheese. "What is the job title?"

Maybe he needed this for his résumé? "Research assistant."

"What is the pay?"

I told him the per-shift rate, which was good for this town. But, I added, there might be tips. I also told him that he would have access to a lot of privileged information that it would be best never to reveal. "Would that be a problem?" I said.

He asked me the schedule, and I told him. He reached for some crackers with a big hand that was attached to a very hairy wrist. He seemed ready to eat the whole plate. With difficulty I stood up in the needle-tipped shoes and extended my hand. "I will call you," I said. We shook again and he left, trailing a wake of some very nice manly soap.

I put a line through his name.

Dairy fatigue was setting in, or else sheer terror was making me sleepy. There were six more candidates and only a few crackers left. I figured I could only disqualify one more. I practiced getting my speech out calmly and with intention.

The next two were fine. They seemed to know what was what before they came in, although Tim Lakewell was so quiet I couldn't be sure. He was also enormous.

I decided to hire him just for that, even if he didn't once look at my face.

The fourth, Janson, listened to my speech, which was getting smoother, and then asked me, "It's sex, right? I'll be having sex with women."

"Right."

"And getting paid, right?"

"Yes."

"Cool."

I offered him the crackers, keeping the plate far enough away that I could see his wrist emerge from under his cuff when he reached. Not hairy.

He leaned back against the leather couch and stretched out his arms. His chest was wide and his wingspan was like that of a condor, magnificent.

"Safe sex," I said.

"Only kind." He stood up. "I have practice now."

I ate another cracker. I was not sure I could stand the interviewing process without cheese.

I used the classy phone to check my messages. Since I rarely had any, this was a form of time squandering. But I did have a message, from someone who identified herself as Granny Bryce. She said she would be happy to rent the lodge off-season. Her voice crackled cheerfully. "Paint it nice and keep the heat going and you can have it for a song, 'Yankee Doodle Dandy.'" She hummed a little of it. "We lost the key, so if you want to see the inside, bring a crowbar." She hung up the phone, still singing.

By the last interview, I figured his teammates must have filled Sidney Walker in, because I didn't even have to give my speech. He already knew what the project entailed.

Without saying a thing to me, Sidney Walker carefully arranged a tiny iPod system with speakers the thickness of two credit cards on the mantel above the fireplace. He turned on a Los Lonely Boys song, "Heaven" and began to strip. It was the most interesting thing I'd watched since they put a mirror up for the birth of Darcy.

I stopped chewing crackers, and they formed a carbo hump on my tongue. He must have practiced in his dorm room, because he had his routine timed out perfectly to end with only socks left.

His body was lovely, like a corn-fed pet, milky and sleek. He was enjoying himself. ("Obviously," as they say.)

"Are you hot?" He let the awkward question hang there. Los Lonely Boys launched into a considerably less good song in Spanglish.

"No," I said firmly, with what I hoped was a friendly smile, as I tried to choke down the half-chewed crackers.

Watching him put his clothes back on, I thought of my lifetime of no's—piled up like every single missed turn on every wrong road I had taken.

"Tell me about yourself," I said.

He looked up from tucking his shirt lovingly into his pants. "Why?"

He's right, I thought. There was nothing more I needed to know.

"You have the job if you want it. We start next month, Tuesdays and Thursdays between noon and five." I'd picked these times so as not to interfere with PTA or soccer. They coincided with band practice and swim team, which all but the looniest mothers skipped.

He pushed his impossibly large feet into his slip-on shoes. I wondered if his was the first generation for which shoe tying was a lost art.

"Why are you doing this?" he asked.

"Science," I answered. He kept staring at me like someone accustomed to the unvarnished truth. "And money." He kept his eyes on mine, open and unwavering as a pair of barn doors.

"No one in this town gets any anymore," I said. "The women don't. They take medications. They eat. They quilt. It's like the Puritans around here."

He leaned toward me slightly. I think I wanted him to kiss me. I think he knew that.

With effort I moved my lips. "You have the job," I repeated.

"Yeah." He said this like someone who was used to being entirely wanted. "Is there a sound system there?" he asked.

"Not yet."

"I can put one in if you let me arrange the mixes."

"Sure," I said.

CROWBAR

When the door shut on the last potential sex worker, I sat, an absolute stone, and listened to the hum of the ventilation system. It sounded expensively quiet. The men seemed extremely nice. Overprivileged, like a lot had been handed to them, but still sweet and solid.

As I was thinking this, there was a discreet knock at the door, and the monitor entered. The person in the nice brown suit who walked into the room and leaned against the leather sofa could easily have been male or female.

"How did it go?" The voice was a smooth tenor, and I was still confused.

"Fine," I croaked, and pushed the nearly bare plate of crackers toward him/her. "Sorry, I ran out of cheese."

"Thank you anyway. I am a vegan."

I wanted to say it had been rescue cheese from a run-over cow, but I didn't.

"Were you satisfied with the room?"

"Yes."

"Will you need to access the research assistant pool further?"

I blushed. We looked at each other. This person might know everything. "No, I am finished," I said.

I swept the cracker crumbs into the trash and limped outside to my car in my pinchy tilting shoes.

I sat behind the wheel and realized yet again that I had no one to share this life with. I was going to be running a cathouse eight afternoons a month, and no one would say, "How was your day, dear?"

And how did I, who did not believe in commodifying people, get involved in selling sex? As I looked at the handsome knobby stick shift of my car, the plain and straightforward dashboard with every gauge serving a useful function, I decided I was not selling sex; I was selling a fifty-minute full-control vacation from your life as you knew it.

I needed to go see the interior of the lodge, to figure out how it could possibly work.

I didn't have a crowbar, so I drove to the hardware store to purchase one. I pulled up beside the door next to a pickup truck. Although it was not yet five o'clock, it was quite dark and I was glad for the light spilling from the display windows. By now my shoes were assassinating my toes, and I limped around to my trunk to see if there were some boots or clogs or anything in there to relieve me.

When I bent over to unlock the trunk, a familiar-sounding bark boomed out at me from the bed of the pickup. Startled, I looked up to see Matilda's huge head silhouetted against the night sky. "Matilda! What are you doing here?" I called to her. She woofed again. "Come, girl!" I tried to sound authoritative. She must have slipped out the side door, which I rarely locked. I couldn't imagine how she had gotten all the way to the hardware store, unless the driver of the pickup had seen her beside the road and loaded her in, presumably to try to find her owner.

Matilda had probably gotten lonely while I was gone the entire afternoon, and had escaped to find me, or more likely, to find John, her idol. "Come here!" I unlocked the latches on the tailgate of the pickup and let it down. She woofed in a friendly way but didn't come. In the gloom I could make out that she was tied or chained. I wondered if the truck owner was in fact trying to steal her.

I had to hike up my pencil skirt nearly to my waist to climb up into the bed of the truck. "It's OK, girl," I said. "I'm here." I squatted down beside her and she licked my face. "I'm happy to see you too."

There was a loud clunk behind me, and I whirled to see a man with an ax standing at the tailgate. He had thrown something onto the bed of the truck and was carrying the ax on his shoulder.

"Where did you find her?" I asked, trying discreetly to tug my skirt down where it belonged.

"She's local," he said. "New breed."

"Was she running loose on the road?" I asked, trying to unfasten Matilda from the chain.

"What are you doing?" His voice was calm but not friendly.

"I am unhooking my dog."

"That's not your dog."

"Not exactly my dog, but I am responsible for her." I had managed to get one side of the chain unclipped. With one hand on Matilda's head, I stood up to go to the other side of the truck bed and unfasten the other clip, but I bumped into something. Someone, rather. It was the man standing way too close to me, his chest the wall I was up against. He had climbed into the truck bed much too quickly and quietly to be a good guy, and he still had the ax in his hand.

"I am taking care of her until her master comes home," I explained. "She must have gotten out the side door." I tried to step past him, but he blocked my way. He didn't move, exactly, he just seemed to widen his chest so there was no way around him.

"Sir," I said stiffly, "you can't just go helping yourself to other people's dogs." The high heels were making it very hard to balance on the uneven surface of the truck bed, and I almost fell.

"Lady." He put his hand around my wrist, steadying me. "It's not your dog."

"Let go of me." This was getting creepy. "I know it's not my dog. I explained that already. It's my ex's dog and I am responsible for her." I got my wrist free. "She's a Bull Dane. It's a new breed."

"I have never met anyone who didn't know their own dog," the man said. He squatted down, laid the ax beside him, and put his face near Matilda's. "Hey, Rex," he said softly. The dog licked his forehead and put one paw on his knee. Matilda never did that to me.

"It's my dog. I've had Rex since he was a pup, almost two years now." He rubbed the dog under its chin. "Aren't you the lady from the ice cream parlor?"

I remembered him now, the carpenter who was supposed to take Penitence's virginity.

"Yes." I tugged my skirt down the rest of the way.

"I have a piece of Upstate wisdom for you, maybe two. The first is get to know your own dog. And the second is never ever get in someone's truck unless he invites you. Up here our trucks are like our homes: private."

"It was an honest mistake," I said. "In the city I would call you an asshole and know I would never see you again, but here I will probably see you tomorrow fixing my fence."

"Your fence needs fixing?" I could tell he was smiling at me.

I was trying to get down from the truck without either splitting my skirt or yanking it way up to my butt in front of Rex's master, the smug ax-toting jerk.

"I don't have a fence," I said, staring at how far down the ground was.

Leslie Daniels

"Maybe you need me to build one for you?"

"No thanks," I said firmly.

"It would keep your dog in," he pointed out.

"My dog *is* in," I said. I sat down in an inelegant plop and slithered off the end of his tailgate.

"Nice work," he said.

"Asshole," I said softly.

In the store I bought a small crowbar to go with my ladylike outfit. When I came out, the truck and Rex were gone, thank goodness. I put the crowbar in the trunk and was about to get in my car when I noticed a piece of paper under my windshield wiper.

It was torn from a memo pad with *Holder Woodworking* at the top. On it was written, *Good fences make good neighbors, buy you a beer? Take our dogs for a walk?* The note was signed, *Greg Holder, asshole.*

LODGE

It was Monday, and I thought I would hear something from Margie about *Babe Ruth,* but I didn't. It was nerve-racking. I wondered if Nabokov had a hard time waiting to hear about publication. Maybe he simply moved his focus to the next project. I wondered if he had absolute faith in the worth of his existence. I wanted to be like that. But he may have had none at all, and felt he had to work extraordinarily hard to earn his place here on Earth. If he *had* written the novel, he would have gone from *Babe* to *Lolita*. That made sense—he would have been trying even harder to make the big world sit up and notice him by writing the most provocative book imaginable. And if his belief in himself did start to flag, he had Vera. Maybe a Vera would appear where a Nabokov existed; maybe the genius brain drew toward it a devoted beauty and helper.

I had Margie, and sometimes I had this dog.

Matilda and I loaded ourselves into my terrible car. It had started to smell like a dogmobile, and I rolled down the windows even though it was below freezing. I drove to the old lodge, crowbar in my trunk. I pried the plywood off the front door. The wooden double door underneath was ornate in a Cottage Gothic style. It creaked open. Inside a little light came in from the unboarded tops of the windows. The wide-planked wood floors were smooth and dusty. The stone fireplace had built-in benches beside it. There was a piece of furniture in the corner that looked like a pulpit. Behind that, the stairway angled upward.

Upstairs were six small bedrooms, each with a sink. Two bathrooms had cast-iron claw-foot bathtubs. The windows were hung with rotted deer-patterned muslin curtains. Deer heads were mounted on the walls. A large stuffed beaver climbed the newel post of the staircase. A closet held ratty braided rugs, covered in plastic to keep them from mice. Matilda padded along after me, as interested as I was in the new finds.

Her nose led us down to the first floor and into a kitchen with an ancient yellow enamel cookstove. The sink was a long, rectangular slate trough, with a hand pump at one end. Behind the kitchen, a porch perched almost directly over the lake. The sun poured into the back of the house, filling the kitchen with light reflected from the lake. Even the the ceiling rafters were lit.

I was so in love with the place I could feel it in my chest.

I called Granny Bryce and told her I wanted the lodge and would like to start fixing it up. She said fine, and to send her "a little check," but she had to get off the phone because brunch was being served. I had never met anyone as easy and trusting as Granny Bryce. Maybe she was a Zen mistress.

I was starting to like Onkwedo. I didn't know how it had happened. Maybe it was meeting Bill. And discovering he was married to Margie. Maybe it was the influence of Matilda. Being around an animal supposedly increases your endorphins.

I drove the winding lake road back to the hardware store, where I opened an account based on my local address and homeownership, with a whopping eight-hundred-dollar credit line. I rented the Buick of Shop-Vacs. I bought primer and paint and drop cloths and tape for

Cleaning Nabokov's House

masking the trim. I still had my father's paintbrushes. He took very good care of his brushes, soaking them in turpentine and wiping them clean after every use. In spite of that, on the handle of one was a smear of gray paint from the porch of my childhood home.

He let me help him paint that porch every spring. We would touch up the worn spots. I would be given a brush and a small can of paint. He showed me how to take plenty of paint on the brush and "butter" it on. The line between work and play didn't exist when I was with my father; there was only doing interesting things and being together.

My father never told me he loved me, but I knew he did because of the way he taught me to paint. I still enjoyed painting. I recalled his big hands, so sure of themselves. My hands looked like his, grafted onto my skinny female wrists. But they didn't have his certainty of movement.

As I was leaving the hardware store, I caught my hand making one of his gestures, an overhand fling that ended with two fingers stuck out. I watched my hand toss the receipt in the trash with exactly his movement. I stopped and stared at my hand. I could not remember if it had always moved like that and I'd never noticed, or if it had its own memory system, activated by thoughts of him and of painting.

At the lodge I plugged in a boom box to play working music. Ollabelle. My father taught me that the longest part of painting was the preparation. I put on an old college T-shirt of John's that I'd decided he would not miss, and the pants before the Pants.

I took the many deer heads off the walls. Matilda nosed them avidly. There were also plaques with deer hooves pointing upward for hanging coats and hats. It was disturbing to think about all their little feet twisted the wrong way around. I hid the plaques in the back of the closet.

The rented Shop-Vac sucked up every cobweb and dead fly.

I spread the drop cloths over the floor and taped off the windows. I primed the dusky green walls with a stain killer. The trim was wood, so I left it alone. The ceilings too were wood. The work was endless. I thought I could do it in a day, but it took the best part of three days. The nights I spent spreading Bengay on my sore shoulders and swallowing Tylenol. I painted the upstairs bedrooms in soft chalky white. It didn't exactly say "cathouse."

By midnight of the third day the lodge looked beautiful. I was exhausted, aching, and proud. I lay on the floor and listened to Olabelle sing "Before This Time" for the seventy-ninth time.

If my father were here, he would still be working. He worked until the job was finished. Most people stop when they feel like it, or when the day is done. He would go till the end of the work.

I tried to picture him up in heaven, not working. I wished I could believe that he was someplace and was happy there. But I couldn't. I was glad that he didn't have to work anymore. He loved work. He did. But he finished his.

I dragged myself off the floor, drank a Diet Coke, and kept painting. By four in the morning I was painting with my left hand. Or maybe it was my right hand but it just felt like my left hand.

I was too exhausted to see my finished paint job. The shadows on the wall looked like big old ten-point bucks. I packed the stuff into my car trunk, the dog in the backseat, and drove home.

It was the quietest time of day, right before dawn. The lake was dark and the hills were darker. My house was cold. I plugged in the space heater and took a hot bath. I fell asleep in the tub and awoke when the water turned cold.

I ate the ideal breakfast of cold plump shrimp dipped in hot sauce and squirted with a lime wedge. I went to bed. Life was sweet sometimes.

IKEA

The horrid part of getting the cathouse ready had arrived: decorating, my worst talent after marriage. My mother promised to help me. OK, she didn't know the full scoop. I billed it to her as "Finally furnishing the house!" She was ecstatic that she had an excuse to shop with me at the Ikea in her neighborhood.

I left Matilda and all her gear with Margie. Bill was happy to have a dog around and promised to take her for long walks. He'd offered me his own personal van. Bill drove a 1999 postal van that had been retired from service. The markings were painted over, but the steering wheel was still on the right-hand side. I drove it around the block a few times to get used to it. I was so broke that I was relieved to see the van's gas gauge on full.

I drove the four hours to Ikea hugging the slow lane, with people honking as they passed me. At Ikea I applied for the revolving credit card that offered a 15 percent discount. I met my mother at the credit desk. I had forgotten how *Town & Country* she looked. She kissed me near the cheek, insisted that she would pay half, and told me that we had to eat first or she couldn't concentrate.

We each ordered a plate of Swedish meatballs cooked in sauce that tasted like grape jelly—seventy-nine cents. It was a big step down from Bistro Moutarde, but it fit the Atkins diet, according to my mother.

"You want a simple color scheme. Something classic like white and blue," my mother said. "Dresden blue is nice. And you want clean and sturdy." She speared a nickel-size meatball and wiped the jelly stuff on the edge of her plate.

"Won't it look like a dorm?"

"Trust me," she said. I did. I'd polished off all seven of my meatballs, jelly and all. When we finished our glasses of pink and fizzy diet Lingonwasser, whatever that was, we hit the linens.

In the oversize pushcart, my mother put six sets of sheets, three hundred thread count, "Wears better than four hundred," she said. How she knew these things boggled me. I'd never wanted these kinds of facts in my head. Seven rugs came next, then art for the walls. Mother chose one print each of the young Scandinavian designer series, with the exception of the Edvard Munch follower. Six sets of towels in blue, eighteen matching washcloths, and two Egyptian waffle cotton robes. I had never owned so much uniformity in my entire life.

We searched hard for the right bedstead. My mother insisted that they be mid-thigh height, and I didn't ask why. She measured the options against her own gabardine slacks. We bought three rustic-looking bedsteads, with near Duxiana mattresses, which, my mother said, "do it for less."

When we got close to the checkout, my mother conveniently needed to find the ladies' room. She didn't overhear me tell the cashier to triple the linens order, and double the bedsteads. I paid with my mother's charge card and my new Ikea credit card.

I was on the loading dock with the mountain of stuff when my mother strolled up chatting to Dr. Groom on her cell phone. She ignored the helper and me, as we jammed a zillion pounds of furniture into the van. She was laughing at something the doctor said that she seemed to find clever. I could hear in her voice a flattering, girlish kind of trill that set my teeth on edge. I vowed to think hard before I paid her back for furnishing the lodge.

She finally clicked off, all flushed and happy looking. He'd bought her a fox fur swing coat for an engagement present, and she twirled in it like she was in an Audrey Hepburn movie.

I kissed her and thanked her, and couldn't wait to get away from her. The van was so full, I drove with a pile of sheets on my lap.

Back at the lodge I unloaded. Because it was Ikea, everything came in pieces that I could more or less lift. Once I had it all in the living room, which took me all day and activated the same sore arm muscles, it was very clear where to put things. But I was too tired to do it. I dragged myself home, gathering Matilda on the way.

The next day I came back with my companion Bull Dane and a bottle of aspirin. I hung the deer heads back on the walls, but high up near the ceiling. I left the deer-foot plaques in the closet. The pulpit puzzled me. I circled it, looking it up and down. I decided to leave it alone and figure it out later. When I was done, I walked upstairs and through the small bedrooms. They were pretty and cozy. The rugs were a pale ashy-blue. The tatty old curtains were gone and the windows bare. I could see the snow melting from the tree branches and beyond that the lake. The effect was sexy, a kind of "We live nude here, so what? We're Scandinavian" feeling. It said, "Take *your* clothes off too, it's OK. You're in good hands."

Mother had thought of everything. I even had office supplies for my hideout in the kitchen. I'd bought a one-way mirror for the pass-through so I could watch the comings and goings in the front parlor. There *must* be comings and goings. I was now in debt up to my eyeballs.

END OF THE YEAR

It was evening and it was also Christmas Eve, a wholly ridiculous time of year if you are not participating. John had the children and I got Matilda for the holiday. That was how my life was unfolding: Christmas alone with someone else's dog. With my own children, I got Easter, Mother's Day, the Fourth of July, and Presidents Day. It was divorce by Hallmark.

John had taken the children to Florida to visit his parents and play golf. I didn't like Florida, I didn't like golf, and I didn't like his parents' relationship, which was based on the jailer-prisoner model.

They lived so close to the golf course that to play outside in the yard safely, the children had to wear bike helmets.

When I'd first met his father, I'd given John enormous credit for his developmental evolution, a leap forward in the human species from his paternal origin. Now that John had taken my children, I could see the similarities between father and son. They now seemed like clones, only his father was as old as Santa Claus.

John's real mother died of skin cancer when he was nineteen. Six weeks later John's father married his deeply tanned executive assistant, Tammy. Every inch a trophy wife still, Tammy was the only sixty-year-old I knew who wore a bikini. On the desk in his study, John's father had a brass paperweight that was a mold of Tammy's left breast.

Every night before they went to bed, Tammy put a padlock on the refrigerator door and gave John's father the key. I had discovered this while trying to eat the hot fudge sundae I woke up needing every single midnight hour of my pregnancy with Sam.

John's stepmother was nearly always shopping. When we first visited, she took me with her, buying me maternity dresses made of wallpaper-like fabric. They went straight from my hands to the Salvation Army without ever coming out of their tissue paper.

It was not that his parents weren't *nice;* they were very nice. It was that they possessed pathological values: overshopping, ignoring everyone who was unlike them, a kind of screw-the-earth-and-its-inhabitants mentality. On their honeymoon to Yellowstone Park, his father started a brush fire with his barbecue that decimated ten thousand acres. His new wife saved the newspaper clippings about the fire, with headlines like "Newlywed Causes Conflagration" and "Hot Honeymoon." The articles were laminated, framed, and hung above the fake fireplace beside an oil portrait of them in wedding clothes. In the painting Tammy is so deeply tanned in her white dress that she looks like something from a minstrel show.

I thought of Tammy and the eager-to-please Irene hitting the shopping mall, hard, John and his dad golfing silently, viciously. I thought of the children eating sugarless Christmas cookies, Darcy in the hot tub in her size 4T black bathing suit, and Sam in the shade reading the recipes in *Weight Watchers Magazine,* both wearing bike helmets.

I called them. "Grandpa's barbecuing," Sam told me.

Darcy got on the phone. "Grandpa's burning meat. There's smoke up to the sky. What are those brown spots on his back?"

"Moles, honey. Tell Grandpa to check the barbecue, OK?"

"Can I catch them?"

"Catch what?"

"Grandpa's moles."

"No. Please have Daddy check the barbecue, OK?" Darcy put down the phone, and I heard splashing and the sound of water running, maybe from a hose. I waited, but no one came. The water sounded louder, and then the phone got disconnected, perhaps drowned. I waited some more, but no one called me back. There was no way to know what was happening there in Florida with my children. I called again, but no one answered.

I felt myself start to panic. Matilda snapped me out of it by drooling on my hand. I called six more times, and finally Darcy picked up the phone. "Are you OK, honey?" I asked her.

"No."

"What's wrong, Darcy?"

There was no sound from the other end but Darcy's breathing. Then, in a tiny voice she said, "I miss my mama."

I told her I missed her too and I would see her soon. I told her to go find Sam and sit in his lap, ask him to read her a story. I asked her what Matilda liked to eat best.

"Cheese."

"I am going to make your dog a delicious breakfast. Go find your brother."

I cooked some cheese grits with extra butter for the dog and me. When we were finished (four seconds for her, four minutes for me), I brushed her coat. I used John's matching set of English boar bristle brushes that had arrived in the house via one of Darcy's handbags. Matilda seemed to like being brushed, raising her nose to the ceiling, closing her eyes, almost smiling. The children never enjoyed grooming like that.

I forced myself to open and read the Christmas cards and letters: a postcard from my mother with Dr. Groom in Boca Raton, and another of Hemingway's house from Margie and Bill, vacationing in Key West, plus the annual morbid rambles from people I vaguely remembered from high school. Matilda was my only source of comfort in the chilly house. She leaned against my legs as I hunched over my desk. The way Bull Danes express themselves is to lean. I didn't know if her leaning was affectionate or if she was trying to push me over.

I decided that the dog wanted to walk, although it was more likely me trying to escape from loneliness.

Outside there was water moving under the ice of the stream. It was cold but not bitter. My breath made a fog around my face, ice crystals on my scarf. Christmas trees lit every window. Matilda walked dutifully beside me, like she was only coming along to burn a few calories.

It was late enough that even Apex Market was closed. We walked through downtown Onkwedo along the central street, looking in the store windows displaying modest goods tinseled and bedecked with greetings. Having sold all they could, the stores were closed for the holiday. It was nice to have a day when no one could shop, not just me.

On Christmas morning I thought about the children, of course. I had not gotten them very good presents, just some stuff I found at the Unitarian church rummage sale; a purse and matching slippers for Darcy made entirely of potholders, and for Sam, *Best Recipes from Down East,* a county-by-county cookbook of Maine. The recipes were everything imaginable you could make with canned milk, potatoes, lard, soda crackers, and lobster meat. The recipe for "Poverty Stew" omitted the canned milk. I hoped never to eat that dish.

I looked on the web at the local free-stuff site, hoping to find a boat. Sam loved vehicles of any kind and he loved the water. I found a pump and a paddle and three boats called handyman specials, but nothing ready to put in the lake.

Still on the local site, I found a posting that I thought was intended for me. It was from a man who smiled at a woman in the Apex Market on Sunday night, and she smiled back. "You had a cart full of dairy products. I had a motorcycle helmet. You are the middle-aged woman who smiled at me. You have a nice smile and nice everything. Even if it is not you, but you want a new friend and some excitement in your life, write me back. I am the handsome guy you went home thinking about."

I remembered a guy in the breakfast cereal aisle carrying a motorcycle helmet. I remembered him smiling at me when I was reading the side of the puffed rice box. (Puffed rice has nothing in it, giving it that texture-only taste, and not even much of that.) But maybe he didn't mean me. I do have a nice smile, but "nice everything" meant big breasts and tight jeans on long legs. I was undoubtedly wearing the Pants and a sweatshirt. And "middle-aged" stuck in my craw. Did I want excitement in my life? I didn't think so. I had a business to run, cheese to move.

I decided to post the cathouse on the "Mothers Only" message board, and the "Girls' Night Out" one too. It was hard to find just the right words. I settled on: *Pedicures don't do it for you? How about a full-release massage? We go till you say "Stop."* I choked on my muesli writing that.

For no good reason I thought of the carpenter with the matching Bull Dane. I looked up "Holder Woodworking" on the internet. There were beautiful photos of cabinets and desks, including a stand-up writing desk that I coveted. The address wasn't far away. From the satellite pictures on the web, the place had a tidy roof with a large blue lump beside it, perhaps a boat.

I wondered if I would ever date again. I wondered what people who were nearly forty wore on dates. I did an internet search for "underpants." Hanro was the only entry. How was it that the Swiss made the only internet-available underpants—could that even be true? At extreme prices, Hanro underpants were a sort of perma-panty, designed to last your entire life. But if I was ever going to go on a real date (big "if" there), I would need some unquestionably good underpants, so I ordered the ecru low rise.

Then I ordered an inflatable rubber dinghy from the nautical supply store, hoping it would fit three people. It was the only boat I could afford.

With the last few days of the worst year of my life to squander, and no chance of hearing about *Babe Ruth* since everyone but me was on vacation, I decided to camp at the cathouse. There was little work to do for Old Daitch Dairy; people seemed to eat more dairy products in the winter but complain about them less.

I packed books, some food, Matilda's leash, and the pair of pajamas Tammy had bought me to save my marriage—still tied with the Frederick's of Hollywood ribbon—and drove to the cathouse. It was cold but welcoming, with a deep quiet grace that seemed suspended, separate from the rest of the world. There was an air of expectancy about it that was real, like anything could happen here and it would.

I made a fire and sat on the couch with a pile of books and the dog at my feet. I'd brought some of Margie's romances, and a biography of Nabokov, so I could look at pictures of him sitting in his car—sometimes writing, or with his wife.

The front door of the lodge was tight, and with the fire going, it was cozy inside. I moved from room to room, getting used to the views from the windows at different times of day. I slept each night in a different bed, like Goldilocks in hooker pajamas.

I read the romances. They played me as if I were a piano, my grandmother's black baby grand. I could feel it happening, like a drug taking effect. The drug was tenderness. It didn't comes from the sex scenes but from right before, right after. The narcotic was not lust but the tenderness between people, the love in spite of their unlovableness. Lust is like a robin attacking his reflection in a pane of glass again and again. But tenderness and yearning seeped gently into me, slipping up around me like water. These books seemed to say, *We know you, we can take care of you, we have what you want.*

The days of reading made me see the world differently. I tried to convince myself that one is enough, one person can be a family, but I failed. To console myself on New Year's Eve, I made a pitcher of what might have been considered sangria, or at least lightly spiked punch. It had almost no alcohol in it, because I was not really a drinker. As I sipped it, I made a list of every person I could remember who had wanted to sleep with me and whom I had turned down.

I could remember at least five. I was pretty sure there were more, but I was being strict about the criteria, not including someone unless he had actually asked. And it didn't count if he was drunk at the time. (I am not sure why I made that rule, since *I* was nearly drunk by now, and it seemed like a perfectly reasonable state.) I started to feel very happy, proud of showing such good sense at least five times in my life.

When the pitcher of spiked punch was empty, I decided the night air would sober me up. I threw on my parka and put Matilda in the car.

Driving wasn't difficult, and I was particularly careful since Onkwedo's entire police force seemed to be on the road or parked beside it, waiting for criminals like me to cross the double yellow line. I drove along the lake road, away from town, and found myself passing a sign that read Holder Woodworking .2 miles.

I pulled off the road at an old white farmhouse just ahead. The windows were dark, but there was an outbuilding, maybe a workshop, where the lights were blazing. I opened the car window to a blast of icy air. I could hear the whine of a power tool. I turned the car off to hear better, and there was the woof of a big dog. Matilda roused herself and woofed back. I turned the key in the ignition fast. Nothing happened.

I bent down, trying to find the manual choke that sometimes stuck open. It was very dark, and the dome light didn't reach the shadows under the dashboard where the small knob for the choke was.

"Can I help you?" said a voice right outside my window.

Startled, I straightened, whacking my head on the steering wheel. The carpenter was standing beside my car, his hand on the open window. "No," I said. Matilda stepped on my thigh. I thought she might be trying to bite him, but she was trying to reach his hand for a sniff.

"You're the lady from the hardware store."

I rubbed the knot on my head.

"Are you stalking my dog?"

"No." I tried to think of something appropriate to say, but the bump had made me a little fuzzy.

"Why are you here?"

"My car won't start?" It came out as a question, which I hadn't intended.

He shook his head as if to clear it. "Are you drunk?"

"No," I said, "not really." Matilda's nails were digging through the flimsy satin cloth into my flesh. "I better go."

"Should you be driving?" he asked. Matilda, recognizing him as the alpha male, was licking between his fingers, trying to get on his good side fast, the slut.

"Of course," I said.

"Would you like to come in and I will make you a cup of coffee?"

"I don't drink coffee at night," I told him. My head was throbbing.

Matilda had started licking his wrist. I stared at the wrist. It was wide and well defined, two big bones with a flat plane between them, some hair but not a lot. I found myself wondering what it tasted like.

"May I ask your name?" he said.

"Barb," I said, "um, Smith. Barb Smith."

"Come in and have a cup of tea, Barb Smith." He said the name like he knew it was fake. "You can bring your dog for protection."

I thought about what I was wearing, pajamas, not even the Pants, but my parka was pretty long. "Pull into the drive there"—he pointed— "and don't touch the manual choke; it messes up the air intake."

"I know that," I snapped. Fortunately the engine turned over, and I lurched into the yard, farting a big cloud of exhaust at Mr. Holder.

The entrance to his house was a mudroom, like most houses Upstate seemed to have. It gave way to a fairly bare kitchen with a round table and four chairs. I sat there, my parka zipped, keeping my hand on Matilda's collar so she wouldn't abandon me altogether for the new man in her life. He put a cup of water in the microwave and took out a ratty collection of tea bags. "I'm more of a coffee person, but see if there's something here that you like." I selected Green Ecstasy Tea. The microwave dinged, and he handed me the nearly hot water.

While my tea steeped, I looked around. On the wall were four small oil paintings of sailboats. Or maybe they were all the same boat. I don't like series art, but I was trying not to be judgmental. The house was wonderfully warm. There was a pellet stove in the corner. I knew this because he was explaining it to me, how it used compressed sawdust, how efficient it was, how well it heated the house. He started telling me this after trying to take my coat to hang it up. I thanked him but declined.

"Where is your dog?" I said when there was a lull.

"In the shop," he said. "I'll get him." He went outside.

As soon as he left, I unzipped my coat and flapped it open, trying to cool off. I looked down at myself in the "hot" pajamas. I looked ready for amateur night at Kumon Fellas, Onkwedo's strip bar. The pajamas had actual break-away bottoms. They came with a DVD on how to strip for your husband that I had never watched.

It was eleven p.m., late enough to have changed into pajamas, but the truth was that I had not taken them off from the night before. Or the night before that. The cathouse seemed the ideal place to do away with clothes. Only here I was in a strange man's kitchen on New Year's Eve, without them. I zipped up.

He came back in with Rex, who was even larger than Matilda. The dogs greeted each other like long-lost siblings, which they might have been. "Are you sure I can't take your coat?" he asked.

"No, thanks. I'm fine." It was at least seventy degrees in the kitchen, and the tea was making me sweat.

"Do you live nearby?" he asked.

"Yes." There was a pause with only the sound of the dogs' tongues lapping.

He took a package of Oreos out of the cupboard and put some on a plate. Matilda stuck her nose over the edge of the table, but Rex did not.

Greg Holder moved with grace and ease. He seemed very relaxed. He was home in his own kitchen with his own dog and his own Oreos, wearing clothes, of course, while I was not.

"Do you live alone?" he asked, pushing the plate of cookies closer to me.

"Yes. Mostly. Sometimes."

"Which is it?" His voice was friendly.

"My kids are with their dad. He has custody. And this is his dog.

I'm taking care of her while they're in Florida." I realized I had a cookie in each hand. I gave one to Matilda, who swallowed it without a chew. She put her muzzle on the table, sliding it sideways toward the plate, the better to engulf the whole pile of cookies. Greg tapped her nose, and she promptly left the cookies alone and lay down on his feet. Rex put a huge paw on her neck. I watched, knowing that this was the language of dogs, which I did not speak.

"I don't have kids," Greg said. "I was married, but she lives in Oregon now."

"Do you cook?" I asked, looking around the kitchen, which seemed very tidy and unused.

"Just the basics: breakfast, pasta, steaks." There wasn't a pot or pan in evidence. The stove was brilliantly clean.

"You cook in that?" I pointed to the microwave.

"Sure." He had on a flannel shirt open over a white T-shirt. His shoulders were wide, and I couldn't help noticing his chest, which looked solid and good. I blamed all my romance reading for making me so stupidly aware of his good looks. He was handsome. Handsome men always made me nervous.

"That's not cooking," I said, "that's warming."

"You're really working hard to make friends with me, aren't you?" He smiled at me. "You try to steal my dog. You're spying on me, maybe to kidnap Rex. I still don't know why you need him—possibly to teach your dog some manners. And you drive to my house at night—a little drunk—to insult my cooking."

"Do you know John Barrett?" I said.

"The rubber guy, inventor? Yes, I know him. Is that your ex?"

I stood up. "Come on, Matilda, let's go." Matilda was uncooperatively sleeping on her new master's foot.

"It's OK," Greg said. "Drink your tea. You seem nervous. You don't know me, but John does. I am a nice guy, I promise. I won't try anything. You can take off your coat, finish your tea, and then go home."

I wiped the perspiration from my forehead. "I wasn't planning on coming here. I was just going for a drive, so I didn't dress." We both looked down at my legs in the pink satin pajama bottoms.

"What are those?"

"Pajamas." I sat down again. "Actually, they were supposed to save the marriage, but I never took them out of the box." I found myself telling him about Tammy, and John's dad, and the children, and losing them. I told him about the house and finding the book.

He put some bread and cheese on the table and cut some slices of each. I hadn't had dinner, and I ate hungrily.

"Is the book valuable?" he asked.

"If it was proven to be by Nabokov, it would be priceless. But the experts say he didn't write it."

"You think he did?"

"I do. I am probably wrong. I am usually wrong. It's an incredible book. Babe Ruth is such a loser in it. There is love all around him, but it's not the kind he understands. I guess it's a tragedy, but it's funny. And it's so weirdly right about this place. I wish someone would publish it. My agent is working on that. Margie." I unzipped the side vents of the parka.

"Margie Jenkins?"

I would never get used to small-town life. I nodded. "I better go." I didn't want to leave, it was so cozy talking to him, Matilda snoozing, pinned by Rex's paw. I clucked to her, but she slept on. I leaned over to fasten her leash.

"Those pajamas might have saved your marriage," Greg said, but in a friendly way.

I hauled on Matilda's leash, trying to rouse her.

"Would you like to have dinner sometime? When you're wearing clothes, of course."

"OK, maybe. Sounds nice." I was still hauling on Matilda.

He snapped his fingers and both dogs sprang up. "Stay, Rex," he said. Rex froze.

"How do you do that? I thought Bull Danes were untrainable."

"They can't learn much. They're faithful, but they're not very bright. You have to work with their nature. They bond very well." He made a clicking sound with his tongue, and Matilda came to his side. "I'll walk you to your car."

Outside the temperature had dropped well below freezing. I opened the passenger door for Matilda.

"How's Tuesday?" Greg asked.

Tuesday was the first day for the cathouse. "No, I can't."

"Is there a good day this week to have dinner together? In a restaurant," he added.

I remembered from what little I knew about dating that Friday was too big a night for a first date and Saturday was worse. "Thursday, but next week. This week I have a new project."

"I'll call you. It's Smith, right?" He tilted his head at me, teasing, but nicely.

"In the phone book I'm still listed under Barrett." Making sure Matilda's nose was in, I slammed the car door, suddenly eager to leave. As I stepped away from the car, I heard a ripping sound and I was bare-bottomed. I had closed the edge of the pajama bottoms in the car door, and the Velcro had given way, just like it was supposed to. I looked down at my naked legs, pale as Popsicle sticks going into my boots.

Greg shook his head. "You live an interesting life," he said. He opened the car door and retrieved the pile of fabric that had been my pajama pants.

"Thanks." I snatched it from his hand. I backed around the car, taking small steps, both hands on the hem of my parka.

"Here, take this." Greg pulled off his flannel shirt and tossed it to me over the hood. "Cover up, you'll freeze."

"Thanks." The shirt was still warm. I realized I hadn't touched a human being in a long time. A week? Ten days? And a man in longer than that. I wrapped his shirt around my bareness and climbed into the car.

It started on the first try, and for that I patted it on the dashboard.

"Happy New Year," I called, and drove away. I peeked in the rear-view mirror and saw Greg Holder's magnificent chest in his white undershirt. He gave a wave before he turned to go back to his workshop.

OPENING DAY

The first Tuesday of the New Year was the opening day of the cathouse. I wore the new jeans and some spike-heeled boots that Margie had outgrown. The young men, all four of them, arrived clean and sweet smelling. (Must remind them not to use aftershave so liberally, I thought.)

It was chilly in the lodge, and Janson and I went out back to get firewood. Janson helped me split the wood. He told me he grew up in Ohio on a hog farm and was attending the Waindell agriculture college, planning to take over the family farm and raise organic pork. He knew how to line up the logs and split them as if they were begging to be cleaved.

I was watching him with so much admiration that at first I didn't notice when a minivan pulled up. The driver backed into the hairpin turn like she was a novice trucker. One wheel ended up off the road entirely. She stepped out and beeped the car locked. I didn't know what she was afraid of out here—bears? I told Janson to come in when he was ready, and I scooted to the back steps and flew inside.

When the woman opened the front door, I was by the fireplace with an excellent newspaper-and-kindling blaze going. She was dressed exactly like she was going to lunch with a special friend: pale lipstick, every hair in place, not a speck on her wool coat. The three young men stretched out, doubling in size for her benefit, their legs extending into the room, their arms along the back of the couch. The woman looked extremely nervous.

"Welcome," I said, "let me take your coat." I had forgotten that detail; there was no deer hoof to hang it on, so I laid it across the pulpit. "Cup of tea?" I asked. Coffee is the opposite of an aphrodisiac, so I wasn't serving it. Instead I had a big samovar of white twig tea. It warmed the yin and balanced the yang, according to the package.

The woman held the handle-less Swedish mug and looked around, anywhere but at the men. "Beautiful ceilings," she said. In the corner of my eye, I could see the men still stretching.

Janson came in with an armful of wood. He rolled it down beside the hearth with a clatter, then crouched and skillfully built a crosshatch of logs over the blaze. "Pine burns fast, but birch is sweeter," he said, opening the two round flues halfway. "That will cook," he announced, and stood up to his full six feet two inches.

The woman looked at me, her eyes wide. "Him, please."

I nodded and watched them go upstairs. Sid turned the music up, and I wondered what the hell the rest of us were going to do for fifty minutes. But I needn't have worried; each man had a plan. You didn't get into Waindell if you didn't know how to make good use of your time. Two laptops appeared, along with a statistics textbook, paper, and calculator.

Before they could get going, there was a soft knock at the door and two more women arrived. I knew one of them by sight. She was an officer of the PTA. She was decisive, picking Tim.

The other woman had a horrified look on her face that I understood completely: she didn't want to hurt anyone's feelings. I didn't know how to help her. The two remaining young men were not helping either. They were equally beautiful, large, strong, and sweet smelling.

One was blond and the other brown-haired. After a very awkward moment covered by the voices of the Shins blaring on, she turned to me. "Two isn't possible?" she asked me in a low voice.

I shook my head.

"I've never been with a blond," she murmured.

I nodded at Richard.

After they went up, I tried to think of something to talk about with Sid. As if he knew what I was thinking, his eyes met mine. I noticed how they glistened like a windshield in the rain, "Don't worry about me," he said. "We're pooling tips."

By the third hour I knew that the spiky boots were impossible to walk in and made a mental note to bring some slippers. I liked to stand by the front windows and watch the women leave, driving their SUVs and minivans carefully up the steep switchbacks of the drive. I considered opening a spin-off enterprise: a driving school. I had gotten the entrepreneurial bug.

At the end of the day, the cathouse had made a cool pile of cash. It was not a lot by Manhattan's Forty-eighth Street standards, but for Onkwedo it was a great start. The workers were taking home a tidy sum.

They looked tired. "Thank you all very much," I said. "And please let me know if you have any, um . . ."—I couldn't find the right word— "issues." No one but Sid met my eyes.

Janson told me to knock the coals before I left and to close the flues. I watched them leave, driving expertly up the driveway. I thought for a moment of how unfair "la différence" was, la différence in le performance of le spatial tasks. Then I tackled the enormous pile of laundry.

All the quarters from redeeming empties came in very handy at the Laundromat. No one asked me why I was using all the large washing machines at once. Fortunately none of my customers frequented the

Laundromat. They were all home making tacos or mac and cheese for their kids and a fast steak for their husbands. I could almost hear their clandestine emails and cell phone calls buzzing with today's adventure. The nail salons in this town were really going to take a hit.

I stared into the circular window of a washer, trying to stretch my mind. I could see Darcy questioning Irene about her new Florida shoes, Sam leafing through the Maine cookbook I got him for Christmas. I saw my mother in the metropolis of Wilkes-Barre, having a Kir Royale with the doctor, her cheeks pink with being adored. I saw Janson and the others at their evening workout in the Waindell crew tanks, the coach—Rudy—yelling at them to pull harder. I didn't know enough about Greg Holder to picture his routine, but I knew his dog would be beside him, behaving appropriately.

Finally, the sheets were clean. I loaded them in the dryers and emptied the last of my quarters into the slots.

At home I ate a sundae of my own creation, Old Daitch Dairy vanilla ice cream and pecan-butterscotch sauce. It was the kind of dinner that set up a deep craving for kale. The butterscotch sauce recipe called for melted butter, brown sugar, and pecans. It came out grainy and odd. The kale was divine.

When I was first living without my children, I couldn't convince myself that the day was done. I would prowl from room to room, picking things up and putting them down, without any thought behind it. My hand would reach out, shaped to grasp a boot, scoop up a sweater, select a pencil, no purpose or task to complete. Now I'd finished a day full of people and work. I was exhausted and somehow less lonely, feeling weirdly part of something. I slept.

THE CHANGE

In the morning I called Margie. After six rings, she picked up the phone. "What?" She sounded extremely pissed off.

"Hi, Margie. What's wrong?" There was a lot of crunching on the other end, like she was chewing glass.

"I'm going through fucking menopause. I am only forty-seven. I hate it."

"What are you eating?" I asked.

"Ice cubes." One of Margie's diet tricks was continuous cold drinks. She liked Crystal Light, the nastiest stuff, and she had it in six different "flavors." Margie choked at the other end of the phone.

"Are you OK?" I was wondering how fast I could drive there, if the paramedics could get there faster, in case she had a cube of frozen Crystal Light caught in her throat. Then I heard her sniff and realized Margie was crying.

"I thought I might still have a baby. Maybe I'm ready now. Bill always wanted one, but my career came first. Now it's too fucking late." She blew her nose longer than I would have thought possible.

"Margie, can I come over? Can I bring you some fresh butter? It's Wednesday." There was a long pause, and I heard her crunching more ice. "You would be a top-flight mom," I said softly.

"Don't come." Margie sniffed again.

"Anybody who has you in their life is lucky as heck. Like me, I'm lucky to have you." I heard the glug-glugging sound of pouring. "Margie, isn't it time for your workout? That might make you feel better."

Margie sighed. "How was Christmas?" she asked.

"Pretty lonely. But I met a nice man, through the dog. Matilda." I switched ears on the phone. "Here's the bad part. Margie, I told him every blessed thing about my life. Now I want to take it all back. Nobody here knows stuff about me except you."

"You trust me?" Margie asked.

"Of course."

"Maybe you can trust him too."

"All I know about him is that he's a carpenter, he's divorced, and he has a Bull Dane too."

"Greg Holder? He's a good guy. And quite a looker." Margie sounded like her regular self again.

"I have a date with him next Thursday. I don't know what to talk to him about, Margie. I've already told him everything."

"His wife left him for another woman. Out in Oregon somewhere. She left town on the back of the biggest motorcycle you've ever seen, driven by one tattooed lesbian. The whole town watched them leave." Margie knew everything.

"Well, I can't ask him about that."

"Nope," Margie said.

"Maybe he doesn't like assertive women," I said.

"Maybe he doesn't like women who change their sexual orientation." The ice clinked in her glass.

"What should I wear?"

"Jeans. Hot top. Not too hot." I heard her putting dishes in the dishwasher.

"What if he takes me to a fancy place?"

"You can't underdress in Onkwedo." Right, I knew that. "What are you going to tell him about your life plans?"

"Nothing."

"Good idea. But what about if there's a next date?"

I hadn't thought about that. "I'll think of something."

"I'm sure you will," Margie said dryly. "Try for normal here, Barb, OK? Greg Holder is a good one. Tell him you write romances, and then write me one like I've been telling you to do."

"I'll try, Margie." She was relentless on this romance book business.

"Go someplace cheap. Go to Café Raw."

"Tofu?"

"It's not about food, Barb."

"Right," I said, but Margie had hung up.

"I love you," I said to the dial tone.

BANK AND LAUNDRY

Week two dawned at the cathouse. It was beginning to feel like a real job. I had on sensible mules and the fire was stoked. I had stopped at two drugstores on my way to work and bought them out of personal massagers. The cashiers didn't even bat an eye. I stocked every room. I could see the fringe of icicles on the eaves beginning to melt in the morning sun. Sid had left me a mix for the day titled "Love, Tuesday." With Al Green crooning and a nice fire crackling, our first customer showed up.

She was a petite dark-haired woman, exotic looking for this town, the features of a larger person crowded together on her small face. I didn't recognize her at first, but when she started talking in a low husky voice, I pegged her as the three-time treasurer of the garden club and wife of the fire chief. She was wearing a pink cardigan and carrying a laundry bag and a pink purse. I told her the price for fifty minutes. "I don't want him to touch me," she shuddered, then glared at me. "But I want him completely naked and I want him to pick up these socks." She opened the mouth of the bag. I told her it would be the same price as a full-release massage. (I got that term from a billboard outside Onanonquit.) "I am not here to economize," she said tartly. "And if he pairs them right, there is a big fat tip." She cinched the bag shut.

I invited her to sit down and have a cup of tea. I checked the kitchen wall calendar to see if by any chance it was April 1; but no, it was still January.

The front door banged and four men arrived: Janson, Sid, Tim, and Evan. Janson did the log thing again, but the woman sitting on the couch with her ankles crossed and her cardigan buttoned was not impressed.

Evan was new, and a friend of Janson's. I hadn't yet talked to him about laundry (all linens in big hamper fast, fresh ones in the drawer), or sex toys (second drawer down), or anything beyond the instructional chat on privacy, hygiene, and basic anatomy. (From the library I'd borrowed an old video in the Human Physiology series, *The Mystery of the G-Spot*. I screened it, but the narrator was slower than Jacques Cousteau.)

Evan looked tidy. Below his pressed khakis, his socks were cuffed; I could see Mrs. Fire Chief noticing this detail. "Evan?" I said. He smiled like he had won Lotto and said expansively to her, "Come on up."

She rose, handed him the sack of laundry, and followed him primly up the stairs.

After we heard their door close, Janson said quietly to the others, "Wack job. I can spot them a mile away."

I excused myself and retreated to the kitchen. I was starting to like my employees very much, but they still made me uncomfortable. Sometimes I blushed just looking at them. I tried to stay out of sight unless I had a job to do. When they thought I couldn't hear them, they resumed their discussion from the week before of who was sexier, fat women or thin women?

"Fat women want it more," said Sid. "They are more in touch with their desire."

"That's crap," said Janson. "Fat women sublimate their desire with food. Food dulls you, man. Food is the anti-sex."

"You ever screw anybody when you were hungry?" asked Sid. " 'Course not," he answered himself.

"You guys miss the point," said Tim. "The point is how good she *feels*."

"To me?" said Sid. "I like some flesh."

"No, you moron, to herself. That's how sexy she is."

In the kitchen, I was scarcely breathing.

The doorbell rang, and the conversation stopped. I opened the door to two women, one fat, one thin. The heavier woman picked Sid, which made me unreasonably happy. I didn't stay to watch who the thin one picked. I would gather the stats from the guys later.

At the end of a busy afternoon, Tim, Evan, and Janson drove away. Sid stayed, fiddling with his iPod and the mixes. I was collecting linen from the hampers.

"This place is too white," he said to me over his shoulder. He was playing some dated-sounding hip-hop.

Sid was trying to get a rise out of me, I could tell. At the very first meeting I'd noticed his confrontational style. "As opposed to where you come from in Connecticut?" I said.

"You need some brothers." He was facing the speakers on the mantelpiece. His striped oxford shirt was coming untucked from his khakis. He had that impossible ratio of wide shoulders to narrow hips that makes women lose their sense.

I swallowed the saliva that was pooling in my mouth because my jaw was hanging open. I knew that I had to take charge, but it had been so long since I stood up to anyone who so indubitably had a penis. "You know someone who's interested?"

"Might be interested. He's a physics major."

"What does that mean?" I managed to close my mouth, not that he was looking.

Sid tapped a button and Public Enemy vanished. Something sad and soulful crooned out of the speakers. "Big study load. Like me."

"Who is singing?"

"Natalie Walker."

"Beautiful."

"Chick singers." I must have snorted my disapproval, because Sid elaborated. "Loving and getting dumped. It's boring." He kept his perfect and arrogant back to me while tapping more buttons.

"Aren't you afraid of the competition if your soul friend comes aboard?" I said.

"You wouldn't hire him."

"Why not?" He was pissing me off.

"You'd be afraid to oppress a black man."

He had an interesting point, but I was not giving an inch. "If you feel oppressed, quit," I said. "You can get a job at RadioShack."

"I'm not doing it for the money," Sid informed me. "I'm doing it for the sex. Cougar riding, that's my hobby." I knew that "cougar" was what some young men called the older women they dated.

I couldn't tell if he was teasing me or not. He glanced at me over his shoulder, but it wasn't casual. His eyelashes curled so far back the effect was startling. His irises glittered a blue-green color. He looked at my mules, my arms full of linen, then up to my attempt at a hairdo, meaningless strata of hair products, twists, and clips. He turned back to the iPod and clicked on Kevin Lyttle's "Dance With Me." It had an irresistible beat. "I have to do the laundry," I said faintly, but neither of us noticed. It had been such a long time since I had danced. I couldn't remember the last time. The rhythm seemed to get inside my tailbone. Sid turned up the volume. The voice was insistent: "Baby come and dance with me." I dropped the pile of sheets. The mules were perfect, slippery on the wood floor and giving my hips a tilt that felt provocative, almost a gesture.

How long *had* it been? Three years? Four? My arms felt stiff, like they didn't know where to go in space. I didn't look at Sid but turned to the windows, which were faintly steamy, above them a deer head with its mouth open like a stapler.

"Dance with me, dance with me." I closed my eyes. My spine seemed to remember what to do even if my arms were clueless. Sid cranked up the music. I was getting almost breathless. I didn't know if my aerobic capacity was poor, or if I was too nervous to breathe. Sid was dancing behind me. I didn't turn, but I could feel the heat from his body all along my back and thighs. I could feel us both on the beat.

As the song finished, I bent over and scooped up the laundry from the floor and held it tightly to my chest. When I turned to face him there was a mountain of crumpled sheets between us. "Work to do!" I said brightly.

Sid raised his eyebrows at me. "You are so chicken," he said. "Absolute bawk-bawk-bawk chicken." He made the noises of someone who had spent quality time around poultry.

"I'm your employer here," I said. "It wouldn't be professional."

"Oh yes." Sid gave me another blast from his glittery eyes. "It would be *professional*."

I dredged up a friendly mommy smile for him, a sorry-the-cookies-are-all-gone smile. "See you Tuesday. Bring your physics major friend if you want."

"Wayne."

"I look forward to meeting Wayne."

He punched a final button on the gizmo, and after the door closed behind him, some weird remix of "Do the Funky Chicken" blasted through the speakers. The windows were completely fogged up and I was sweating. I sat down on the mountain of sheets to gather myself. I was trembling a little. It was the sex jitters; I remembered them from a long time ago.

Bank and laundry, I said to myself firmly. Bank and laundry.

My safe-deposit box at the bank was quickly filling up. For two years it had held nothing but a gold bracelet of my grandmother's and a short strand of graduated pearls, a gift from my cousin. You are supposed to wear your pearls or they lose their luster, but I am not a pearls kind of person. I was saving them for Darcy.

The cash was a problem. I didn't want to draw attention to myself by depositing it in an account, but it was bulky. Onkwedo women seemed to use mostly small bills, as if they had been saving their change from the car wash and the supermarket.

Apex Friendly Market had become a major no-fly zone for me during the day. Each aisle was likely to be filled with my own customers. I had taken to shopping at midnight with the stoners, the insomniacs, and the newly divorced guys. With no kids to cook for, I barely ate dinner at all.

At the bank I stared at the small metal drawer with a stack of five-dollar bills in my hand. I tried again to wedge the money into the safe-deposit box. In vain. I contemplated asking for a bigger box or changing all the fives and ones for hundred-dollar bills. Both seemed too attention grabbing. I sighed and packed the money back into the inner pocket of my parka. I was saving the parka for next year when Sam's arms were longer. I wondered if his fatness was gathering for a growth spurt and he would outstrip his father in the years to come. The thought pleased me.

I forced myself to march up to the counter. I announced to the teller that I needed to deposit some cash. She looked at her computer screen and informed me that my account had a negative balance of six dollars and six cents and was scheduled for closing.

Her eyes widened at the messy stack of bills I pulled out of the parka pocket. "Is it counted?"

"Not exactly," I said. She put the money in the trough of the counting machine and evened the sides of the stack. The bills began to flip, manipulated by rubber-tipped mechanical fingers. She filled out the amount on the deposit slip and slid it over to me, her eyes on the figure.

"Did you open a business?" she asked, a little too eagerly.

From her candy dish, I took one of the red Valentine's Day Tootsie Rolls. It had the stale coppery taste of an old penny. "Yes." I forced myself to meet her eyes. "Scrapbooking—it's a cash cow."

I vowed to make all future deposits in the overnight slot after banking hours were done.

MATURE ROMANCE

On Wednesday morning I tried to make my agent happy. I sat on the floor of Nabokov's house with some lined paper and a pen. It was early in the day and I'd had a good night's sleep. There was no reason to be tired, but the mere thought of writing a sex scene for the boomer market exhausted me. I couldn't remember sex. I told myself it was like riding a bicycle, but that didn't help because I was a lousy bike rider. I took out Greg Holder's shirt and laid it across my lap.

I closed my eyes and held it to my face, inhaled. I imagined the carpenter's open mouth, smiling. I could almost smell his upper lip, the remnant whiff of shaving cream and coffee, smell his chest, the heat rising from the V in his shirt. With my eyes still closed I started to write: *She can feel his thumbs on her upper arms, their lower bodies leaning into each other, yearning. His pants are worn denim. She knows this because her fingertips are learning him, memorizing. His lower spine curves toward her, two thick ropes of muscle flanking it. She can feel them through the flannel shirt, feel the elastic ridge of his boxers.* [Note: Must find out if boomers wear boxers. Google this?]

He is breathing into her open mouth whispering, "I want you." Their tongues touch. Heat spreads inside her body, honey poured on a hot side-

walk, oozing into all crevices [Note: Find alternate less urban image: *blind ribbons of heat unfurl . . . meadows? Corn rows?*]

"*Sit up here,*" *he whispers. Perches her on the edge of his workbench, nestles between her knees. "This is good," he says. She has lost her tongue, lost it in his mouth. She undoes the buttons of his shirt and peels it back, off his shoulders. They are round with muscle and bone, thick. He stops to unbutton his cuffs and free his hands, tossing the shirt over his stepladder. "Come here," he says. "Please." His hands tilt her rib cage up. He nuzzles her breasts. She has lost her mind, lost any sense of where she is, of time. She lies back, ignoring the sawdust. The handle from a tool pokes her in the back.* [Note: Must find out from Margie if the target audience is retired, or if they would still be working, maybe hobbyists?] *He is efficient with his clothes and hers, and they melt. He scoops up her body, one arm under her hips, the other under her shoulders, and lifts. She wraps her legs around his hips, locking her ankles. Holding her, he walks into the bedroom and, bending down, lays her on the bed.* [Note: Must ask Margie if reader would be concerned here for old person's back?] *She can feel his hardness pressed against her.* [Note: Is erectile function addressed?] *His thumb is stroking her, his mouth on hers, his other hand caressing her breasts. He seems to know exactly what to do to melt her.* [Note: Overusing "melt"?] *Her heart is beating fast and her breath is ragged. She presses herself up against him and stretches her legs open wider, rocking her hips against his hand, against his . . .*

That was as far as I got, because even though the sun was shining brightly on my face, I fell asleep. When I awoke, I found I had been napping for half an hour. My pen had made a squiggly line down to the bottom of the page, and I had drooled onto Greg Holder's shirt. I roused myself and came up with this bland offering: *He feels incredibly good inside her, better than anything she can remember.* [Note: Must check about condoms used?] *Dizzy, she lies back on the bed, letting him steer the boat, get her to the other shore. He takes his sweet time, and just as she thinks her mind is gone forever, they arrive.*

Reading this over, I feared it was impossible to tell if the people had orgasms or not. I was not sure how important that would be, so I added a note to Margie: *Dear M, can you tell if the people came? And does it matter?*

Using the options my ancient Daitch Dairy computer offered, I formatted the scene like a real book, a scrolly header with a small heart on every page. When I printed it out and inserted it (fattened with many blank pages) into one of the covers of the mature romances, *Matched at Last,* it looked like an absolute genuine published book. This was a visualization technique I learned at my old job. Make it look real, and it will become real.

I placed the mock-up senior romance book on my coffee table, where I would see it frequently, and made a plain copy for my agent. I hoped the scene would get me some work, as Margie had suggested. I couldn't imagine who would want to read about elderly people doing the nasty, but then I don't like watching the animals in the zoo either.

I put Margie's copy of the Mature Romance Scene in an envelope and sealed it. Then I put it in another envelope in case the first one lost its stickiness and flew open, exposing the contents. I decided to drive it to the post office rather than wait for Bill to pick it up. I would be mortified if Bill were to read that scene.

On Thursday (date with Greg Holder day), I didn't wait for Margie to call me. I called her right after lunch.

"Margie, how does that scene work for you?"

"Hold on, Barb." I heard "Bye, Sweetheart," and a kissing sound that would be icky if I didn't know they loved each other.

Margie came back to the phone. "Jesus, Barb, this is your idea of a love scene? These people are screwing on a bench! On top of nails and hammers! This isn't a love scene."

I was blushing into the other end of the phone.

Margie paused to take one of her deep, raspy breaths. I recognized this as my agent gathering herself to explain life to me. "Barb, you know how you're with someone you like, and all of a sudden you realize he's the one? That's the scene to write. Only these people are older; they have their whole lives behind them. Well, most of their lives," she amended. "Or you could write the scene where they finally decide they are meant for each other, the commitment scene."

These sounded like the same thing to me, and like nothing I knew from life experience. "Margie, I can't do it. I think I should stick with the day job for a while."

"The *milk* letters?" Margie sounded outraged.

"The whole love and destiny business, I just don't understand it," I said. "I am OK with dairy products."

Margie snorted at me. "You're passing up a gold mine."

DATE

I thought about calling Rudy to find out more about current dating practices. Particularly I wanted to know if people kissed on the first date nowadays. I also wondered if people, particularly older people like us, did more than that on the first date, or was it sometime after the third, as it had been when I'd last dated. I stretched my mind over in Rudy's direction instead of calling. It seemed safer.

If I was Rudy's date, there would be two Rudy-sized depressions next to each other on his couch. I'd be in one. His big body would be slanting the couch, pulling me toward him. I'd feel his heat. The remote would be nestled conveniently by his left hand. A game would be on TV. It would be narcotizing to sit on Rudy's couch and watch the game. I'd feel my mind shut down, a good feeling.

That would be Rudy's foreplay, I thought. He wouldn't have retooled it since college. The date, whoever she was—glad it wasn't me— would be doing what Rudy did: watch TV and go to bed. There would be so much gravitational pull that the woman would simply get sucked into the vortex of his habits.

Rudy's fourth Scotch would have done its work, and he'd begin an efficient preparation for bed, as if she/I had already left: untying each shoe, stripping off socks, unbuttoning shirt, unbuckling wristwatch and laying it beside the remote, removing creaky leather pants. He'd say something in my/her direction that might be "You coming?" or might be "You going?"

In my mind, I retrieved my shoes from under the couch and tiptoed out, closing his front door quietly behind me. There hadn't been any kissing at all on Rudy's date.

When I got to Café Raw, Greg Holder was standing outside, leaning against his truck. He had on new-looking jeans and a corduroy shirt under his ski jacket. After we greeted each other, he said, "Please let me take you to a better restaurant than this, OK?"

Café Raw had been my suggestion, but I was not about to insist on cold tofu. I climbed into his truck, which was nicely messy, a stash of paper coffee cups rolling around on the floor.

He was even more ridiculously handsome in the candlelight of the restaurant than he had been under the streetlight. The weird thing was that I didn't feel nervous. He ordered a bottle of something great from an Upstate vineyard called Whitecliff. "These folks are my friends," he said, but not in a snobby way, just matter-of-fact. Then he suggested I order for us both. "Can't go wrong here," he said.

My mind registered this good news: no control issues around food. Either that or he was excellent at faking it.

The food was so delicious it was hard not to hum while I chewed. Seared herbed tuna with a ball of wasabi and a rose of pickled ginger. I asked if the cook was from New York.

"Plattsburgh," Greg said. We talked easily about Upstate and Down—he sold his furniture pieces there occasionally—about movies, and even about my kids. "You sound like a good mom," he said. That made me want to kiss him right on the spot.

I felt more and more relaxed as the evening went along. He drove me back to Café Raw, where my car was parked. He turned the motor off and got out. At my car door, he stood close to me, but not too close. He didn't kiss me, although I thought he would. I held out my hand and he took it. I'd never known what the rules were for handshaking between men and women on a first date, but Greg clearly recognized the shake as a non-kiss. He held my hand firmly, looking a little bemused. He asked if he could come and see me sometime up in Nabokov's house. It was his nice way of saying that things would go as fast or as slow as I wanted them to. I liked that, the idea of being in control, of going slow. It seemed very adult.

But there was part of me that was saying fast, fast, fast. I dove for his lips. I hadn't meant to, but suddenly I did, an almost spastic puckered-up mouth slam of a kiss. And then I jumped in my car and drove away fast, fast, fast. It was only luck that I didn't run him over.

At home in bed, I tried not to think about Greg Holder. Thinking about him was—well, hot. Hot hadn't been in my life in a very long time. But my mind had never been obedient, and I could see Greg pull his shirt over his head, in the one-handed way that men do, could see his chest—mmm, his chest. I could see how easily his jeans fell to the floor once unbuckled. And then I couldn't see anything else, darn.

UNDERPANTS ARRIVE

Margie had made it clear that there was nothing to hear yet about *Babe Ruth* and that I should not bug her, so I went about my work. After yet another trip to the Laundromat, I was back in my house, folding umpteen sheets and pillowcases and screening erotica on the computer. The film was in the new (new to me?) "femmeporn" genre. The actresses were real looking, but the actors looked like gods, or at least gym kings.

I missed the plot setup because the phone rang. While the action on the screen was getting warm, I was having a conversation with Darcy's new kindergarten teacher, Ms. Sugarman, about my daughter's unwillingness to join the group.

As best I could understand it, Ms. Sugarman's concern was that Darcy refused to be a princess. All the other girls were in a princess club, and Darcy didn't want to be a princess. She'd said she wouldn't mind being "a real princess" because they got to live in France, but "stupid pink princesses are fake." The teacher wanted me to make Darcy apologize to the girls. And she wanted to know if Darcy had any clothes that were "lighter colored."

I had the feeling that this was a screen issue, because John would have been their first call. Sure enough, there was one more thing: Darcy had called Ms. Sugarman a "behemoth shit."

"She doesn't know what it means," I told Ms. S. without taking my eyes from the authentic-looking fake climaxes. "I'm not even sure what it means." There was a long pause that I realized I was obliged to fill. "'Behemoth,' does that mean large or grandiose?" There was a tooth-sucking sound from Ms. Sugarman. I turned the volume on the pornography down, and remarked on Darcy's smooth transition to her new school and her great improvement in her numbers and letters. This was not true. Darcy went into kindergarten knowing the alphabet and caring not at all about numbers—hers or anyone else's—and she was still in exactly that place. A nine to her was as irrelevant as Pluto the planet or non-planet.

Ms. Sugarman wanted me to come in for a meeting with Darcy and her father after school. It happened to coincide with my most lucrative time slot at the cathouse, Thursday at two. Driving to Oneonta and back would take me five hours and the same number of quarts of oil. I wanted to refuse—I knew how unproductive it would be for all of us— but I tried to be nice for my daughter's sake. I could almost smell the teacher's minty fresh breath over the telephone. (Why was it that everyone was better groomed than I?)

"Sorry, Ms. Sugarman, I am working then. Is there a morning time available?" My schedule had completely flipped: supermarket, laundry, bank, and cooking in the nighttime, sex all day (not having any, just facilitating).

This request caused her to sigh and page through her day planner. I could hear displeasure in her silence.

I tried to appease her. "I know that Darcy is an unusual person." There was more silence on the other end. The femmeporn was getting steamier: one actress on the couch eating chocolates while the gym god dogged her roommate. I suppose it was hot. How different from manporn, I didn't know. Fewer fake breasts maybe, and in manporn they'd be smearing the chocolate on their bodies rather than eating it.

I wanted Ms. Sugarman to leave us the hell alone. Let Darcy be a Goth tot, just teach her to count, for goodness' sake. But I didn't say this. If there was a special hell for passive-aggressive mothers, I was going there. I heard myself agree that February is such a short month! And then I promised to explain to Darcy that fake princesses have real feelings. And that certain words didn't belong in school. I hated the thought of squandering my precious Darcy time dispensing conventions to help her fit her wonderful self into the conforming world of kindergarten, but I would try.

With *Bad Girls Finish First* reaching its three-way apex and the endless pile of sheets folded for the next day's cathouse trade, I thought about Ms. Sugarman's life. Maybe she lived alone like me. Maybe she had no roommate. It made looking after pretend princesses and teaching bad spellers a noble kind of duty, let alone while suffering insults.

I wondered what the men would think about the femmeporn, what Sid, the cougar rider, would think about it. (I'd had the pleasure of telling Margie what "cougar" meant. She had never heard of it.) Sid was in my thoughts way too often, his unbelievably smooth skin and low body fat, the way he always managed to match the music mix to the mood of the day.

Ms. Sugarman made a Monday morning date for "both the parents and the concerned teachers" to meet. What a behemoth pain in the neck that I would have to sit in a room with John. She gave me a wind-down paragraph about "the effectiveness of team effort." I made some appropriate mmms and hmms while I watched the roommates dominate the gym god. Chocolate was involved there too.

"Have a nice day," we said simultaneously.

The doorbell rang and it was my special-order ecru underpants from Hanro. They were an atrociously drab color, sort of a pre-pissed-on beige, but wonderfully soft and light. I put them on and looked in the mirror. They were anything but sexy. As usual, I was a lousy consumer. On me the Hanro ecru low rise looked like nun panties.

WEEKEND

After school ended on Friday, John brought the children for my custody weekend. I handed off Matilda and all her stuff, a good trade. "See you at the school meeting," he said. John was probably looking forward to it; unlike me, he loved authority figures.

Wearing her large backpack, Darcy looked like a very beautiful turtle. She slogged into the house without speaking and dropped it inside the door along with her coat and boots. She went directly to the cupboard and got herself a handful of crackers, which she ate, glaring at me, daring me to tell her to wash her hands.

I didn't. Sam had gone dutifully to the sink and then to the fridge, which he held open, staring inside.

"Let's play school," Darcy said when she'd finished chewing and wiped her hands on her pants. "I am the teacher." She directed me to sit on the rug and flanked me with Barbies. "Listen up," she said, and then, leaning meanly into my face, she made the zip-your-lip gesture. She left to find a piece of chalk.

I could hear Sam getting a bowl out of the cupboard. "Can I make something, Barb?"

"Sure, what are you thinking of?"

"Soufflé."

On her small chalkboard Darcy wrote b-u-t-t. This was too much for her and she giggled, but quickly regained her stern teacher face. "Stop whispering," she said. "It's rude." I took Barbie onto my lap. "No touching!" She stood very close to me. With me seated on the floor, we were eye to eye.

"Why do some ladies wear black stuff right here?" She touched my eyelid.

"Mascara," I said, "it's for their looks."

"Do they wear it in the city?" Darcy asked me.

"Yes."

"No talking," she said in her stern teacher voice. "Today we are cutting with scissors." She pointed at the one-armed Barbie. "Take turns or you will go to the principal's office."

I asked Darcy if she had any new friends in kindergarten. "Boys are jerks," she informed me. "Sarah stepped on my shoe." She burst into tears. "And then Trudy did it too." She was sobbing. "I hate them." With the scissors she lopped off a chunk of two-armed Barbie's hair.

I could hear Sam whipping egg whites in the kitchen.

"The teacher treats me like a maid. I have to paste all day long." She sniffed. "The snacks taste like poop." She looked at me. "I want it to stop." Darcy leaned against me, her nose running onto my shoulder. "I need some mascara." She looked at me craftily. "When you buy me the mascara, I will keep it here in this house."

I gave her the mascara from my purse and watched her find the perfect hiding place: a black zippered change purse inside a sequined shoulder bag. She showed me her money collection in there too, three separate wallets: one for dollars, of which she had two; one for pennies; and the third for silver coins, all of which she called "nickels."

We ate soufflé for dinner, and a fruit salad. Sam had written down the recipes for both, with notations on mistakes to avoid: "Do not cut fruit too big," and "Check for shells in the egg whites."

At the table Darcy asked me if I knew Jesus.

"No," I said, not sure where this was heading.

"Irene does." She was eating only the bananas from the fruit salad.

"Shut up!" Sam said. He threw his spoon down on the table. "Stop being a weirdo for once."

Darcy looked stunned. I had never heard him speak to her like that. I watched her little face shut down. "Sam, take it easy," I said. "I think she had a question." He pushed back his chair and stomped out of the kitchen.

Darcy pushed her bowl away. "Why don't you want to live with us anymore?" she asked me.

"Oh, baby, is that what you think?" I opened my arms to her and she climbed into my lap. I kissed her hair. I tried to explain to her that it wasn't up to me. She didn't believe me. To Darcy, adults did whatever they wanted, and her mother wanted to live away from her. I held her and rocked her, swaying from side to side. "Mama loves you," I crooned. "Mama is so proud of you." She leaned her head on my shoulder, pressing her face into the curve of my neck.

After a while, I carried her to bed and laid her small body on top of the coverlet. She let me dress her for bed, limp and unhelpful as a tired infant, but never taking her eyes from mine. I brushed her teeth and smoothed her hair back from her face, noting the spiky patch in front where it was growing back.

"I'll always be your mama," I said. I fluffed her pillow.

"Will Sam always be my brother?"

"Yes, even when you are all grown up."

"Where *is* Grandpa?"

"He's gone, Darcy. But we all remember different things about him, and we keep those memories all of our lives." I pulled the blanket up to her chin and tucked it around her shoulders.

"Did he know he was going to die?"

"Yes. He was ready, Darcy. He had a long, good life."

"Did Grandpa take one last blink at the beautiful world?"

"I'm sure he did." I kissed her eyelids closed.

I tiptoed away to find Sam. From behind his bedroom door, I could hear nothing. I knocked, but he didn't answer. He probably had music playing through his earphones and couldn't hear me. I knocked louder. He cracked the door and looked out without removing his earphones. "What?" he asked.

I motioned for him to pull out the earphones, and he did—one of them. "Darcy thinks I wanted to leave you guys. You know that isn't true, right?"

"I know you do whatever Dad wants you to do." He stuck the plug back in his ear and closed the door.

Our drive to school on Monday was nearly silent. I wanted more than anything for them to know how deeply I loved them and longed to live with them, but here I was following orders and returning them to their life without me.

Near their school, a highway patrol car passed us with its lights flashing, and Darcy screamed.

"They're not after Barb, you dummy," Sam said.

They let me kiss them goodbye at the school entrance, and I watched them walk away, neither acknowledging the other.

I parked in the visitors' lot. The school was decorated with construction paper hearts in preparation for Valentine's Day. John and I had to sit on same side of the table to accommodate all the teachers in the room. He looked perfect, of course. I was wearing my good mommy accessory, a scarf I'd liberated from my mother's closet. The art teacher, the district psychologist, and both Sam's and Darcy's homeroom teachers were assembled.

They talked about Darcy first. Instead of the Valentine's Day cards that were the curriculum of the past week, she'd been writing misspelled notes of loathing to students in her class. The art teacher displayed some of them, lumpy hearts with lines through them. And something that might have been a bad word, but hideously misspelled.

The kindergarten teacher said meaningfully that Darcy wore only black and gray to school. John didn't refute that.

The art teacher wanted to discuss Sam as well. She showed us a self-portrait he had done. It was a circle with a snout and two specks for eyes. There was a knife sticking out of the neck.

The teacher wondered if there were pressures at home.

John said no.

I mentioned the low-carb diet.

Everyone agreed that it was important to watch children's weight. I guess I lost *that* point. I could tell from John's complacent exhale that he knew who'd won.

The district psychologist wondered aloud if Sam had outlets for his feelings. John piped up with the ice hockey regimen.

Everyone agreed that athletics were a central part of a young boy's life. That seemed to satisfy the requirements of the meeting, because the teachers stood up. While John was shaking all their hands, I swiped my children's artwork: the portrait and the hate mail. There was a plate of Mint Milano cookies set out for a staff appreciation luncheon. I stuffed two in my mouth on the way out. It gave me something to do with my own hands that wasn't criminal.

Driving home, dodging the crazed Valentine's Day shoppers, I realized I had been so wrapped up in my feelings of loss about the children that I hadn't understood what it meant to them that I was gone. Darcy thought I had wanted to leave her, and Sam thought I only did what John wanted me to do. Furthermore, they weren't each other's allies anymore; my children were not a team.

I felt powerless over the circumstances of my life. When I met John, I had one superpower: the Walking Away Power. I lost that when I gave birth to my first child. Now all I had was the Making the Best of Crap Power.

At home I found the family court checklist of the conditions I must meet to establish custodial fitness. It read like a business plan on How to Bring Order to Your Fucked-Up Life: steady employment, mortgage paid on time, average balance in savings account, low credit card balances, evidence of social activities, friends, hobbies, clean house. Why couldn't I do these things?

STEADY EMPLOYMENT

Word was definitely out about the cathouse, but it was for the most part a deep secret in chatty Onkwedo. Women spoke of it only to their most trusted friends. The word of mouth was coming mostly through beauty salons, from client to beautician to other client. Most women appeared at the door of the lodge with their hair and nails freshly done like it was date night.

Thursday was the first time I had to go upstairs during working hours. The day began fine, with Janson laying the fire and Sid cranking up some faux-nostalgic Motown remixes. The music made me happy, though I think it was his homage to his parents' generation. Evan had a human development paper to write, so he wasn't there, but the handsome Wayne and the very quiet and enormous Tim occupied the couch. It was Wayne's first time, but he seemed more relaxed than anyone except Tim, who sat with the stillness of a side of beef.

I started my day the way I always did: in the kitchen, gathering the data from the previous workday. It was up to the guys to note down the information, and they were thorough and reliable about it. I suspected that none of them had ever turned in homework late. On slips of paper they noted customer preferences by code and filed them beside the cashbox in back of the pulpit.

Sid had helped me set up a simple statistical model, enabling me to make comparisons between visits and observe choice patterns. One thing I'd noticed was that, except for a few customers who were working their way through the entire staff, the women seemed to choose the same person over and over again. My theory was that the women were being "faithful." It was sweet. I didn't know if it was because the women were concerned about hurting their person's feelings or if they were reluctant to seem promiscuous by adding more partners to their list. ("Partner" might not be the correct term.)

Ginna, the bookkeeper for Old Daitch Dairy, was a regular. So far, we had only nodded at each other. She came every week. She was one of the exceptions to the data, having no particular pattern of preference, unless you considered "innovation" a pattern.

I was recording some anomalies in a special notebook. Dr. Gladys Biggs, tenured sociology professor and cougar, went upstairs with Tim for a Standard (fifty minutes). I didn't need to check who she picked, because his tread on the steps was heavier than the others'. Tim had never made any requests of me, or even spoken except in a monosyllabic greeting or farewell. But he did seem to stay busy. He was so huge; it may have been the novelty of his size that appealed to my clients.

They hadn't been gone more than a quarter of an hour when Tim came thumping back down the stairs. He didn't look agitated, because it was not in his repertoire of facial expression, but his loafers were off and his belt buckle undone. He came straight to the kitchen, where I was trying a new way to manipulate the data that was supposed to give a predictive model, and informed me that Professor Biggs wouldn't use a condom and she had her legs up against the wall and it was giving him "the creeps."

It gave me the even bigger creeps, because I knew that was the ideal position for conception to occur. I ran up the stairs and pushed open the door to room 5. Sure enough, there was Professor Biggs in the classic sperm-facilitation pose. I saw so much more of her than I ever wanted to. "Please get up," I said, keeping my eyes on the baseboard. "We are expecting a visit from the chair of your department." (Fortunately I knew from my workers that the acting head of the sociology department was a woman.) I closed the door and waited outside it while she scrambled into her clothes.

She emerged with her short hair askew (bed head or a self-cut, I couldn't tell), and pushed a fistful of twenties at me. I could see close up that she was old enough that conception was most likely only a fantasy. But I felt that I had to stand up for my men.

"Dr. Biggs," I said, "we welcome you back, but condoms must be used at all times for everyone's protection."

She grunted at me, pounded down the stairs, and rushed out the door, pulling on her fleece. From the upstairs window, I watched her race her Prius up the drive before her boss's Prius arrived.

I lingered in the upstairs hallway, listening. Behind the door of room 2 I heard quiet moaning that might have been soft crying. I slipped off my shoes and tiptoed along the hallway. Behind another door a woman's voice was slightly raised, the man's rumbling and low. I couldn't make out any words, but an intense discussion was going on. In the last room I heard giggling and the sound of a slap and more giggling. I stood in the middle of the hallway, proud. Everything was cooking.

I slipped on my shoes and returned to the kitchen/office to bring out bread and butter. I found things worked best if I served a late-afternoon snack. Everyone's mood stayed more pleasant, and there was less talk of pizza and beer.

In the living room, when the clients had gone home and the men were reassembled, I delivered a lecture about standing up for yourself and insisting on safe sex. I had been practicing this speech to give to my son and daughter when the time came. (As far in the future as possible, please!) The men had heard it before, I could tell, and barely looked up from the food.

They had never tasted homemade butter. Tim pronounced it "good" on his fourth slice.

Someday he might reproduce, but I hoped he wouldn't be rushed into it.

After they left, I made my final data entries, knocked the coals apart, and sat by the fire. I wanted to share my workday with someone. I called Margie.

"Hi, Barb." Margie sounded cheerful.

"How was your day?" That was the question I missed most from marriage. Not my marriage, but a good marriage.

"Fine. Making money hand over fist in the romance market." That's what I was doing too, in a way. The fire crackled. "Where are you?"

"That's what I wanted to tell you, if you have a moment."

"Sure, I'll feed the cats. They know when it's five o'clock." I could hear the whine of her electric can opener.

"I started a business, a kind of spa for women." I poked the fire with the tongs, watching the coals brighten and then dim.

"At the Bryce lodge? I heard about it, but I didn't know you were part of it."

"How did you hear? No, what did you hear?"

"Barb, it's a small town. We all get our pedi's at the same three places. Women share a good thing."

"You heard good things about it?"

"Excellent things. Hot things. Nobody is telling the men anything."

"That's good."

"Good? Are you crazy? That's essential. What in God's name were you thinking to try and pull that off here?" I could hear the cats calling for food.

I tried to explain to Margie how I thought of the cathouse business and why Onkwedo needed it. She cut me off. "Barb, it's better if I don't try to follow what goes on in your head. The important thing is that you don't get caught. So far women are keeping it absolutely hush-hush, but I don't know how long that can last. You better not piss anybody off." She was right, of course. "How is business?"

"Fantastic. Full up every Tuesday and Thursday afternoon. We book ahead nearly a month and we're at capacity."

"How's overhead?"

"Low."

"How is the action? No, don't tell me. You have no idea." Margie knew everything.

"I try to keep it professional."

Margie snorted. "You are my oddest friend."

"You're my friend who knows everything." I didn't say she was my only friend; I think she suspected that.

"It's not a life plan, Barb. Get an exit strategy."

I banked the fire and went home.

LEMONADE

On Saturday afternoon, well before Greg Holder was due to arrive, I was cleaning Nabokov's house. They say Nature abhors a vacuum, and I did too, but I was using it. Cleaning was how I dealt with anxiety. I put things in order. It's boring, but better than berating the dog. Anyway, the dog was gone.

I was anxious about Greg Holder arriving and what would happen after that. I was not sure why I'd kissed him. I remembered reading an article in *Psychology Now* (page 27) that said some women can launch into slut mode without warning. It's a little like being a werewolf, the right conditions—say, a full moon—can bring it on suddenly. I was thinking about that as I sucked invisible dust from the baseboards.

The example in *Psychology Now* involved a woman on a date, her first ever, at the age of twenty-six. They were parked near a lighthouse, and when the beam of light swept the car, she suddenly dove for her date's lap. He was startled, and there was no second date.

I'd kissed Greg and I had not meant to do it. I don't remember the lighting conditions, but I remember him standing very close to me with his mouth slightly open, and I remember my thought—if I *had* one: This is how a date ends. And it did. It was not the same as diving for someone's zipper, but still, I wondered about myself.

I stopped vacuuming the clean house and tried on sweaters. I found a fluffy blue one that I had forgotten I owned, and the jeans of course. The outfit followed one of the principles of sexy dressing, the only one I could remember: Soft on top, hard on the bottom.

Then I emptied all the wastebaskets and spritzed them with Lysol. The smell of Lysol makes people behave in a tidier way. I remembered that fact from my old job too. Even if it is a faint whiff, it will cause people to clean up after themselves. It is the opposite of patchouli oil, the scent of which makes people leave their stuff all over the floor. Here I was *cleaning,* just like the other Onkwedo women; maybe I was becoming a repressed native.

The doorbell rang and Greg Holder stood there, looking totally handsome, like he got out of bed in the morning handsome and stayed that way all day. I didn't want to start zipper diving, so I turned on all the lights and went to the kitchen to fix us a snack—cheese and crackers, lemonade—and put it on a tin tray.

While I was flipping light switches, spilling, dropping things, and trying to compose myself, he called from the living room. "Are you reading *Matched at Last*?"

I walked in with the tray and saw that my mock-up mature romance book was lying open in his hand. "This stuff is like sex fantasies for the retarded," he said. He saw me looking at him, stock-still, tray in my hands. "Sorry," he said, clearing books off the table so I could put the tray down. "I meant 'mentally challenged.'"

There was an awkward pause during which he studied my pinkening face. "Are you reading this book?" He spoke slowly, like he was talking to a—well, mentally challenged person.

"No," I said stiffly. "I wrote it."

There was a very long gap in the conversation. "Maybe you need to do some research," he said finally. "When was the last time you kissed someone?"

"Last week." I couldn't believe he had forgotten already. "I kissed you."

"That was more like a drive-by shooting." He took the tray from me and set it down on the table.

"You are—"

"I know, you told me. I'm an asshole." He poured two glasses of lemonade. "You made this from scratch?"

"Yes."

"Please sit." I sat. He sipped. "This is great lemonade." I was staring at him. He seemed totally relaxed, while I was tensed up like a bunch of wire coat hangers. "There's no point in rushing the good stuff, right?"

He looked out the big picture window and asked about the hawthorn tree. I didn't know it was a hawthorn tree, and I had not a clue how he could tell it was a hawthorn without a single leaf on it. Greg talked about wood. He had harvested a fallen European willow from the Waindell trustees' private burial ground. It had come down in an ice storm. "I sawed it into slabs on New Year's Eve. That's what I was doing when you came by. It needs to cure for about ten years."

"Then what?" I sipped the lemonade. It was very good. I had pressed thinly sliced lemons into a small pile of sugar with the back of a wooden spoon, and when it had macerated into lemon syrup, I added water and ice. It had just enough of the bitterness from the zest to counter the sweet. My grandmother had taught me to make lemonade; she'd learned how from her cook.

"I'll build a long dining table, maybe some desks." He finished his drink. "I can't keep up with the demand for stand-up writing desks. I had to triple my prices." He put his glass down. "Where in this house did you find the book?"

I showed him Darcy's room. With his thumb, Greg rubbed the wood of the built-in drawers. "Well made," he said.

At the threshold of my bedroom he stood and looked in, but did not enter. I backed away, feeling uncertain, and called to show him Sam's cookbook collection, which he admired.

I stopped awkwardly by the front door, not sure what to do next. Leaning toward me, Greg touched my lower lip with his finger, and then his lips brushed mine. They were just right, salty and smooth. My eyes closed like one of those plastic dolls that you tilt. It sounds sappy, but I melted. I felt the heat in my belly and all that trite stuff.

I had forgotten kissing. Was it possible to forget kissing? How very wrong to go on in life without remembering kissing.

I stood there with my eyes closed and my mouth open, and Greg said something to me softly that I couldn't make out. I opened my eyes and he was looking at me. God, he was handsome, and his eyes were kind, and so smart. "Pay attention," he said, "this is for your book." He cupped my cheek with his palm and traced his thumb over my lips. It was sexy and sweet and my lips parted. He kissed me tenderly, with a lovely unpushy readiness. Oh yeah, I thought, he is right there. It was hot and soft and I could have gone on for a lot longer, but he stopped. "Slow is good, right?" He had his coat in his hand. "I have to go, but let's pick this up next time?"

After he left, I felt confused. Did he like me? Did he think I was slutty? Was I? Were the rules different since I had last dated? Did I even like him, such a confident, overly handsome person? And why did he leave so fast.

WEDDING PLANS

My mother emailed me a photo of herself in her wedding dress. She let about five minutes elapse before she called me. She had decided to have her wedding on the birth date of my father, in three months. She explained it to me like this: "Barb, the day your father was born was the luckiest day of my life." I was speechless.

Mother filled the silence by informing me that the wedding would be a good opportunity for me to meet a "nice doctor." I reminded her I didn't like doctors. She said, "What is the matter with you? You used to hate lawyers, now it's doctors. You are so opinionated."

"I never hated lawyers, that was someone else. But I like your dress." That shut her up. Her dress was a beautiful silvery mesh. In the photo she looked like a petite mermaid of a certain age.

Mother agreed to let Darcy wear black and silver as the flower girl, as long as it was mostly silver. (The wedding colors were watermelon and silver.) She was having my father's tux cut down for Sam. He would be fancier than the groom, Dr. Gold. I planned on standing next to Sam in all the photos, slightly in front of his waist.

She told me she planned to invite John to the wedding and he could bring a date. My mother always liked John. Even after the custody judgment, she refused to say bad things about him.

"Irene?" I said.

I could hear her writing it down. "Is she thin?"

I had to shout at her to get her attention. "They can't come! If they come, I stay home."

"Calm down," she said. "Fine, I won't invite them. But I have a real problem to discuss with you." She explained her wedding quandary. She wanted to invite my cousin's widow to the wedding, but she was concerned that his widow had no escort. Didn't I think it was a terrible problem? Was there anything I could do to help that situation? And how should she address the invitation?

My mother had arranged my wedding to John without all these inane questions, although I might have been too pregnant to notice, or too sad.

The month before my wedding, at my cousin's funeral, five of his ex-girlfriends sat on the facing benches of the Quaker meetinghouse, weeping. Each one was more beautiful and bereft than the last. His first love arrived and departed in a limousine, never lifting her black veil.

I told my mother to include my cousin's widow, that there must be an extra doctor somewhere. She insisted that I try to find "a nice man, a friend" for the widow. She said that there would be an open bar. Maybe she thought I should look for a nice friendly man in alcohol rehab.

"And what about you?" She got back to her favorite embarrassment, her divorced daughter.

I decided to get her off my back, and at the save time save myself from being paired up with a physician or a drunk or both. "I might bring someone too. He's a carpenter. I don't know him very well."

"Has he met the children?"

"No."

"They could pass as John and Irene's kids, and you could be single."

"John's not coming. If you want your daughter and your grandkids at your wedding, John and his yard worker cannot come. That's my last word."

"Barbara, you do not have to shout at your mother."

I breathed deeply. "I think I have a DJ for you, but he costs a lot."

"That's fine, dear." To my mother, expense equaled quality.

I left a message on Sid's voice mail about being the DJ for my mother's wedding. I told him to name his price. Then I called Rudy about being an escort for my cousin's widow. I plonked the words "open bar" into my first sentence.

Rudy said he could come.

I decided to wait to invite Greg, which seemed like a really bad idea now that I thought about it.

BUTTER

Each day at the cathouse had its own feel. There was a close relationship with the school calendar, I noticed. It was the Thursday before Easter vacation, and I had all but given up on *Babe Ruth* ever selling. Wives were frantically getting ready for trips to see their in-laws or buying massive hams to bake for twenty family members. In between they decide to do a little something nice for themselves and come here. The nail salons were practically empty. The day before, I had gone for my first Onkwedo pedicure. They seemed to know exactly who I was and treated me like a celebrity, bringing me tea and throwing in French tips for free. In the high-heeled mules, my toes looked like strangers.

I set hot bread on a rack to cool and put the fresh butter in the fridge. It was an ancient, slope-shouldered, energy-inefficient refrigerator, but Granny Bryce was very fond of it and had given me specific instructions on its care, including monthly defrosting without the use of an ice pick.

Most afternoons Janson arrived early and laid the fire. The days were getting milder, but we still had an occasional snow flurry and the fireplace was a good source of comfort. When a new customer came in, she always remarked on the fire, as though she was expecting a wet-vinyl interior or red fake fur. Janson took the opportunity to throw on a log, which earned him the first look and often led to a trip upstairs.

I opened the data program and started reviewing the predictive model. It looked like sooner or later everyone would get spanked. Weird. Another pattern was that the women didn't seem to know what they wanted at first, but as they kept coming back to their "person," they got more specific in their requests and more daring. There was also a "T" notation on many slips, but I had no idea what that meant. There were a surprising number of entries that included no sexual activity of any kind, just the "T." I wasn't sure whether they were coded wrong or I was missing something.

Ginna, with her bent for variety, was always an outlier on the graph. I suspected that the knowledge that people were having sex in the room next to them was more of a turn-on than anyone admitted, but there was no way of measuring that.

The men were coming in the front door, calling out greetings. I could hear Janson piling logs on the hearth.

I hated to be profiting from the racism that defines the United States, but Wayne was certainly outearning everyone but Tim. I think it was not only his skin color that engaged the curiosity of my customers but also his impeccable grooming. The other men managed to look slightly disheveled next to him. It must have been the ironing. Very few men in Onkwedo understood the value of ironing.

One thing that was obvious was that the cathouse was absolutely at maximum capacity for the hours we were open. I'd even had to give some women rain checks.

There was no way to add rooms, and I didn't want to hire more people anyway; I liked the men and they got along well with each other.

I decided to raise the prices, just like Greg Holder, to keep a lid on the demand. I decided to go up by half for spring fever, to take advantage of the seasonal restlessness and spousal neglect that sets in with the opening of baseball.

I wondered if Greg Holder was a baseball fan. Greg Holder. The feel of his lips was disconcerting, too hot, too full of something that felt very destabilizing. Oh, right, desire.

As I was thinking this exact thought, Margie walked in the front door. I could not have been more horrified if it had been my own mother. She took in the fireplace, the neat crease in Wayne's slacks, the span of Sid's shoulders. Tim and Janson were already upstairs with some Easter cooks. Margie looked beautiful, as usual, but her clothes seemed tighter, more obvious. I could see the men take her in, not as a customer but as something else entirely. Sid uncoiled. Wayne smiled the nastiest, hottest smile I had ever seen.

"Margie!" I practically shouted. "Come in the kitchen!" She crossed the room in the disturbing way that long-legged women on high heels could manage; her hips displaced the air in heat waves. I hustled her into a kitchen chair and put the electric teakettle on. "What are you doing here?" I said. "Does Bill know you're here?"

"Bill is at his mother's," Margie said. Bill's mother lived in a cottage at the north end of the lake, and Bill was often there fixing things or keeping her company.

I heard the front door open and close and glanced through the one-way mirror to see Wayne go upstairs with a regular. Sid put on his favorite music, the sound track from the Bond movie *Goldfinger*. It was corny, and the other men teased him about how often he played it.

I didn't want to demand that Margie tell me what the hell she thought she was doing here, jeopardizing her good marriage, just when she and Bill should pull together to help each other. I was not Dr. Phil. I trotted out the only skills that I felt confident about, the mommy ones. "Snack?" I asked. And before she could answer, I had sliced some homemade bread, popped it in the toaster, rustled her up a cup of hot tea with lemon, and pulled up a second chair to block her access to the front room. Sid had just gone upstairs with the only woman I had seen in the cathouse who could pass for twenty-two. Tim came lumbering downstairs, and I invited him to join us.

I introduced him to Margie, explaining that she was my agent and an investor. This last part wasn't true, but it flew out of my mouth with no warning to my brain. I wasn't sure if that made her off-limits, which was my intention. I didn't want Margie anywhere near the action. It violated my feeling of anonymity, of being a simple service provider. And besides, I knew Bill. I *liked* Bill. The whole idea of Margie going upstairs with one of my workers bothered me greatly. Maybe it was hypocritical to make the distinction with a marriage I knew, but Margie and Bill were happy together; they were a rare good thing.

I smeared the toast liberally with butter and smacked it down between them on two plates. I was counting on Tim's lack of conversational skills to discourage Margie from thinking of herself as a potential customer. "Tim is majoring in botany," I said, since he was engaged in chewing and could not talk. Margie looked at him with friendly curiosity. It was too friendly and too curious. "Have some toast," I urged. "I made it." Margie looked at me like I had lost my mind—of course I'd made the toast, she'd watched me—but she took a bite anyway.

I watched the butter have its way with her taste buds. Her brow smoothed. The crease between her eyes that showed up every six months when the Botox wore off began to ease. She took a larger bite, chewed thoughtfully. I noticed that she bit the toast upside down so the butter side was touching her tongue.

"Oh my freaking god," Margie said. "This is good. What do you call it?"

"Butter," I told her. "From a cow that lives up the road. She eats hay from the field on the bluff, right up there." I pointed up the drive, deliberately waving my arm between her bosom and Tim's eyes.

Tim was staring at her. I had never seen him focus directly on a person, but he was gazing at Margie like she was a new species of orchid.

Margie leaned back in the chair, lengthening her neck, and pointed her chin toward me. "I think we have a home for the *Babe Ruth* book."

Tim had a piece of toast cradled in his big hand. Butter was dripping through his fingers to his lap. He was looking at Margie, his pupils dilating till they were ready to give birth. Margie may have known the effect she had, the way she crossed her legs and leaned in to rest her chest on the table amid the crumbs.

"Who?" I said.

Tim echoed me. "Who?"

"Don't you have homework?" I snapped at him.

He stood up slowly, unfolding his big body, prolonging the moment when his zipper was level with Margie's ear.

After he left, Margie smiled at me. "Who would have thought you had such a head for business."

"Margie, don't make me wait any longer."

Margie said she had one publisher willing to do it, Sportsman's Press. It generally published sports books, in particular on baseball, she told me. The editors wanted to get the book out fast to coincide with the baseball season, because a good portion of their sales took place at concession stands in the ballparks. Margie explained that Sportsman's Press didn't give advances, but that the royalties were fair. "You won't have any input as to how they publish it."

"Will it be a hardcover book?" I asked.

"I can make sure of that," Margie said kindly, like a mortician granting a closed casket.

Her hips swinging on her way back to the front door, she turned. "Your work is done. The rest is up to fate."

I was glad to see her go. The men watched her every move. I could feel their readiness. Rudy would say they were "on deck."

After the door shut, I asked the guys what the "T" meant.

"Talking," Wayne said. "They talk a lot."

"And what do you do?"

He looked puzzled as to why I would need to ask. "Listen."

Sid said, "I hear some amazing stuff. Secrets. Never been said to anyone before."

Janson nodded. "It started when one lady first told me what she wanted," he said. "Then she started telling me everything she'd ever wanted."

"I wonder why?" I said.

"She says I get her."

DEAD CAR

My car died on the way back from returning the children to Oneonta. John had offered to pick them up, saying my "junker" wouldn't make it, but I wanted every possible minute with them. I made it to Oneonta, but the car started making grinding noises as I backed out of his driveway to return home. Before I hit the Welcome to Onkwedo sign, the car seized up with such a definitive sound that I knew it was the end. I did what you are not supposed to do: unscrewed the plates, stuffed them in my purse, patted the car on the hood, and left it on the side of the road. Walking away with my purse clanking, I was a little sad, but I wasn't surprised my father's long-ago gift car had made its last trip.

It was late afternoon and chilly, the first thaw. The harbinger of spring in Onkwedo is mud. The gutters beside the road gushed with salty snowmelt. Worms floated in puddles, filling the air with their drowned smell as I walked along the deserted road. I walked hard and fast like I was in the city still. I wasn't sure how far I was from home and whether I could get there before dark.

Then I recognized Waindell's experimental potato farm, and beyond that the woods I'd explored with Matilda. The fertilizers Waindell's agriculture department had tried out the year before caused all the frogs in nearby ditches to turn light blue. This year the edges of the

farm were posted with signs warning about shoe washing and no pic-
nicking. I skirted a potato field and headed into the woods.

The woods were brown and gray; green had yet to appear anywhere. Branches were bare. Layers of mud and ice coated the ground.
If you took the mud tones out of the palette, the entire landscape would
disappear. I realized I knew the way home, knew the paths through the
woods from my walks with Matilda. I even knew the iced-over stream it
followed, the bends and the flat rocky places. I could hear the ice creak-
ing to accommodate the movement of the water underneath. A flicker
poked its head out of a hole in a trunk and stared at me. I stopped
and stared back. I could feel my blood moving like the water under
the ice.

There were no people, and for once I didn't mind. It seemed right
to be alone in the woods. I wasn't frightened. It wasn't that I belonged
to the woods, but unlike the manicured town, the woods were wild, un-
ruly, unregulated. I thought about this. My home was near woods, near
wildness. That suited me, matched the inside of me. Anything could
happen here.

I came out on the other side of the woods into my neighborhood.
On the sidewalks people were glumly walking their dogs. It was the
exact time of year when people's behavior was at its worst. Everyone's
resolutions for the New Year had given way. No one was jogging at all.
I could hear gym membership cards gathering dust, chocolate cakes
being defrosted, spouses being yelled at. It made me happy for a moment that no one expected anything of me, thinness, or even niceness.

At home, without taking my coat off, I made a cup of tea and steeled
myself to call Greg and invite him to escort me to my mother's wedding. I planned to leave a message for him with my phone number
and then not answer the phone when he called back. I knew it was all
wrong: a bad date idea, an impossibly bad *third* date idea. He'd be

meeting the kids and my mother and seeing me in a stupid dress all at the same time.

Still, I didn't stop myself. The tea loaned me a temporary kind of courage. I called. I peeked inside my purse at my license plates for inspiration—what a good long ride that car had been.

Greg answered his phone.

I started right in. "Hi, I know this is a bad idea, but my mother is getting married again. This time it's to my father's doctor. I was wondering if there was any way you would be my escort."

"Are you paying me?" I could tell he was amused.

"I could," I said.

"You're right, it is a bad idea." There was a pause. "I'll go if you'll go sailing with me first."

"It's cold," I said.

"Yes." He waited.

I sipped my tea, thinking. "Do you have a suit jacket?"

"You're dressing me now?" He pretended outrage. "Yes, I have a suit jacket. I even have the pants that go with it. But if I am putting it on, you have to sail on my boat *before* the wedding."

"I hate to be cold," I said.

"I can take care of comfort, trust me on that one."

"Can you dance?" I asked.

"Don't push your luck," Greg said.

I gave him the date for the wedding and hung up. I liked the way his voice sounded. I liked that he teased me. I poured my lukewarm tea down the sink, smiling.

ON THE LAKE

Wednesday was the day I had to meet Greg for a ride on his sailboat. There was nothing bad about this. I even knew what to wear. But instead of putting on my jeans and my white-soled shoes, my windbreaker and my shades, when it was time to go, I was kneeling by the front door looking at the photographs of my dead people, my cherished and departed men with their two paths to the end: one fast, one slow. I knew this was not productive. I knew this was the way to stay alone forever, but I had to see their faces before I left the house. I didn't kiss the pictures. There is nothing about a thing that is even close to being a person. The shiny flatness and curled edges of the photos reminded me that the past was gone; I had only now to live in and be happy—or not.

I put the photos away and dressed. My jeans were snug but not stupidly so. I didn't have a muffin top or panty lines—I checked. My butt was what it always had been, my third-best feature (I could never decide on the top two). I had packed us a picnic: hard-boiled eggs, a baguette, marinated bean salad, early strawberries, two brownies. I didn't want him to think I was a show-off cook, but the brownies were good, and I felt like eating one out in the middle of the lake with the wind on my face.

When I finally left, I tried to stuff down my ambivalence by talking to myself: *You like boats. You might like Greg Holder. You like being with people. You like leaving your house.* Those last two might not be true, but I was repeating them to myself as I took the city bus to the marina.

Greg's boat was nice and not too big. He got it out of the slip without much fuss. I reluctantly admired people who were good sailors. All it meant was that they grew up rich, but still, it was a good thing.

The far end of the lake disappeared into mist. There was not much wind, but he made the most of it, gracefully coaxing the boat up the lake. He was wearing a wool overshirt, and I found myself wondering if it would be scratchy to the touch. I also wondered if he was warm. Not warm enough, as I customarily worried about my children, but if his body would feel warm were I to lean against it, that is, if his shirt was not too scratchy. I looked away, at the shore slipping past with its summer cottages and the occasional glimpse of railroad tracks.

"This is my place," Greg said when we were near the middle. He let the sail out and turned toward me. He looked at me carefully from under his eyebrows. I knew he was measuring me to see if I got it.

"Because we're equidistant from both banks?" I can speak Man if I have to.

"You answer only to yourself here, it's freedom."

Freedom, yes—we shared that value. I nodded. He'd told me something important about himself and I'd recognized it; we both knew it. I unwrapped the picnic and we ate in the middle of the lake, the wind on our cheeks and the sail fluttering. Out here with water all around us, the brownies tasted like treasure.

On the way back, he offered me the tiller. I knew that they taught this etiquette in summer camp for rich boys, but it was polite and I accepted it. He walked to the bow and stood with his feet apart and his hands on the rail. If he was allowing me to admire him, I did. The shore view was much less interesting than his back, his legs, the way his ankles were bare and his pants cuffed. For a moment I wished we would capsize so we could save each other, cling to the keel, share an adventure. I felt too impatient for the incremental way that relationships are built, a dinner at a time, a movie, the stray party or outing.

He walked back toward me, looking down at the water. I wondered if there were rocks under the surface here—unlikely in the deep narrow lake. He sat beside me, without offering to take the tiller back. His shoulder rested against mine and I could feel his warmth. He put his arm across my shoulders. His shirt was soft.

"Are you warm enough?" he asked.

"Mm." I didn't want to wreck the moment with talk. I leaned my head back against his arm and closed my eyes. Behind my eyelids, without intending to, I saw sex. I could see him over me, the thickness of his green shirt, the unused button mid-sleeve for rolling back the cuffs. I could feel his weight, held partially on his strong arms. I could almost smell the scent of his body—not soapy, just live and good.

But then I remembered this part: how men are bigger than we are, how they are inside our bodies and not the other way around, how they are stronger than us. How we suspend knowing all that—with trust, with willingness, with what we sometimes call love. I opened my eyes and looked at Greg.

He was watching me. "You don't need to worry, I am a good guy." He was teasing me a little. His tongue peeped out between his teeth. It was a combination of tenderness and amusement, like a kiss and a laugh together and also a holding back, like he wouldn't do anything to embarrass me or to ruin the moment. I had never seen anyone make that expression.

The rest of the sail was smooth. I helped tie up the boat, using the two good knots my cousin had taught me. We made a plan for the morning of the wedding.

I walked toward the bus stop, and when I knew I was out of his sight, I skipped the rest of the way.

WEDDING

Just after the children had finished dressing in their wedding clothes, the doorbell rang. Darcy rushed to answer it. Greg stood on the threshold. She looked him up and down from shoes to eyebrows and back. I invited him in, and he stepped around her and into the living room.

Darcy grabbed Sam's hand and dragged him to the opposite end of the couch from where Greg sat. "Sit here." She pushed him. Sam sat. Darcy wedged herself between them, her feet swinging. "I like orange." She stared sidelong at Greg. "Do you like orange ice pops?"

"Yes." He nodded politely.

"We need some pops over here," she said to me. She took a pinch of the hair on Greg's arm. He looked down to his arm, where her small fingers gripped him. He remained still. "Were you born like that?" she asked.

"No, I was more like you," Greg replied.

Darcy held her smooth, pale arm next to his, comparing. She gave his arm a little pat.

I handed out the pops. Darcy said proudly, "Sam made these ice pops from a recipe."

"They're very orange," Greg said.

"Food coloring," Sam said, blushing. "Red and yellow, six drops of each." Since he had put on my father's tuxedo jacket, Sam had taken on the stiff decorum of a young butler. "Darcy, you'll get orange ice on your dress," he said.

"My dress is dark, silly." Darcy started to lick her pop.

"But you'll get sticky." Sam leaned over her, Jeeves-like, no creases in his attire.

"We could all sit at the table," Greg said.

I left them at the table and went to put on my dress. Darcy and I had found it online. It was a gray silk sheath with a matching jacket. Darcy said it looked French but not Paris. I don't know where she gets her ideas. The caption described it as "classical chic," which became Darcy's adjectival phrase du jour.

I had brought the dress to Margie's dressmaker and had it taken in, fitted just right. It was what I thought Vera would wear, not Vera Wang, Vera Nabokov. Darcy had wanted to fix me a "fancy hair-do" but I'd resisted, opting for a simple chignon, the only "do" I knew. And my spectator pumps were beyond pretty, almost kissable in their perfection. I took them out of the box and slipped my feet into them.

Rudy called as we were walking out the door. "What time are you picking me up?" I had forgotten him.

Greg, of course, knew Rudy the coach. He was building display shelves for all the crew team trophies. "Good guy," Greg said. We drove to Rudy's apartment on the Waindell campus, and Rudy climbed in the back between the children. Darcy grudgingly moved three purses to accommodate him.

As soon as Rudy had buckled his seat belt, Darcy asked him, "Who are you?" Rudy proceeded to tell her about his coaching job. I could see that Greg found it interesting, the part about breaking the ice for the sculls for morning training in early February. But Darcy interrupted him. "Don't you find that sports is *disgusting*?" Another word of the day.

Sam was staring out the window. I asked him if he was OK. "I'm worried that the salad greens will wilt in the trunk." Sam had planned the menu with the caterer and had arranged to do a special spring salad course of his own.

"Are those your real shoes?" Darcy asked Rudy, but he ignored her.

Greg turned the radio on to the oldies station.

Darcy pointed to Greg. "He could be the groom." She paused for effect and then leaned right under Rudy's face. "And you could be the bride." She sniggered.

"Are they all like this?" Rudy asked me.

"All five-year-olds?" I said.

"Darcy has a good sense of the absurd," Sam said, defending his little sister.

Rudy leaned into the front seat. "Is *he* normal?"

I glanced at Greg, who was smiling.

"Children are people," I told Rudy. "And all people are different."

"Not *that* different," Rudy said.

"Great kids," Greg said. He rested his hand on my leg. The imprint of his hand went right through the silk sheath like it was designed to transmit heat. The warmth spread to my inner thigh. I could feel my pulse slow down. My breath deepened. Greg gave me the slightest caress with his thumb before taking his hand back.

I closed my eyes. Maybe this egregious event would go all right.

In the back the children were singing along to the radio. I was pleased to hear that they knew all the words to "Yellow Submarine."

My mother's wedding to Dr. Gold was being held at the Wilkes-Barre Country Club. It was his club and close to her home. We pulled up in front under the silver and watermelon pink bunting festooning the portico. My mother was not going for originality. We unloaded the salad greens, and Sam took them to the catering kitchen.

My mother greeted me in the golf lounge. Taking my face in her hands, careful not to smudge my makeup, she said, "You look better, darling. I knew your marriage wouldn't last." Then she pointed out that Greg was handsome. "Looks are important," she said, "remember your father." That remark trailed over her shoulder as she rushed off to meet other arrivals.

As if I could forget.

Greg did look spectacular in a suit. He'd gotten his hair cut, shiny and precise. Darcy sidled up to him and did a pinch test of his jacket. I could tell she approved.

Sam had made sourdough rosemary croutons for the salad and had selected the greens: baby arugula, early lettuce, as well as other leaves that I think were weeds from the lawn. Some discriminating diners pushed the dandelions and burdock to the edge of their plates, but most chewed them diligently with their balsamic glaze.

Dr. Gold's starter wife was there with her current husband, Dr. Something Else, a surgeon. She told me that she and Dr. Gold had raised four children. She pointed out four young Turks in matching blazers. "Lacrosse," she said, which might have been some kind of code. I now had siblings, all brothers.

She leaned up against my new dress and whispered moistly in my ear that her new doctor-surgeon-husband had found her G-spot. He thrust out his hand to introduce himself. I beamed brightly into his face, unable to compel myself to touch his G-spot finder.

Dr. Gold, my mother's groom, was not handsome, but he seemed stable, and he enjoyed food. He even finished the salad. He made a special point of speaking to me before the dancing began, seeking me out near the hors d'oeuvres bar, where I was standing with Greg. He asked me to stop calling him "Dr. Gold." I gave him the happy drunken smile I had perfected for such occasions. He leaned in over the hors d'oeuvres to be heard above the music. "Your father was a great man," he said to me.

I looked up at the ceiling of the tent, trying to keep my mascara on my lashes and not running down my face. "Yes," I said, "I know."

In trying to make his point, Dr. Gold had planted his elbow firmly in a wedge of the Brie en croûte. The first-dance music came on, the flagrantly schmaltzy "Bésame Mucho." Sid, the disc jockey, had all the right cuts for this crowd.

I peeked over Greg's shoulder to watch Dr. Gold cross the dance floor to the bridal table and invite my mother to join him in the first dance of matrimonial life. On his navy pinstripe morning coat, the Brie made a lone beige elbow patch.

I nestled closer to Greg. "I'm not going to fix that."

"It looks fine on him," Greg said.

My mother and the doctor were dancing cheek to waistcoat. Her dress fit, but barely. Although she was the thinnest person in the room, the dress was tight enough to give her a twin ripple of back fat.

When "Chantilly Lace" came on, my cousin's widow danced with Rudy, the extra man, matching his Lindy step for step, not a wasted inch between them. She looked happy. Rudy looked positively sexy, something I'd never thought possible.

Darcy appeared near the DJ platform wearing a different frock from her flower girl attire. It was pink and satiny, more appropriate for a little girl going to her grandmother's wedding, but I had never seen the dress before. When I looked closer, I saw that it was one of the watermelon pink swags from the Wilkes Barre Country Club decorations, an off-center neck hole cut with nail scissors, I suspected, by Darcy in the powder room—and belted with a silver ribbon from the golf lounge. Darcy had insisted on doing her own coiffure. The tips of her ears glowed pink below her ink-colored hair, upswept in a knotty lump on top of her head and bristling with hairpins. She looked like a wild rose with a very beautiful black center.

She was doing what she considered to be ballet in front of Sid and the electronics. The music stopped abruptly after Blondie sang "Eat to the Beat." I saw Darcy talking to Sid, her toe pointed in an exaggerated ballerina fashion. I overheard her saying that Sid's shoes were "classical chic."

Sam was talking to a friend of the doctor's, the restaurant critic for the *Wilkes-Barre Bugle*.

Sid knew enough to play Motown to get the dance floor filled. The beginning of "You've Really Got a Hold on Me," came on the speakers, and I turned to Greg. "You can dance to this, right? Anyone can dance to this."

"You don't give up," Greg said. But he put one hand on the small of my back and we turned out onto the parquet floor. My beautiful smooth-soled shoes slid on the wood with the slightest of friction.

Greg's arms went all the way around me. I felt I was inside something almost sacred, like a hollow tree, warm and still.

I knew my children might be watching, so I didn't lay my head on his shoulder, as I wanted to. I could feel the heat between us, and the carefulness too. The music got louder as Sid spun the Neville Brothers' "Brother John Is Gone," which was the signal for the bride and groom to lead a conga dance, a line of half-lit people from the medical profession.

I snagged Darcy's hand as she aimed for the back of the line and led her out to the checkroom for our coats. Rudy found me there, a drink in one hand and his other on the arm of my cousin's widow. "Estelle will give me a lift," he said.

We met Greg in the parking lot. We waited while the valet got his car, and we piled in. My head was still pounding from the music, and I leaned back on the seat. I thought of what it would have been like to be there alone, answering questions about my work and making chitchat with doctors. I shuddered.

As we pulled onto the main road, Greg told Sam that the food was excellent. I could see Sam's cheek brightening with pleasure. He had the tux jacket folded carefully on his lap.

Darcy curled up in the back in her car seat, and I covered her with a blanket. I unfastened my hair and let it loose. My mother's new happily-ever-after with Dr. Gold had begun. I was glad to have the wedding behind me.

I looked out the car window at the dark land slipping past. It was still my father's birthday. I thought of his favorite dessert, coffee Bavarian. It was a simple dessert, as much air as taste. It had the potent nothingness of the foam on an espresso that you drink standing up in a train station in Italy.

"Thank you for coming with me," I said to Greg.

"You look beautiful with your hair down," he said. I couldn't remember anyone calling me beautiful, but at that moment it felt true.

"Rudy said you opened a business recently." He glanced at me.

It was a question, but my brain unhelpfully supplied this: *Oh shit oh shit oh shit.*

From the backseat Sam piped up, "You know the big old dairy on top of the bluff? My mom answers their mail." He sounded proud of me.

"People write letters to the milk company?" Greg asked.

"Lots of letters," Sam informed him.

"Is that enough to live on?" Greg looked at me.

"I do OK," I said, fiddling with the car heater, turning it down, then up.

"What about your business by the lake in the old Bryce hunting lodge? Rudy said he hadn't seen it but he'd heard it was innovative."

I couldn't breathe. I coughed, trying to get air down to where I could use it. Greg went on: "I was in the lodge with my dad once when I was a kid, my first and only time deer hunting. Rudy said he was coming next week, maybe I could come with him?"

"Our clients are all women," I squeaked out. "There wouldn't be anything to interest you. It's a day spa, essentially." My hands were making big meaningless gestures of their own accord.

"Haircuts?"

"Body treatments." This was almost true. My fingers found the radio dial, and I turned it on at full volume. The Rangers game blasted into the car. "Sam," I exclaimed shamelessly, "ice hockey!"

When we arrived at my house, my old car was parked in the driveway. The antenna was tagged with a neon orange ribbon, and there was a matching sign stuck on the back windshield. Sam got out of the car to read it. Darcy was fast asleep. "I could carry her in," Greg offered.

"All right," I said. Greg carefully lifted Darcy up against his chest. In sleep, her face still held the baby she had been: perfect brow, rounded cheeks, petal lips.

"Officer Vince Vincenzo of the Onkwedo police force left his phone number. I think he wants you to call him." Sam was reading the sign. "Sergeant Vincenzo does the SOD program at my old school." Sam had been devoted to the Stay Off Drugs program, which had filled him with zeal and misapprehensions. Kerosene, he once informed me, is highly addictive and leads to harder drugs.

In Greg's arms, Darcy stirred, making a small sucking motion with her mouth.

"Follow me." I led him into the house and to Darcy's room, where he passed her to me and I laid her sleeping body on the bed. I slipped off her black patent leather Mary Janes and covered her with a comforter.

Sam went into his bedroom, calling, "I'll brush my teeth."

Greg and I stood in the hallway by the front door. "You have good kids," he said.

"Thank you." My beautiful shoes were numbing my toes.

"Are you free for dinner some evening this week?"

I was alone all evenings. "Yes."

"Does Tuesday work?"

I nodded.

"I'd like to kiss you, but not with the children in the house." Greg leaned in and brushed his lips across mine. "See you soon."

"Yes," I managed to say before sucking in my lower lip to capture the sensation.

After Greg drove away, I slipped off my shoes and stockings and padded outside barefoot to look at my car. Except for the sign, it looked the same as when it had died, just a little dustier. I opened the door and climbed in. The key was where I had left it in the ashtray. I put it in the ignition, slid the gearshift into neutral, turned the key. It started, but when I tried to put it in gear, there was a loud grinding sound like metal meshing, and it shook all over. I turned it off. It was the end of a long, mostly good ride.

FIRST COPY

Tuesday began as one of those heartbreaking early spring mornings. The sun was out and I was on my knees in the gravel, screwing the license plates back onto my car. Above me the hawthorn tree budded chartreuse clusters. Nearby the birds feasted on worms. A pregnant deer tiptoed past, proud to have thwarted Waindell University's seven million-dollar forced-sterilization program.

Bill's postal truck drove up. Margie's long legs climbed down, followed by Bill's shorter ones. "I thought your car died," Margie said.

"It did, but the police brought it back." I stood up and dusted off my hands. I tried picking at the edge of the neon-colored sticker, but it wouldn't come off.

Margie was looking at it. "Officer Vincenzo? You better call. He's in line for chief of police." She handed me a book.

There on the cover was a wooden baseball bat and a butterfly, looking like it had just landed, wings open. I sucked in my breath.

"It's the first copy," Margie told me. "They did a super-rush job. Never seen anyone in the book biz move that fast." She draped her arm on my shoulder, and together we stared down at the gorgeous thing. On the jacket was a brief paragraph about the finding of the book in Nabokov's house in Onkwedo, and the possibility that he had written it. Lucas Shade was the name of the author, though, and appeared in every place it should.

It was thinner than I had envisioned. "Is it all there? Did the editors change anything?"

"It's an artifact." Margie sounded scandalized. "They wouldn't dare." She seemed to have forgotten that I had written some of the book. "There are reviews too."

Bill held out a couple of newspapers. On top was the *Onkwedo Clarion*, folded open to the sports section. Between golf news and a squib about Yankee spring training was the banner "Hometown Home Run: Novel Found Here in Nabokov's House." Margie gave me a squeeze. "Where the hell did they get that picture of you? It looks like a mug shot."

I looked at the paper. Above the cover of the book, the newspaper had printed a photo of Nabokov in his study at Waindell, looking professorial. His forehead shone, a round and brilliant dome. Beside it was a snapshot of me with my address listed underneath. The photo credit read, "on file." Even with the poor quality of the print you could see in my eyes a look of horror. It *was* a mug shot, "on file" from my booking on the kidnapping charge. The only change had been to crop out the black line measuring my height, 5'4".

"We're on Bill's morning route and we have to go," Margie said. They climbed into the truck and waved goodbye.

Hugging the book, I leaned against my bumper and read the review. The piece was a long discursive ramble on Babe Ruth. The *Onkwedo Clarion* viewpoint on whether or not the manuscript was genuine seemed to be that since it was found here in Onkwedo, where Nabokov once lived, of course it was. For that I was grateful. There was no mention of the quality of the writing.

As I stood reading, several cars drove by, slowing down as they passed the house. One man stopped and held a camera out the car window. I went inside.

Away from the prying people, I read the other review. The *New York Times* called it "a minor work about a major league player," stating that the ballpark scene was as flat as the field itself.

Assholes.

Here Upstate there was no shame in its being a lesser book by a great writer, Onkwedo didn't mind that. Onkwedo was not one of those "you can't go home again" kinds of places. In Onkwedo, you *can* go home again; it's leaving that's the problem.

I read the first page of the book in the beautiful type on the real paper, and I couldn't stop smiling. I had done it. The book was out there for people to read. I didn't care if they bought it or only borrowed it from the library. Nabokov didn't need to make any money from it, he was dead. If he had wanted to publish it, he wouldn't have crammed it behind the bureau drawers and abandoned it there while he wrote *Lolita*. And I didn't need the money either; I was running a lucrative cathouse.

Funny how Nabokov went from sports to sex, just like me.

I read the *Clarion* review again. I wondered whose idea it had been to print my address. I hoped people wouldn't start digging around in my house trying to find another manuscript.

At the bottom of the page was another photo, a smiling couple announcing their engagement. Lydia Vincenzo, known as "LeeLee" to her friends, was marrying one Derek Townsend next Christmas. They looked handsome and without a speck of doubt, like life was simple if you were they. And maybe it was. The menu for their wedding was printed below the picture, the food in red, white, and green. I cut it out for Sam.

I looked again at the girl; she seemed familiar, but I couldn't place her. LeeLee Vincenzo. She must be related to the cop I'd been dodging, the one who wanted to pin me down for abandoning my car. He'd called a couple of times.

Onkwedo police. Nothing to do, so they had to bust people like me for kidnapping or car theft. Ridiculous. I called Officer Vincenzo. His recorded voice instructed the caller to leave a message "for the assistant chief of police, SOD Program, and/or Deer Population Reduction Program" (DPRP). I left my name and number, dreading the umpteen-hundred-dollars recompense I would have to pay for towing and the big stupid lecture I would get about personal and civic responsibility.

BOOKSTORE

Greg called me on my cell phone. "Hey, Famous, I saw your picture in today's paper. Are we still on for dinner tonight, or are you going to ditch me for someone better known?"

I pretended that I hadn't forgotten. There wasn't time to go home and change, so I took the bus downtown in my madam clothes. I was beginning to really like my madam clothes. I wore very starchy shirts over my Good Times jeans, and shoes that hurt my feet a little, but not too much.

I was to meet him at the bar and grill near the bookstore. I didn't usually go to that bookstore because it wasn't anonymous. The clerks knew the customers and the customers knew the clerks. There were even shelves stocked with the staff's favorite books. (The clerk Selina liked *The Red Tent* and all the vampire books.)

The bus let me off across the street from the bookstore. Even from there I could see in the window a display of *Babe Ruth*. The deep blue cast of the cover matched the late evening light of May. Along the street the ornamental pear trees were in blossom and a recent rain had brought down a circle of white petals under each tree, like a slip fallen from under a woman's dress. The perfume of the blossoms overrode the oil smell of the wet pavement.

Onkwedo was proud of its own, and it considered Nabokov its own. Never mind that Nabokov had left as fast as he could, never to return. The bookstore had devoted the entire front window to *Babe Ruth*. The *Clarion* article was taped to the inside of the glass. I breathed in the moment of all those book covers: baseball bats and perching butterflies, each poised to take flight into someone's mind. It was a perfect moment.

As I was staring at the window display, another person arrived. I could feel him before I saw him, the density of his body displacing air. I could sense that he was larger than I was but he didn't awaken my usual flight response. "Are you a baseball fan?" he asked. It was Greg. "We could take in a game sometime."

I didn't turn. "Would you please buy the book?" I asked him.

After a moment of looking at the display with me, Greg went into the shop. In his absence there was an unseasonable smell of green walnuts. I could see him through the window taking a book off the top of the stack beside the cash register. I watched him pull his wallet from his back pocket and take out some bills. It thrilled me to watch the transaction. Nabokov's book was being purchased, here in Onkwedo where he had lived.

Greg came out, tucking a paper bag under his arm. He pointed to my picture in the *Clarion*. "Lovely photo," he said.

While we were waiting for a table at the restaurant, I told Greg about holding the first copy of the book. He listened like he was completely interested. He was so *there*. I felt absurdly happy and comfortable in his presence. I counted in my mind how many times I had seen him. Only four. Seven if I included the chance encounters.

After we'd ordered, I excused myself and went to the ladies' room, where I called Margie. "It's Barb. How do you know if you're ready to sleep with someone?"

"Where are you?"

"I'm in the ladies' room at the Grill House."

"Classy." I could hear Margie opening a pack of cigarettes. "Are we talking about Greg Holder?"

"Yes." I could hear the crack of a match striking. "Don't tell me it's like riding a bicycle, because I never learned how to ride a bicycle." Someone was knocking on the door.

Margie exhaled. "How does your body feel? Ready?"

I thought for a moment. "Yes."

"Oh, honey, you will be fine. Trust your body; it knows more than you do."

"Thanks, Margie." I hung up. The woman waiting outside gave me a filthy look.

I don't know what I ordered or ate, only that we talked and laughed, and most of the food was still on my plate at the end of the meal.

We left the restaurant, and Greg asked if I would invite him to my house.

I nodded.

Later still, when we were in bed together, Greg said, "You are beautiful without your clothes on."

I started to make a joke about my awful clothes, but he hushed me. "Don't joke, not now." He stroked my face with his hand, so lightly, the way you might pet a bird. "You feel a little bit safe, right?" He looked at me in the near darkness. "This is going to be OK."

I wondered how he knew that. It had been such a long time for me. But I put my hands on his powerful back and his skin felt porous, like the heat inside him and the heat inside me were part of the same fire.

His touch was wonderful, the feel of his strong hands on me, of his fascinating mouth, but then I came to a place where I wanted to stop. My body wanted to keep going, but I felt that going forward would join me to him. He still felt . . . not like a stranger exactly, but still *other*. So I began to make some noises that could be interpreted as an orgasm.

As I was finishing up my totally authentic-sounding moaning, he put his lips next to my ear. "Barb," he whispered, "I don't think we're stopping here."

And we didn't. It was gorgeous. And afterward I felt connected to him in a way I had no intention of feeling.

I turned my head away and leaked tears onto the pillow. Tears for my defenses being down, for the vulnerability of feeling connected with someone, for shame, for loneliness, for wasted time, tears of pity for my own body and everyone else's too. Greg cradled me against his chest and stroked my hair. "It's just us," he said, "you and me." I didn't exactly cry, I just dripped tears till the pool inside me emptied.

Greg offered me his shirt. I blew my nose on it, thinking it was a hankie.

And then I slept.

Around midnight I awoke to Greg gently disentangling himself from me. "I have to let Rex out," he said, and kissed me on the forehead.

THE DAY AFTER

I woke up alone in my bed in Nabokov's house. I buried my nose in the pillow where Greg's head had been.

Nice.

In the kitchen there was a scrap of paper weighted down with a glass. It had two *X*s on it and a *G*.

I made myself the perfect breakfast: a soft-boiled egg on buttered toast. While the egg boiled, I quartered some wrinkly-looking root vegetables, drizzled them with olive oil, sprinkled them with salt, and put them in the oven. Since I had the oven on anyway, I put in a bone to roast in case I got to see Matilda or Rex.

Margie came by with jelly doughnuts. Right, Wednesday was her eating day. I had a second perfect breakfast with her on the picnic table outside. The sun was out and nearly hot, flowers were opening by the hour, two rabbits chased each other across the grass.

Margie reached over and wiped a smudge of jelly from my chin. "How'd it go with Greg Holder?"

"Great, I think." I ate the last of the jelly out from the spongy dough.

"Don't screw it up." Margie handed me a napkin. "Speaking of progress, Waindell University wants you to participate in a panel discussion at the Nabokov conference."

"What?" I stared at beautiful Margie, purple curds of jelly on my tongue.

"The panel is called 'Desire and Reciprocity: *Lolita,* Nabokov, and Current Fiction.' "

"Why in heck do they want me?" It occurred to me that the academics wanted to make fun of me, the silly counterpoint to their serious investigation. Or maybe in this ridiculous culture I was now considered an expert on Nabokov. I—because I was a housewife who straightened her daughter's drawers—deserved placement on a panel of academics whose life work had been to study Nabokov. Only in Onkwedo would this happen. In Paris or Moscow, I would be checking briefcases at the door.

Margie tossed the uneaten half of a doughnut back in the box. "They pay a small honorarium and a night at the Onkwedo Hilton." How did she know I loved hotels?

I didn't want to expose myself to vicious academics, but Margie said I had to go to the symposium. She said, "You are invited. You show up. You sell books. That's the whole story." Licking caramel glaze off her fingers, she told me what to wear.

After Margie left, I pretended to myself that I wasn't waiting for Greg to call. I vacuumed so I wouldn't hear the phone if it rang. I put the vacuum away and washed all the mirrors in the house so I *would* hear the phone. It didn't ring. When I couldn't stand it anymore, I went out to the woods for a ramble.

As I walked among the newly leafing trees, my body felt all soft inside, squishy like the doughnut. I knew perfectly well from my old job that women fall in love with men with whom they physically merge. It's another sick trick that biology plays on us. For men it's like they tried a new restaurant they may or may not go back to, and for women it's like they'd opened their own restaurant. Maybe that wasn't a good comparison.

I wanted to guard against the love business, but I could replay the whole evening, every caress, and the hot tenderness felt so fresh. Why did it have to be like that? I resented the surrender, the joining. It changed everything. Not to other people—their world was still go to work, buy a sub and a soda for lunch, check the internet to see if they had a life—but my world was different.

Greg's world was probably the same as it always had been. I could see him sliding long boards into the table saw, pencil tucked behind his ear, Steve Miller Band playing on the sawdust-covered radio, drowned by the whine of the saw, Rex licking his paw in the doorway.

I could see Greg going about his life unchanged, his body just as solid as ever, no boundaries crossed, no deep tender jellyness awakened inside him. It made me almost hate him.

The world was different. *My* world was different. I had just had sex with someone maybe for the first time since Darcy was conceived. My mother was on her honeymoon. My father was still in heaven. Furthermore, my stupid birthday was the next day, my stupid fortieth birthday.

All of which was nothing beside my children being gone.

BIRTHDAY

It was late afternoon, nearly dusk. The sky reflected dully pewter in the lake. In the cathouse, three women sat on the couches, one talking, one knitting, one emptying her purse, throwing crumpled cigarette packs in the fire, tissues, receipts. Purse lint snapped and sparked in the flames. Between the women, Tim and Evan were studying, laptops open. Sid was prowling between his laptop and the iPod. He played a schmaltzy alternation between Rod Stewart and Bruce Springsteen, songs filled with longing and domination.

It was my birthday and Greg still hadn't called me. It was better not to celebrate your birthday with a new-date kind of person, I rationalized, even if you had already been "intimate." (My language for this stuff sounded fusty to me. What did middle-age people say? Not "hooking up" surely.) And more germane was the fact that he might not want to see me. Maybe this was what dating when you're older was like: You'd already turned into who you were going to grow up to be, so there was no uncertainty, no promise, and the other person simply said to himself, Well, I don't want one of *those*. Or maybe he was busy, or had been struck by lightning. Or maybe he wasn't a good guy after all.

I wanted to see him. I very much wanted to sniff him. It was not a lofty wish. I called Margie and told her what had happened with Greg. I didn't tell her it was my birthday. "So call him," she said. "What's your plan here, life as a solo act?"

I hung up on her.

I was turning forty. I hadn't told anyone it was my birthday. It was a risk to tell people; they might buy a cake, and I had never liked bought cake. When I was a child, my mother would buy the square frozen Sara Lee layer cakes for my birthday parties. The lard-on-frozen-lard texture never tempted her to have a piece. She'd send the guests home with goodie bags holding any leftover pieces. There would be no cake for breakfast the next day. I liked the option of a slice of cake for breakfast, although I was fine with a piece of toast and jam. Or two pieces, if there was butter melting under the jam.

I was now forty and my youth was gone. I should have had more sex when it was offered, I thought, it might not get offered again. I told myself that growing up is being able to delay gratification. I could wait for homemade cake. I could wait for sex. Even if neither happened. And I didn't care if anyone sang to me or gave me a present that once unwrapped would force me to pretend I actually wanted it.

I wanted a stand-up writing desk, and there was a certain carpenter who made them very well. I told myself that I was good at being alone. I knew it wasn't true. I *was* getting pretty good at running a cathouse.

The Purse Lady interrupted her sorting to hold out her cup for more tea. The purse was a faux Prada that Darcy would love, bold, black, and asymmetrical. As I poured the tea, the Purse Lady smiled at me reflexively like I was the waitress. And I *was* the waitress. I was also the person who recorded the data, so I happened to know that she liked some nasty stuff in between her bouts of handbag housekeeping.

Spanking was weirdly popular, and I didn't know why, though it might go along with the cleanliness obsessions. But the Purse Lady didn't want to be spanked. When she started visiting us two months ago, the Purse Lady had caused a major flap. Janson had come downstairs looking appalled. "She wants me to . . ." He couldn't finish.

Sid had had her once before. "Degraded," he explained. "She wants to be degraded." I had told them to refuse, but it didn't stop her requests.

Ginna had come earlier in the day to say goodbye. She had brought a bag of expired dinner rolls and an armful of flowers from her garden, daffodils and tulips. She didn't book a room but stood with me awkwardly till I walked her out to her car. There she told me that she wasn't coming back. She said her marriage was going well. There was shyness in her voice, and wonder. "We're . . . It's the way it used to be, close."

There was a feeling of peace, even happiness in the moment. Soon we would all go our separate ways: crew practice, Apex Market for a roasted chicken and a tray of ready-made corn bread, home to walk the dog. For the first time in Onkwedo, I felt part of something, even felt the "sense of community" that people here talked about. I'd brought something good into this bland potluck of a town. You could say I'd brought the love, but maybe that was overstating it.

Although I hadn't gotten Young Mr. Daitch to agree, I decided it was time to start giving the people more of what they wanted. Back in my office in the kitchen I drafted an answer to the letters that I had put aside.

Dear Person,

I too miss the cherry vanilla ice cream, even though I've never tasted it. All the letters imploring [Note: Too strong? "Suggesting" maybe?] *us to reinstate it have paid off. On July 4th, cherry vanilla ice cream will make its comeback!*

Enclosed please find a certificate good for one cone.

Sincerely,

I tried another version:

Dear Fan of Cherry Vanilla Ice Cream:

I agree, cherries are the perfect fruit—so pretty and with that sweet snap when bitten.

We are planning a cherry vanilla ice cream redux on July 4th. Please join us.

Enclosed please find . . . etc.

I came home to the blinking lights of the answering machine. My mother had called to tell me that I was not middle-aged yet because the women in our family lived into their "deep nineties." That was my mother's style of comfort.

Greg had called. "Hey, it's me." He sounded solid and good, his voice filled with warmth. "Call me back." He left his cell number.

And then there were my children singing "Happy Birthday." The audio fidelity of the answering machine was poor. Darcy sounded breathy and Sam tuneless. I turned it up as loud as I could, till they were roaring "Happy Birthday" into the bare kitchen. And then it was over with a loud mechanical click.

The emptiness of the silence was as deep as the lake. Almost as deep as the day my father died and then we had to do ordinary things without him: make dinner and go to bed.

I sat with the emptiness, my hands open on my knees, waiting. I stayed like that for I don't know how long. And then I stood up. My feet, planted on the floor of Vera Nabokov's kitchen, touched the bottom of the lake bed, the bottom of the emptiness, and I had to act. I might not have a plan, but I had to act fast.

I ate the wizened vegetables without tasting a thing, chewing through their earthy husks; they could have been lumps of dirt.

I lay on my bed without sleeping much, eyes open, ready. The next morning I was up and dressed at dawn, waiting by the front door till the world awoke. I went to the bank, withdrew cash, and paid down an entire year of my mortgage. The nosy teller was surprised. She wrote me an affidavit stating that I had met the terms of the loan through the next tax period. I asked for their financial planner, and she turned out to be that too. I opened a college account for each child with more cash.

I had now paid for two weeks' worth of any New York state college.

I walked into the car lot next door and put a down payment on a completely nondescript car. I drove it off the lot.

I took the last two hundred dollars of my money with me in a nylon eco-friendly grocery sack, like a robber. I drove to the hardware store and bought an eight-foot sheet of pegboard and a set of hooks. I installed it on the wall of Darcy's room and hung her forty-seven purses.

For Sam's room I bought a bookcase from the furniture store that they strapped to the roof of my car. At the bookstore I bought every readable and original cookbook that Sam did not yet own, plus one called *Repurposing Your Kitchen Appliances,* probably a mistake.

At home I hauled the bookcase into his room and shelved his new collection.

I photographed these improvements in my children's rooms.

I put on my nice-mommy scarf, a sensible skirt and sweater set in a warm peach, and shoes with small stacked heels. I looked like a supermarket muffin: bland and sweet.

I drove downtown to family court with my documentation: letters from the bank showing that the mortgage was paid for a year and college funds had been started, a photo montage of the children's wholesome rooms featuring their interests, a copy of the *Onkwedo Clarion*'s review of *Babe Ruth,* a copy of the letter from the Waindell University archives thanking me for the loan of "the disputed manuscript of arguably our greatest modern writer." (Why were academics always arguing?)

With my portfolio under my arm, I walked past the guard and up the steps till I found the right offices. On one tall wooden door a plaque read "Judge Q. L. Teagarten." A different judge was presiding from the one who'd taken my kids away. The door was ajar and a receptionist was sitting at a desk behind a massive in-box.

I waited till she was off the phone and explained why I was there.

She reached for the materials without looking up. "I can leave this for the judge to review, but the other party must be notified. You can do that yourself, or the court will do it." She dumped my portfolio on the top of the pile. "Make sure you leave the correct number and address." She looked harried, with a thick band of stress-fat around her middle— a good candidate for regular pampering, I thought.

As I was making that assessment, she glanced up for the first time. "Have your lawyer file his plea for review as well, hon."

No way in hell was I going back to that dolt of a court-appointed lawyer. I'd need somebody with actual teeth in their head. I thanked her and left.

I went back to the car, parked under an oak tree just budding out in leaf. I climbed in and opened the glove box, where I'd put a copy of *Babe Ruth*. I wondered if the book was in ballparks across the country next to the corn dogs. I touched the shiny blue cover. The book thrilled me.

I could do it. I could take on John. I was stronger than when I first got to Onkwedo, less sad. I had accomplished things. And I knew people.

It was time to call Greg. Still holding the book, I dialed his cell. "Hey, there's something I need to do here. It's important. I have to do it before I see you again."

"OK, Barb."

"That's all? You don't need me to tell you more?"

"Tell me more."

"I'm working on getting my kids back."

"You versus John?"

"Wish me luck."

"Hang in there. And Barb, I'm here."

"I know." I smooched into the phone. But first I clicked off.

JOHN AT WORK

I gassed up my car and drove all the way to John's new office. Why retired people needed offices was beyond my understanding. Maybe to hold the smugly visible position of not needing to work but still doing it.

There were several late-model trucks parked alongside John's building. I pulled into the newly created handicapped spot, probably reserved for Irene's father. I knew John took lunch at noon and broke for the day at five o'clock. It was ten minutes to five.

Inside, John had his back to me and was talking on the telephone. He was hand-grooming his dark brown hair. His hair was the only part of himself that he was vain about, getting a sixty-dollar haircut every month in an actual salon, rather than the eight-dollar standard at the Onkwedo barbershops.

His office was immaculate. There was a long table with piles of papers perfectly trued at the corners. Each pile corresponded to a John-invented rubber object for use in the automobile industry. Each pile was weighted down by the actual gizmo.

I knew John had seen me enter. A mirror hung over his desk so no one could sneak up behind him. I waved to him in the mirror, and he stopped smoothing his perfect hair. Into the phone he said to make sure the sample tires were there by Monday, and then he hung up.

"Barb," he said.

I had never seen John surprised, and this was no exception.

I sat down, though I had not been invited. My chair was too close to him, and he inched back. I had trapped him between his desk and the door, intolerable for John.

I perched my nice-mommy purse on my knees and I told him that we needed to talk about the children. He looked at me warily. I could see him girding himself with experts—the lawyer, family court, Irene— assuring himself he didn't have to talk to me.

"The children don't seem happy," I told him.

He waited.

"I am ready to revisit our custody agreement. I think they need to spend more time with me." I wished I smoked cigarettes or chewed gum or even bit my nails. There was nothing to do but breathe.

"What do you know about happiness?" John fitted a chuckle into the question. John used to be right all the time. It was a cornerstone belief of our former relationship: we both knew that John was always right. Only that was no longer true.

"I am doing much better," I said. "My circumstances are different."

John slid back his chair, putting the maximum possible distance between us.

"Anyway, it isn't about me," I said. "Children need time with their mother to feel secure, to feel self-acceptance." I was casting around here, using the mushy words from my old job. "You can see from their school behavior that they aren't doing well."

He stood up and edged around my knees and large purse. I didn't want to leave before I made some progress, but things were not going my way. John picked up his keys and a new windbreaker jacket that I suspected Irene had helped him select. It was purple. John wouldn't know that, because John was a little color-blind.

"You have nothing new to say to me. You live in chaos. You have no plan for the future. How can you know what is good for children?" He unclipped his cell phone from his belt and placed it in the inside pocket of the florid jacket. "Even Matilda comes back from your house with the runs because you feed her god knows what."

What could be wrong with a little toast? I thought animals had an instinct for self-preservation that kept them from poisoning themselves.

I thought of my children and how sad they were: my Sam, my little Darcy. I stood and faced him. "We could live in a way that's fairer to them and to me. To all four of us," I said.

John jingled coins in his pocket. I didn't remember him being so fidgety. He told me that we'd been through "exactly the same territory a hundred times." He leaned in close and took my forearm the way you might grasp a chicken by the neck, hard. He told me to call a lawyer and "spend some more money you don't have."

I had forgotten that about John; how he always went for the gut punch to make sure his opponent knew not to get up off the mat.

I snatched my arm back. "OK," I said. I stood up in my dopey nice-mommy-goes-to-court clothes and walked out of his office.

We couldn't do it without a fight, so we'd fight. I was ready. Some women stayed all their lives with people who told them what to do. It's seductive to have someone tell you what to do, it lulls you into a state of not having to think for yourself.

GIRL

The next morning I bolted tea and oatmeal, the breakfast of sheep herders, and went to work. I could compartmentalize, just like a man, pretend it was an ordinary day, eat breakfast and hit the job.

I liked many parts of my workday but the time alone in the lodge before we opened were particularly sweet. I readied the upstairs rooms and front parlor, then went to my record keeping. I'd started keeping the data only as a cover in case anyone challenged me about the research involved, but the information itself was fascinating.

I'd filled out most of the data for the last week, with the customer code name on each row, and preference by column, and entered any notes from the staff. I noticed that the sock lady had come back twice but had moved from laundry to more conventional activities. Professor Biggs had not come back, I was relieved to note, but her department chair was here weekly for a Clinton (no intercourse). By customer selection, Wayne had a slight edge overall, but Sid and Janson had the most repeat business. And Sid had the highest muffin rating, as in he got the most muffins baked for him by clients. His muffin rating was off the chart. They all had increasing numbers of "T" entries.

A girl came once a week and slipped upstairs with Sid. I had never spoken with her, and I noticed that the other guys seemed to be in on some kind of conspiracy to distract me when she arrived. I only saw her leaving, her white Lexus fishtailing as she tore out of the gravel drive. She always got a Special, two hundred dollars, ninety minutes. She was the only one in this frugal town who treated herself to a Special once a week. That was not what interested me. What interested me was her age, and the secrecy, and that she looked familiar to me.

She came on Tuesday afternoons at four. It was two now, and Sid was warming up, doing slow shoulder rolls while he stood by the fireplace. He did this at the beginning of every workday. I didn't know whether it was for his job here or for crew practice, and I hadn't asked. Janson had built a fire and gone out back to chop more wood. I doubted we would need it for warmth, but the flames were lovely.

Sid stretched his neck, first to one side and then the other. The crew team had started racing season, and I could see the thickness and tone of his neck muscles, like cables connecting to his shoulders. "Who is the girl?" I asked him.

He stretched a powerful arm overhead. The room got a little smaller. "Are you jealous?"

There it was again, that man thing: the best defense is a good offense. It reminded me exactly of John. I decided to play the same game. "Yes. I am in love with you."

He stopped and glanced at me. He couldn't tell if I was joking or not. Neither could I, exactly. "Who is she? She can't be more than twenty-one."

"Nineteen." He was doing his tongue exercises. Some ridiculous yoga business that Janson swore by. "She's a townie."

All these young men had such privileged lives, but it rankled me to hear him name the class division. "How did you meet her?"

"Here. She requested me. She'd heard about my sessions."

It sounded like Sid was lying or covering something, I didn't know what. He was stretching his hamstrings, which meant his face was hidden. "What does her family do in Onkwedo?"

"Law enforcement."

I thought I'd recognized her. "Is she by any chance the police chief's daughter?"

Holding his ankles, Sid arched his back. His muscular body looked both complacent and proud. I felt a strong desire to tip him over. "This could close the place down, Sid." He shifted his weight slightly to his left leg, stretching his right.

"She leaves happy," he pointed out.

"What about her fiancé? What about her parents? You aren't naive enough to think this will end well, are you?" If I were a real pimp, I would have had some powerful trick up my sleeve, violence or a threat. I could only reason with Sid, there in the prime of his life, too handsome for his own good.

"I give her what she wants."

"What *does* she want?"

"The same as all you ladies; total control." He put his palms on the floor, just outside his feet, and in one amazing gesture shifted his weight to his hands, bringing his knees in to his chest and unfurling his legs straight up to the ceiling. I was eye level with his absolutely perfect butt.

The view made me tired. I was tired of being around gorgeous young men. I was tired of people having great sex all around me. I was tired of being in charge. I wanted to smack his ass. I didn't know if it was aggression or lust. "Please come back up here where I can talk to you."

He righted himself and stood just close enough to me that I could smell his sweat. It was a great smell. It was the kind of smell you inhaled and for a moment you believed you could run a marathon, swim across the lake, make a charlotte russe for forty people. "Her or me." I didn't dare look up at his flushed face. "If you want this job, you break it off. Screw her on your own time." I realized this was the first ultimatum I had given a man. My stomach tightened.

Sid cut his glittery eyes at me. "Come upstairs," he said. It was a challenge.

"No. We can't. Even if I wanted to, I'm not going to. You're a student and I'm a—"

"Cougar," Sid finished for me.

I think I wanted to go upstairs with him. I could feel the prickling in my belly and between my legs. "No," I said. "You and I are—"

"We're adventurers, Barb. We're sex warriors." Sid was leaning over me, and I was holding on to the back of the couch behind me (the expensive down-filled plush couch, my biggest purchase at Ikea, the "Ingrid"). I didn't know how he had backed me into this position.

We both waited to see what I was going to do.

I was his boss, I reminded myself. And then my brain supplied a perfect 3-D picture of Greg Holder's face. I could even see his eyes, the way he watched me, kind, but not missing a thing. I mouth-breathed, so I wouldn't get any more olfactory input from Sid.

"When she comes today, you are not available," I said. "If you are not upstairs already, I want you to go there the minute you see her car."

"You think hiding solves anything?" Sid stood six inches from me. I knew this body tactic, I remembered it from John.

"This is my business," I said stiffly. "I am your employer. If you don't want to follow my directions, please leave now."

"Barbara," he almost crooned, "take it easy." He reached out his hand, perhaps to touch my arm, but I was turning away and his fingers brushed my breast.

My ridiculous slutty nipple was erect and we both knew it. Sid exhaled and I inhaled, our mouths open. I could feel the heat from inside his body. Heat again, there it was.

I put my hand on his chest and pushed. He was solid as a refrigerator, but he shifted back. I extended my arm fully until we were two feet apart. "This," I said, "is the right distance between you and me."

Janson came in with wood, and I escaped to the kitchen. The other men arrived and I called out a greeting. I heard someone, probably Janson, go upstairs and into the shower. In the kitchen, I collected myself, combed my hair, drank a glass of water, put lipstick on, wiped it off.

There was no music playing in the front room, and I could hear the low murmur of voices. It stopped when I crossed the threshold. They looked up at me, and there was a unity in their gaze that was discomfiting. I was the outsider. The bell rang, and two of our regulars arrived and went upstairs with Janson and Sid. It was three o'clock when they came down.

I served a snack—toast of course. For myself, I was done with toast. I'd decided to go on a raw-food diet, raw bread anyway, the toaster was a sinkhole for time. Sid fiddled with the iPod. There was a tension in the room that had never been there before, even on the first days. Sid didn't look at me. Neither did anyone else, except Tim to ask for more butter, please.

There was a flash of light from outside, sun reflecting off a white Lexus hood as it wove down the drive. I looked at Sid to see if he'd noticed. He had, but not a muscle in his hard young body was moving except for his thumbs twiddling with the iPod.

"Sid—" I started to warn him, but the door banged open and there stood the girl. She was blond and her eyes tilted up at the corners. She had the perfectly huge breasts that girls get from doting daddies for their sweet-sixteen birthday. She giggled and reached out for Sid. I didn't think she had even noticed that I was in the room.

I'd recognized her from the newspaper photo, the yuletide bride-to-be, LeeLee Vincenzo. And of course, since we were in Onkwedo, her father had to be the same Officer Vincenzo—now Chief Vincenzo—who was looking for me. I stepped forward. "Sorry, he can't today. He pulled a hamstring." (I remembered this injury from *Rowing and You*, page 167.) She looked around uncertainly.

"OK, him then." She pointed to Tim. Behind me I could hear a rumble coming from Sid. It sounded like a growl.

"He has a prior commitment. She'll be here shortly." Tension filled the room. I stepped toward her, blocking her view of the men. Up close she was sexier than she was beautiful, awesomely clean and fresh, with clingy low-cut jeans and no muffin top below her short cashmere T-shirt. The diamond on her finger was big enough to be gaudy.

"We can't help you today, I am sorry. We are full up. If you want to book, please call ahead." I put my hand on the doorjamb so she was obliged to back up slightly and stand outside the open doorway.

"Did my father call you?" She gave me a look that was one part innocence and two parts entitlement.

I was about to close the door on her fresh and collagenated self. She didn't rattle me—what rattled me was what I saw behind her: a Miata parking beside the Lexus, and Rudy inside it. I grabbed her by her lovely wrist. "Please come in." I yanked her in and slammed the door behind her. "Upstairs," I said to Sid. "With LeeLee, now."

As LeeLee and Sid went up the stairs, I turned to the others.

"Your coach is here. You're having a statistics study group. Now." They scooped up laptops and other electronics, and spread out on the couches, orderly, breathtakingly confident.

I peeked out the window. From the Miata the thinning crown of Rudy's head emerged on top of a new leather jacket. He unfolded to his full height, chest slightly puffed as if about to receive a medal.

I welcomed him from the doorway with a wave and a fake smile. "Come in," I called out in someone else's voice. Then I dashed across the room and poked at Sid's iPod till Sade was blaring from the speakers.

Rudy stepped inside, greeting his crew team. From behind his back I heard something about statistics and "evening workout."

I made my face smile. Dialogue from *Gone with the Wind* fell out of my mouth: "To what do I owe the pleasure?"

"Hey, Barb," Rudy said. He was taking in the old beams and the granite chimney stones, the new furnishings. "You're running a study hall on top of the beauty business?"

"Full service," I said. Rudy crossed to the mantelpiece and picked up the iPod. Sade's voice diminished to a whisper that did not cover the sounds of loud moaning from upstairs.

He looked at the stairway, then back at me.

"The treatment rooms are upstairs," I said.

"Sounds painful."

"Body waxing hurts." This was a true statement. "Come see the lake from the back porch," I said, hoping to get away from the sex noise.

Rudy followed me into the kitchen, stopping in front of the old refrigerator. "Uses as much power as four new ones." He opened the door and looked at the worn rubber seal. "These gaskets are obsolete—can't get a new one for love or money." Rudy shared my ex-husband's fascination with rubber-gizmo function.

I opened the back door onto the little porch, which balanced high above the sloping ground. A railing with narrow slats surrounded the warped wooden floorboards.

Rudy stepped out behind me. From where we stood we could see clear down to the south end of the lake. "That dock is massive." He leaned over the railing. "It's a little busted up, but we could pull a longboat up to that." I heard the window sash slide open above us. "We're two miles from where my team puts in." With his thumb raised, Rudy sighted down the lake toward the Waindell Boathouse. "We could aim for your dock on our stamina row days. It's plenty deep," he said.

LeeLee's voice picked up again, breathy and rhythmic, as she unmistakably reached her finish above us.

Rudy pointed questioningly to the porch ceiling.

"Brazilian bikini waxes are close to torture," I said. This might be true too.

He cocked an eyebrow at me. "Are you running a whorehouse?"

I didn't deny it.

"My team is mid-season. We have a shot at the All-Ivy. I see my top rowers here except for Sidney Walker. To be winners they can't be doing this. Ruins concentration."

The front door opened and I heard two female voices.

Shoot, I had forgotten that Professor Biggs's boss often came after the Tuesday departmental meeting she chaired.

"Stay," I said to Rudy as if he were Matilda.

I scuttled out, intending to explain to the chair and her companion in the nicest way I could think of that we'd had an unexpected interruption and to please come back on Thursday and I would make it up to them. But they had picked their regulars and were headed upstairs.

When I turned to go back to the kitchen, Rudy was standing at my shoulder.

"Those are the plainest hookers I have ever seen," he said after the faculty of the sociology department had disappeared.

Sid and LeeLee came ambling down the staircase. Sid's hands were on her shoulders. The lipstick was gone from LeeLee's lips, which were even more pouty than before, a bruised-looking plum-red. The lace of her thong was visible above her low-rise jeans.

"That's more like it," Rudy said.

LeeLee ignored him. "See you next week," she said to Sid, sounding like it would be hard to wait that long. She slipped out the front door, everything on her round and jiggly-perfect.

"Hey, coach," Sid said. "What are you doing here?"

"Right back at you," Rudy said.

"Back waxing," I said firmly, and the men stared at me. "See you next week, Sid, and don't forget your music."

"Yep, she sure is hairy," Sid said, standing still.

We looked at him.

"Go home," I said to Sid, but meaning all of them.

"It's a whorehouse," Rudy said to himself, "and Barb is the madam."

"Day spa," I said. No one was listening.

"You *pay* for it?" Rudy said to Sid. "Are you kidding me, a stud athlete like you?"

"Staff," Sid said. "Best gig I ever had."

"*She* pays for it?" Rudy pointed to the parking lot, where the white Lexus was peeling out. His voice had risen to a squeak.

"Onkwedo needs this facility. We are always full up." I stuck my chin out at him.

"My team," Rudy sputtered, "you're wrecking their stamina, draining the testosterone clear out. This could destroy the whole season. We'll lose our chance at the Ivy cup."

"That whole business about sex diminishing athletic performance is old science," I said. "The new science says that more sex means more testosterone, better drive, better stamina. Better everything, in fact."

"If anyone misses practice tonight, they're off the boats." Rudy stomped off to his car, wagging his balding head from side to side. "She *pays* for it," I heard him moan.

I sent the men home as soon as the dust from his Miata had vanished. I found a board and made a discreet sign to alert any customers who happened to show up: "Thank you all for your patronage. Have a nice day." That didn't sound right, so I flipped it over and wrote, "Regretfully, we are on hiatus." I gathered up my notebooks and closed the front door behind me. I tacked the sign up on a porch pillar where it would be clearly visible.

Sitting in my car, I looked back at the lodge. It was a beautiful place, serene and graceful. So much had happened there. So much had changed for me. I had come a long way from only being OK in my car. In the photos of Nabokov working or just sitting in his car, he looked very comfy. He may have felt at home with mobility, with perching lightly, not putting down roots. I understood that.

My car would have to be my office for now. I called the entertainment lawyer in the city. Max the assistant answered. I explained that I needed a lawyer up here for an appeal to my custody decision, and could he recommend someone nearby?

"*Where* are you?" Max asked, as though his mental map dropped off its western edge at Tenth Avenue.

I told him.

"Is there an airport there?" he said.

I assured him there was. I didn't tell him it was only for tiny aircraft.

"I'll do it," he said. "The firm will count it toward my pro bono credits."

It seemed rude to inquire if he knew anything about family law, since he was offering his services for free. At least I thought that was what pro bono meant. I didn't want to have to lean on scrawny young Max, but there I was.

I told him the date of the hearing, thanked him, and hung up, but not before he did. Time is money. Somebody's money, not mine.

CONFERENCE

With trepidation, I readied myself to be on the panel with the Nabokov experts. On Margie's instruction, I'd bought a push-up bra. It's strange to have your breasts suddenly closer to your face, like you are trying to get your own attention. Margie said the pencil skirt would do, with a tight sweater, chunky heels, and one very big piece of jewelry, the more crudely made the better. She explained that academics deeply admire primitive culture and its artifacts. I looked through my meager jewelry and found the brooch Sam made me for Mother's Day long ago: dry macaroni, painted gold. I pinned it on.

The professors on the panel were all good-looking. You would think academia would not be so shallow as to promote the best-looking professors. Each one was polished, honed by the scrutiny of a thousand nineteen-year-olds.

There was a table near the door of the auditorium with piles of books. Each of the panelists, except for me, was represented on the table by several serious-looking volumes. In a single stack was *Babe Ruth,* rumored to have been written by Vladimir Nabokov, found by me (authored by the phony Lucas Shade, about whom nobody seemed to care), and published by Sportsman's Press. The shiny blue cover looked garish next to the other books.

From my seat at the far end of the dais, I could see the panelists' faces: two male, two female. I could feel them watching me. I crossed my ankles, and they all crossed theirs. I drank from my free bottle of springwater; down the row all panelists sipped.

The talk began.

As I'd feared, I couldn't follow. The words and inflections drifted in spirals around my head. I was concentrating so hard I found that I could actually move my ears. My thinking muscles must have been connected to the vestigial ear-shrugging muscles, suitable for shooing flies if your hands are full of bananas.

There I was in my herringbone-patterned stockings, borrowed back from my daughter, waggling my ears in total concentration. I became aware of the moderator focusing on me. "And now we come to the tricky issue of Ms. Barrett"—everyone else was "Dr."—"and how her wonderful find may or may not fit in the oeuvre of Vladimir Nabokov."

The discussion had landed in exactly the area I dreaded, whether *Babe Ruth* deserved inclusion. There was a long pause that I was supposed to fill.

Flap, flap, went my ears.

As I floundered, silent and twitching, a large male Ph.D. jumped into the silence. "We think"—academics often are "we" thinkers—"that *Babe Ruth* might have some Nabokovian influence. But then there are sentences like this one . . ." He quoted a sentence from the baseball scene, penned by me. "God knows he couldn't have written it, particularly in that brilliant and fecund epoch of his output." He opened the book to a page he'd marked with Post-its, and read another sentence of mine. "It's very close to gobbledygook," he said.

They turned to me. I nodded sympathetically, earnestly, for what was probably a little too long, trying to convey my compassion for the difficulty of figuring all this complicated stuff out. I looked at their handsome smart faces. I could almost see their fangs come out.

My brain let go of my ears for a second, and in some fear-driven adrenal surge offered up a perfect visual of the found index cards, one after the other. They were so clear to me that I could have read the words aloud. My ears calmed down. "Listen, maybe those sentences aren't great. But the book is beautiful. It's a love story. It's baseball. It's funny, for goodness' sake. What more do you want from a book?"

There was a long, empty silence. They clearly wanted much more from a book. I kept going. "I know about his sentences. His sentences are impossible to imitate, but I know what they do." I told them what I had discovered about Nabokov's sentences: Because the word string and the thoughts behind the words are so original, the reader's brain can't jump ahead. There is no opportunity to make assumptions, no mental leapfrogging to the end of the sentence. So the reader is suspended in the perfect moment of now. You can only experience now. The sentences celebrate the absolute instant of creation. "It takes your breath away," I said.

I could tell from the silence that laypeople weren't supposed to know these things just by *reading*. But reading is as close as you can get to communing, closer than face-to-face, closer than sharing breath. I pushed my chair back, not waiting for the moderator to dismiss me. The free bottle of springwater toppled onto the table, splashing my shoes as I stood.

The moderator thanked us. People clapped politely, which meant not much. I climbed down from the speakers' platform and walked to the table, ready to pack my books and go. As I started filling the cardboard box, a person from the audience came up and said, "I'd like to buy a copy." It was a ticket seller from the bus station, the one who was

Cleaning Nabokov's House

always reading. I thanked her and signed the book, *Found by B. Barrett*. She gave me a lovely private smile, as if we shared a secret.

Others lined up behind her. "I read the book. I liked it a lot. Well, not the sports scene, but the rest of it." A student was addressing me.

"Thank you." I wanted to say something smart, but my shoes were soaked. I leaned over to dry them off. The oddest thing about a push-up bra was that it inverted your relationship with gravity.

At the end of the line of people was the moderator. I signed her book and accepted the envelope with the honorarium. I'd sold out of *Babe Ruth*.

HOTEL

I checked into my hotel room. I took off my wet suede shoes and put them on the air vent to dry. I unhooked the push-up bra and stuffed it into the trash.

Outside the window was a view of Onkwedo from on high, the buildings tidy and even more insignificant than from the ground. I didn't really need a hotel room, since I lived three miles away, but it was the only perk offered besides the fifty-dollar honorarium and the bottle of water I'd spilled.

I ran a hot bath in the long hotel tub and eased into it. The custody hearing was the next day. I lined the edge of the tub with the small bottles from a wicker basket of beauty products. There was a wall phone beside the tub. I leaned back against the porcelain and called Margie. She sounded peaceful. I asked her what she was doing. She said she was cross-stitching a pillow for Bill's birthday. I asked her what it said.

" 'To know me is to love me.' Winston Churchill. Brown embroidery silk on a cream background."

That was true about Bill.

She asked me how the panel went. I told her I'd sold all the books. That made her squeal. I didn't tell her about the ear-wiggling thing. It's better if your agent doesn't know all your inadequacies. I opened one of the little bottles and sniffed it. I told her I was closing the cathouse.

"Good," Margie said. "You got away with it, but hell, Barb, that was a disaster in the making."

I didn't tell her about taking on John in court, not yet. I was too afraid of failing. After we hung up I tried all the hotel products, including a body buffer that seemed to be a combination of perfume, axle grease, and sand. Once I had rubbed it onto my skin, it didn't come off with soap and water.

I used up all the hotel room towels trying to de-grease and de-grit myself. I think I loved hotel life as much as Nabokov did—no laundry ever.

Still sticky, I called Rudy. I reached him on the team bus on the way to the regatta at Princeton. I could hear one of Sid's music mixes in the background. "How's life as a pimp?" Rudy said.

I told him to stuff it and let me talk to Janson. He handed the phone over.

"Hello?" Sweet, strong, wood-chopping Janson.

I talked to the All-Ivy crew team one by one: my handsome, generous, talented, dedicated sex workers. They took the cathouse closing news in stride; they were champs in every way. Sid Walker was last. "Hey," he said, "don't tell me why. I don't need to know. Just tell me this: Was it good for you?"

"Yes, Sid," I said. "It was good. You are good." Then I said something lame: "Call me if you need a reference."

I ordered breakfast from room service even though it was nearly dinnertime. The hotel food presentation was perfect: silver domes over the plates, a bud vase with a daffodil. I pushed aside the greasy home fries and chilly scrambled eggs. I took a bite of frigid toast but found I couldn't swallow it. I was thinking about going to court the next day.

I gave up on the food and lay in the hotel bed, tense. My people paraded through my head. But this time it wasn't the ones who were gone, it was the ones who were in my life now: Darcy and Sam. Margie, Bill. I thought about the man I didn't want to fall in love with, Greg Holder. I thought of what Margie had said when I first met her, months ago: "There's someone out there for you, someone wonderful. The universe is just getting him ready." I'd imagined some poor man, his wife being struck by lightning, or run over in a supermarket parking lot, or—as I now knew—driving out of town on the back of a lesbian's Harley. I fell asleep.

RINGER

I drove to the Onkwedo airport to meet Max. When he got off the plane, I noticed that he had bought himself some fuzzy socks for his tasseled loafers and a navy fleece vest. The genius of lawyers: he planned to fit in. I was wearing the peach twin set again, more rumpled.

Max brought me an enthusiastic greeting from his boss, who had just left for Bolzano, where, Max informed me, spring skiing was at its peak.

In the courtroom Max and I sat together, waiting. Most of a lawyer's life is spent waiting but making money at it, like a parking meter.

John and his lawyer strode through the door like Wyatt Earp and whoever, or Paul Newman and Robert Redford, or Ben Affleck and Matt Damon. Two guys, a bromance. You know before you even watch the opening credits of the movie that women come and go but male bonding is forever.

They sat down in unison. John looked great in a suit: rich and powerful, younger than me, as if we were on different aging trajectories. John. The man I married. The man I divorced. The man who held my children hostage.

I noticed Max discreetly lining up feet with the other lawyer, fuzzy sock for fuzzy sock, smooth shoe for smooth shoe. He winced involuntarily.

As we waited, I rehearsed my attitude for the judge: pleasant and appealing, not begging, simply stating the facts. Not an unstable mother desperate to share her children's lives, but a reasonable person who was mildly and clearly showing the improved circumstances of her life. "All please rise for Judge Teagarten," the clerk of family court blared out. I stood up in my boring clothes, chest lifted in my nice-mommy brassiere.

The chamber doors opened and the judge rustled through. I could hear the robes, but the high desk obscured my view. Judge Teagarten mounted the steps behind the desk, and in the respectful hush that spread through the room, I found myself looking into the eyes of the Purse Lady.

I was having the essence of the small-town experience: I knew something about someone that I had no business knowing. I remembered Judge Purse Lady Teagarten heading up the stairs of the cathouse, her face fiercely anticipating what was to come.

In light of the fact that Judge Teagarten was an elected official, her predilections made sense. As with many politicians of an authoritarian bent, humiliation was what got her going. It was the shady side of craving power, or one of the shady sides.

We endured Judge Teagarten's postponement of the three cases in front of us. Finally she called *Barrett v. Barrett*.

We all stood and waited while the judge reviewed the original custody decision. Apparently it was a waste of her precious time for Judge Teagarten to read anything while no one was watching.

When she had finished, the judge turned to me. "This court issued a judgment very recently, Ms. Barrett. It is unlikely that it will be reversed. However, I will review the appeal and we will reconvene in my

Cleaning Nabokov's House

chambers tomorrow at nine a.m." She looked at me, her face showing not a flicker of recognition.

I let John and counsel precede me out of the courtroom. He and his lawyer matched strides, wheeling around the corner toward the elevators like a pair of ice skaters.

I drove Max to his motel. He'd booked a room at the Swiss Chalet Motor Inn, only it had changed hands and the new owner had renamed it the Alpine Inn. Other than the sign, it looked exactly the same as when I had stayed there, dismal. I guessed Max's firm was not carrying the pro bono thing too far.

He wanted to see where I'd found the manuscript, so I took him back to my house for lunch. I'd anticipated his visit, and the house was spruced up, books on the shelves and wooden floors buffed. "Nabokov lived *here*?" Max said as he crossed the threshold.

"Yes, he did some of his finest writing here," I said, trying not to sound defensive. "Also some of his worst."

I showed Max where to plug in his laptop so it wouldn't blow a fuse, and went into the kitchen to fix us some lunch. I made a salad of early greens and warmed an onion tart.

Max worked on his computer till lunch was ready. We sat down at the table. Forcing himself to make small talk, he asked me how I had adjusted to living outside New York City. The underlying question was how could anyone stand it here? "Onkwedo is a good place for children," I said. He looked absolutely blank. I added, "And for entrepreneurs. It's a great town to start a business." We tucked back into our tart. I knew the lunch was at least on par with the popular bistro down the street from his office, the one beside the original cathouse.

"Nabokov changed my life," Max said. "I was going to be a writer, and then I read *Lolita* and I decided to go to law school instead. It looked easier." He gathered the crust crumbs on the back of his fork.

SCIENCE

When I got back from taking Max to his chalet, the message light on my phone was blinking. The mechanical voice reported that there were four calls. I played them back: Yale, Harvard, U Penn, and the Waindell Department of Psychology. While I was writing the numbers down, another call came in.

It was a secretary announcing that Dr. Fenster from Princeton was on the line, and would I take the call?

"Sure."

Dr. Fenster introduced himself as the chair of the Department of Human Ecology. I don't think that department existed when I went to college. He began by complimenting my performance on the Nabokov panel.

I thanked him, saying it was nothing. I knew this to be true.

Then, with a little fumferring, he let me know that he understood I had access to data that would be extremely useful in their work on human development. He paused.

I asked him how this information had come to him.

He cleared his throat in a practiced-sounding way and launched into a description of the spring regatta just held on "beautiful and serpentine Carnegie Lake."

I waited.

"We hosted the Waindell crew team," he said. Then he waited.

I tried clearing my throat, but it sounded like I was choking. Because I was. I looked at the call list again. "Were there other universities at the meet?" I asked him.

"Certainly," he said, naming the exact colleges from the list.

"Would there be any compensation or grant money for the material?" I asked. There was a shocked silence at the other end of the phone. "Because," I continued, "there seems to be other interest."

"I see," Dr. Fenster said, sounding furious, especially for a psychology professor who should be more skilled in processing his rage.

"Let me take your number, and I will have my associate call you," I told him. He gave me his office, mobile, and home phone numbers. As an afterthought, he gave me the number of his weekend house.

I called Margie and explained to her about the cathouse information leaking out, and the calls from the universities.

She made a hmmm noise, like she was not surprised.

I asked her if there was any money in it.

Margie refused to speculate about money. She thought about money all the time, I suspected, when she was not thinking about her cats, or Bill, or what clothes I should wear. "I'll let you know," she snapped. "Give me the phone numbers."

I was too restless to stay home. Still in my court clothes, I got in my car and drove to the bluff overlooking the lake. From there I could see the roof peak of the lodge between veils of new tree leaves. The bluff was halfway between my house and Greg's. I wondered if he was home and working. I wondered whether he wanted to see me. I looked at my phone for answers, but it didn't ring. I did have his number, though, written on the scrap of paper he'd left on my windshield, and stored in my ridiculously visually retentive brain.

I dialed.

"I'm glad you called," Greg said.

"You could have called me," I said.

"I'm done being with women who don't want to be with me."

I was silent. Was it really that simple? I remembered the one thing I knew for sure about men: sometimes it really *is* that simple.

"Where are you?" he asked.

"I'm at the bluff." There was a small opening in the clouds, and a square of light appeared on the far hill, like a trapdoor.

"Come over," Greg said. "I have cookies."

When I got there, he was walking toward the house from his workshop with Rex at his heel. I climbed out of the car, only then remembering my outfit.

"Are you here to convert me to your faith?" he said, looking at my clothes and my large nice-mommy purse.

"I don't have a faith," I said. "I am wearing these clothes for a reason."

"Of course you are," he said. "Come have tea." He held the front door open for me, and Rex waited politely until I had gone through.

He put the kettle on and slid a plate of cookies onto the table. They looked homemade. "My neighbors are always trying to fatten me up," he said.

I bit into a cookie. It tasted like sawdust and peanuts. I decided to get right to the point. "I used to run a cathouse. I just closed it down."

"I know all about it," he said. "I was hoping I'd hear it from you." Greg took a cookie from the plate and broke it in half. "You don't know me very well yet. I don't have a problem with your choice of work." He took a bite. "I care about other things, like how people treat each other. Loyalty is important to me." He continued munching the non-food cookie. "Sex for money doesn't bother me. I wouldn't do it, but that's my choice." He smiled at me. "I do want to know one thing."

"What?" I tossed my nasty cookie to Rex, who caught it on the fly.

"Did you ever get it on with the help?"

"No."

"Why not?" His voice was low. There was no judgment in it, only curiosity.

"I didn't want to."

He was waiting for more of an answer.

"I need to feel a connection."

"Love?"

I was silent. No one ever said the "L" word this early. Not these days. Not in my lifetime. Greg touched a finger lightly to my face. "I could go for you," he said.

And I said, "Don't stop yourself."

He put his arms around me and started kissing me, or I may have started it. "You're not going to cry again, are you?" His voice rumbled up from some open place deep in his chest.

"No." I don't know why it felt fine for him to tease me. It made me feel known. We kissed again. Our mouths understood each other. After another kiss or three I pulled back. "What do you eat for breakfast?" I asked him.

"Cereal mostly. Eggs, grits, and bacon on the weekend."

I freed myself from his arms and carried my saucer over to the sink. The dishwasher was open and there were dishes in the racks. "Do you care how I put this in?"

"Why would I care about that?" Greg said.

"Don't you think God is in the details?"

"No," Greg said. He was watching me. "Is there anything else?"

"Do you want to kiss me some more?"

"Yes," he said. "Come here." He opened his arms to me, pulling me down onto his lap. "You say things out of left field, and the field beyond that." He kissed me.

"You too with the baseball stuff?" I took advantage of his closeness to sniff his good smell.

"I'm American, and I'm a guy."

Later we were naked. Right in the middle of things I told him to stop and he did. He stopped, and folded himself, handsome and patient, and watched me. I thought I might grab my dopey clothes and leave. I think Greg knew that. But we both waited. In the dim light of his bedroom, on the bed he had built himself, our nakedness was muted and soft. He stroked the side of my face with a long finger. "If it's all right with you, I'm going to set a ground rule here: no faking it. You don't have to pretend for my sake, I can take the truth." As he said this he was touching me slowly with great deliberateness and skill. He spoke into my waiting mouth, "The truth will set you free."

I scooted up on his pillows. "May I ask an inappropriate question?"

"Sure." Greg traced a pattern on my chest.

"How did you get to be so good?"

"I was married to a lesbian. I had to work harder than most guys."

Later still I found myself saying, "I don't want to fall in love with you."

Greg's face was right over mine. "We could stop this," he said, not stopping.

"Don't," I said. And he didn't.

CHAMBERS

After breakfast with Greg—if you call cold cereal breakfast—I sat in Judge Q. L. Teagarten's chambers, all the chairs in a respectful arc around her desk. Max passed out his business card to the judge and John's lawyer. I took one too. On the back of the creamy linen stock I wrote the address of the cathouse and the name of the act Purse Lady had requested most persistently, and handed the card back to Max. He looked at me questioningly and I shrugged.

Judge Teagarten opened my portfolio. Without looking up from the photo essay on my children's rooms, the judge said, "The issue at hand is whether Ms. Barrett can demonstrate a change in her circumstances significant enough to warrant a review of the original decision." She leafed through the pages, unimpressed. She paused to take in Darcy's wall of purses. "Nice collection," she said. She sounded slightly covetous to me. I spotted her same "Prada" shoulder bag beside her chair. "You have a position as the correspondence manager for the Old Daitch Dairy?" she asked. "Ms. Barrett, what does that entail?" She still hadn't looked up from the papers.

I started explaining my work, the nuances of the dairy inquiries, but she cut me off. "Do you have an income sufficient to provide for your two offspring?"

"I started my own business this year," I said, and nodded at Max.

He reluctantly slid the card facedown across her desk. The judge looked at it, and I could see her stiffen. For the first time, she looked in my direction. I could tell that she didn't recognize me in my peach muffin attire. She'd never bothered to notice what I looked like during her three months of cathouse patronage; I was irrelevant to the satisfaction of her desires. But now she'd guessed who I was.

"That's a very nice purse," I said, pointing to her Prada, which I realized was probably real. "Tidy too, I bet."

There was dead silence.

John's lawyer started to say something, but the judge held up her hand to stop him. "I need to speak to Ms. Barrett and counsel." She turned to John and his lawyer, sitting with their legs crossed man-style, ankle at knee, so clearly and confidently unaware. "I will review this matter and make a decision promptly. Please let my secretary know where I may reach you." They filed out, and I heard John give the secretary his office phone number and his lawyer's number, which I knew by heart from the seven times I'd sent nuisance extra-cheese pizzas his way in the first weeks after I'd lost my children.

Once the door had closed behind them, the judge turned to me. "What do you want?"

"Full custody. But I will accept joint custody as long as it is irrevocable." Max stepped hard on my toe, but I ignored him.

The judge reached for her purse and stopped in mid-gesture. "I've just quit smoking," she said apologetically. "I miss my Marlboros."

Max looked shocked. He probably knew people who did recreational heroin, but nobody who would invade their lungs with nicotine.

"Write a proposal," the judge said to Max. "I will give it serious consideration."

Max didn't know what had just happened. I could have explained it to him, but it would take too long, and besides, he would never believe me about the cathouse.

"You will have it this afternoon." Max and I stood up, and the judge swiveled her knees out from behind her desk. "My secretary needs to buy me some gum," she announced, and walked out of the room.

From his laptop in the lobby of the Alpine Inn, Max sent the document to the judge. We waited till his computer signaled her response. She had read it, and if we could provide a custody agreement, she would approve it and file her judgment the following day.

Max stared at me in disbelief that it was happening so fast.

"Things are simpler here," I explained.

Max wasn't up for hashing out the custody and visitation business; pro bono had run out. When I asked him for any tips, he shrugged. "I would think you two could work it out yourselves." Clearly Max had never been married.

I drove him to the tiny Onkwedo airport and waited while the person at the ticket counter raced around the security barrier, putting on her orange security vest so she could perform the second part of her dual job as ticket seller and security personnel.

She made Max take off his big blazer so she could move the security wand closer to his scrawny body. I waved and called my thanks, turning away so he wouldn't know I had seen how young and small he looked without his jacket.

I jumped back in my car, grateful to know it wasn't going to break down, and raced to John's house, dodging speed traps, trying to get there before he and his lawyer cooked up something horrible. As I pulled up in front, I saw Irene in the garden filling a large hole. There were other holes dotting the lawn and flower beds, each one at least a foot deep. She straightened when she saw me, leaned on her shovel, wrists cocked to keep the dirt away from her pristine lavender gardening slacks.

"Hi," I said.

She greeted me, clearly puzzled, since it was not my "day."

"Where are the kids?" I asked.

At that moment, Darcy came around the side of the house holding a rope. She didn't see me because she was walking backwards, tugging hard at whatever was at the end of the rope. "Bad dog," she called out. "You dig too many big holes." She planted her feet and gave the rope a stern yank. Sam came into view around the corner of the house, the rope tied around his waist. He was holding his hands up at chest level obligingly and gave a soft woof that broke off when he saw me.

Darcy turned to see what her dog was staring at and took me in. I was still wearing my nice-mommy-goes-to-court clothes.

She dropped the rope and came over to touch my sweater set. "Is that one piece or two?" she asked, lifting the hem of the cardigan.

Sam approached, the rope still tied around his big waist. Darcy looked at him. "Sit," she said, but he ignored her.

"It's not the first Saturday of the month yet, is it?" Sam asked me.

"Not yet," I said. "I just wanted to see you." I put my hand out and stroked his soft cheek. He had grown. We were a scant year from being eye to eye.

Darcy put her little body between us. "He is my dog," she said firmly, "but you can pet him." I petted them both.

Just then their father drove up. He had bought himself a large new pickup truck that ran on methanol. It smelled atrocious when the motor shut off. He got out, smoothing his hair. "Barb," he said, "you got here fast." I watched him take his warrior stance: body weight centered perfectly, right hand free, almost cocked.

"Have you heard from your lawyer?" I asked.

He nodded at me, too wary for speech. He stepped forward, still on the balls of his feet. "May I talk to you?" He took my elbow and I let him steer me back toward my car. When we were out of earshot of the children, he let go of me and stepped back to his personal comfort zone (three and a half feet away from me, preferably more).

"In here?" I opened both doors to my car and climbed in, leaving the driver's side to him. He hesitated, but he couldn't quite stop himself from getting behind the wheel.

The last time we had been in a car together was ages ago. He'd always insisted on driving. John, like most men, thought he was the greatest driver in the world. It's like the myriad schizophrenics who think they are Jesus Christ—they can't all be right.

John held the steering wheel in the correct two-handed position. "My lawyer took me out to Loro's for lunch, cheap bastard." He scanned the lawn as if on watch for tractor-trailers. "He said that Loro's won't deliver to his office anymore."

I was pretty sure that was my handiwork from my anonymous pizza days. I hoped so.

"He said I had to comply." The last word came out like a curse.

I didn't know what reason Judge Q. L. Teagarten gave John's lawyer to make him cave, but it was effective. Nothing like shame as a motivator. I took the court papers out of my purse and laid them on my lap. "I think we can make a fair agreement here. We failed at love. That's OK. We have these great kids and we're moving forward."

John's eyelids fluttered. "Irene and I are getting married," he said brusquely. "The children don't know yet."

"Congratulations," I said. Without missing a beat I asked for custody of the dog. I pointed out that Matilda did less damage at my place because I worked from home.

"I'll consider it," John said and patted his beautiful head of hair, as if to reassure himself that no one had taken it.

"You're getting married, and I'm getting . . . I'm changing my line of work." I was, too. Even if Princeton didn't pay up, I was done forever with the sex trade. "We're moving on." I took a pen from the glove compartment. "The kids need both of us. Each of us. What do you want?"

"Christmas." He sounded belligerent.

"Fine." I wrote it down.

"Easter." Still Mr. Assertiveness Trainer.

I didn't know John was so religious. "Fine."

"Father's Day."

"Sure." Why would I want to deprive him of that silly holiday?

"My birthday."

So he wouldn't miss any presents? "Fine." I wrote it all down.

I waited. "That's it?"

John seemed to be thinking about what he might miss from the other 361 days of parenthood. "I want Sam to go to intensive ice hockey camp."

I chose my words carefully. "Sam doesn't seem motivated by sports."

"He needs to put the time in."

That old saw. "I think Darcy's our best hope for competitive sports."

He thought about this. "I am keeping them till the school year is over."

That was two more weeks. There was a moment when I could have taken revenge, and we both knew it. I didn't. The holidays were not what I wanted from parenthood. I wanted the deciding what to eat for breakfast, the lazy summer mornings, and the amazing questions before sleep. I wanted as much of that as I could get.

"You can see them whenever you want, you know that. And the dog too. There's no wall here." I held the pen out for John to sign.

He looked at me with a question in his face. He was wondering, as he had many times before, why he'd thought breeding with me was a good idea. He took the pen from my hand, signed, and got out of my car.

IVY LEAGUE

Halfway home I pulled over and called Margie.

She answered the phone on the first ring, as if she had been expecting my call. "Academics are worse than book publishers in every way," she said, without giving me a chance to speak. "Stingy, and with too many darn people on their decision-making committees. They have to answer all the way up to God, and beyond that, the trustees."

"Margie, I got my kids back." I told her about going to court, leaving out the part about the judge/Purse Lady. I told her about the agreement with John.

"I knew you could do it, Barb," Margie said, her voice gruff, as if she was not letting herself cry. Ice cubes rattled, the constant background noise to Margie's home life. "Good times, Barb. Good times ahead." She sounded choked up.

Margie collected herself. "University of Pennsylvania offered four hundred dollars. Yale and Harvard tied at one K." ("K" was agent speak.) "Princeton is the highest bidder at twenty-five hundred."

"That doesn't sound like an auction," I said.

"No," Margie admitted. "It was simply a discussion." I knew she wouldn't tell me any more.

"What about Waindell?" I asked.

"The chair threatened a lawsuit, but I mentioned the release forms signed by their heavyweight men's crew team, who just took the All-Ivy title, as well as patronage by several faculty members, some from his own department."

"But did Waindell make an offer?" I asked. (What a slut I really am!)

"Yes, but I turned them down. Too close to home."

"Go, Tigers," I said, and I honked my horn.

Back at home, the phone call I had been dodging caught up with me: "Chief of Police Vincenzo here."

"Barbara Barrett here," I said and waited silently for the nonsense to begin. That was my passive-aggressive side, my cop-loathing inner self showing.

He started talking, and I listened for the charges, for what bad thing I had done and how much it was going to cost me. But Chief Vincenzo wanted to borrow my old car. He was helping at the high school's auto-tech class, and they needed a transmission to rebuild. "Yours is shot," he said cheerfully. "I tried that key there in the ashtray. Couldn't even get it into gear. The kids might not fix it, but they sure won't make it any worse."

"Then I'd get it back?"

"Sure. Three days tops."

This town was odd, no doubt about it, but it was growing on me.

That evening Greg stopped by with dinner. Everything was well packaged, wrapped in wax paper and secured with precisely knotted string. I suspected one of his neighbor ladies had made it.

"How did it go with John?" he asked.

"Good, I guess. He has Christmas and Easter and Father's Day."

"That's it?" Greg unwrapped a slice of unsquished strawberry rhubarb pie.

"Pretty much. I wanted Halloween, and the Fourth of July, and everything else."

The grilled veggie wraps were tasty. "I got the dog too." I gave Greg a slightly sticky kiss. "Are you thinking what I'm thinking?"

"Rex gets some?"

"No. Well, yes, but I am thinking about puppies."

Greg took a big bite of pie so he wouldn't have to talk.

GOODBYE, CATHOUSE

In the week before school ended I'd ordered five loads of gravel to repair the erosion on the driveway to the lodge. It was my thank-you present to Granny Bryce.

I went for a last look around and a straightening. I made a fire to keep me company. I'd decided to leave everything for Granny Bryce and the hunters: furniture, bedding, even the sex toys.

There was a mountain of clean laundry in the basket, and I started folding sheets. At the bottom of the basket were the Pants. I put the folded sheets away in the linen closet. I stuffed the Pants in the fireplace and held them on the embers with a poker until they smoldered. When the Pants were ashes, I smothered the remaining coals.

I closed the shutters and nailed the plywood back over the front door. I removed the sign; my patrons had all gotten the news by now. Word spread fast in Onkwedo.

MORE MAIL

One morning Bill brought me an envelope from Princeton University. Unsurprisingly, their check cleared.

I gave it to Onkwedo Feed the Children, saving out enough to buy myself a two-hundred-dollar pair of jeans (OK, on sale for forty dollars). They practically kissed me when I put them on.

I called the Waindell archivist and offered the manuscript as a permanent bequest. She was "most interested" and asked if there was an endowment to go with it.

No.

I gave young Mr. Daitch my six different form letters to handle the correspondence. I think the conversations with me had pried open his social side, because he made a tiny bit of eye contact while I explained to him the application of each template. Maybe he was ready to interact with his public a little. I promised to come back for the cherry pitting every summer if the customer demand kept up.

I finally finished the Amish romance for Margie. She liked the scene where the man, as he reached climax—called *"the heights"*—bellowed, *"Marry me!"* Margie thought it had strong female appeal. The market for romance seemed to be insatiable, so I wrote another and another. I recycled all the baseball words I had learned. Writing sports scenes and scenes of lovemaking is nearly the same. It might be turning into a career. My mother was appalled that I would spend my days writing. "Think of how your backside will flatten out," she said.

I heard from the guys occasionally. Tim asked me for a letter of reference. Wayne wrote me a note on monogrammed stationery when he was accepted into the Harvard MBA program. He expressed his gratitude for the opportunity I provided to assist him in developing his interest in entrepreneurship.

Sid sent me several music mixes, all of which had themes that might be considered insulting. He sent Darcy a pair of black ballet slippers. Wearing them, she danced for Sam and me her own version of *The Nutcracker,* using a pliers-type nutcracker, the ubiquitous Barbies, and several plastic mice.

CHERRY VANILLA ICE CREAM

A month after the closing of the cathouse, we set up an ice cream stand on the route of the Independence Day parade. Because all the firefighters were needed for each nearby town's celebration, Onkwedo had its parade on July 7. It was the same parade every year: antique fire engines clanking along, then tractors pulling hay bale floats with the New York State Dairy Queen and her court, waving.

Granny Bryce was there, watching the parade from her wheelchair beside old Mr. Daitch. She wore a T-shirt proclaiming her "Onkwedo's Oldest Resident."

I gave her a dish of cherry vanilla ice cream. Sam and I had stayed up till midnight pitting the cherries. "Thank you, dearie." She ate it slowly, her head bent over her lap, where she had carefully spread a paper napkin. When the small dish was near empty, she rested the wooden spoon and turned her head to look up at me. Her eyes were a well-washed blue.

I knelt down beside the chair. "Well done," she said, nodding at me, "just right."

Sam liked the commerce of scooping ice cream, but Darcy glowered at the customers till I took her away to have her own dish of ice cream. She picked out the cherries, whispering as she did so, "Be gone, be gone, be gone," leaving the ice cream nicely plain, the way she liked it.

I counted: one was Darcy, two was Sam, three was Greg, four was Matilda, five was the sun through the leaves, six was the smell of ripe cherries that drew water to your mouth, seven was the people of Onkwedo all around us happily licking their cones.

After the parade, we watched the Yankees farm team play ball. I sat with Greg and the kids. It was a beautiful day. For the moment, everyone was happy. It was playtime. But then the baseball game went on. And on. And on. I put sunglasses over my eyes to hide my boredom. Greg held my hand and traced on my palm with his finger, making a map of the bases and the players. I wish I could say that there was a breakthrough, that, like Helen Keller, I got it, I suddenly got it: baseball was a beautiful dance, full of grace, power, and individual prowess. But I didn't get it. I just sat there, hoping my sunglasses masked my alienation.

I tried picturing a tall silver-haired Nabokov sitting in the stands, Vera beside him in a straw hat. I could imagine the ripples in the air around his head from the thought waves of his brain. But he wasn't here, and the magnificent patterns that his mind imposed on the world—discerned in even such a lumpen thing as men in uniforms swinging bats—that was gone too.

PASTRY

Near the end of the summer I took the children to the city for a visit. Wandering along an uptown sidewalk, we came across Pierre's patisserie, Ceci-Cela in its new home. Darcy was pressing her nose against the glass case of pastry creations when I got a call from the Princeton professor who'd bought the cathouse data. He was a little blustery. "We paid a lot for this data."

I agreed.

"I've gone through it all very thoroughly." He cleared his throat and continued. "The conclusion I am approaching, from the statistical entries and the predictive modeling we have assigned to them, is that what women want is to be understood." His tone was accusatory.

"Yes," I said, "they do."

"That's impossibly vague," he said. "It could hardly be called conclusive."

"Women will settle for being listened to," I informed him. And I hung up.

Darcy was ogling the apricot tarts. Sam was on his knees in front of the napoleons, counting the layers of pastry.

"Croissant au chocolat. Café, pas de lait," said Pierre when he saw me.

He remembered my order.

"Je t'aime," I said, since it was almost all the French I knew.

He gave a plosive little Gallic puff that expressed it all. It said, "Piss off." And it also said, "I might sleep with you if you wore better shoes."

We ate the pastries at a little table on the sidewalk. I watched my children's faces change, fresh rapture with each bite.

AUTUMN

We made a place for Greg in our lives. Darcy said he could have my room and I could sleep with her. Sam wanted to convert the garage to a woodshop for Greg. I settled on a shelf in the cabinet for his toiletries and a few hangers' worth of shirts in the closet. I bought his favorite breakfast cereal and the wrong kind of beer. (I didn't want him to think I was trying too hard.)

Greg measured me for a stand-up writing desk.

For now it was going well. I knew life with Greg wasn't going to be like the romance novels. I was going to have to learn to say things carefully, and over and over again. And worse, I would have to listen to things like this: "When you dented the fender and pretended you didn't know who did it, and I didn't find out till I got the police report, that made me feel like you don't trust me."

But then there were the times of wide-open ease, like when he built a beauty salon for Darcy to trim the hair off the balding Barbies, or when we were cleaning up after supper and we were dancing along to the radio, and he folded his arms around me from behind, and I thought, He's got my back.

FULL TERM

Nearly four months after the closing of the cathouse, the Purse Lady called me. She explained in her Judge Teagarten voice that there was an unusual situation. A young woman whose father was "a pillar of the community" was pregnant, and the biological father of her unborn child was not her fiancé. The young woman had asked the judge to handle the adoption. The judge said that the young woman claimed not to know the last name of the biological father, but that I would know who he was.

Judge Teagarten editorialized, saying that in her day the girl would have kept the baby, but now she (the judge almost slipped and said her name) wanted to arrange an open adoption so she could see the child occasionally but not have to raise it.

We had a confusing discussion, with the judge speaking law and me speaking English.

The upshot was that she arranged an adoption for Margie and Bill. The nasty things I knew about Judge Teagarten may have bumped my friends to the head of the line of prospective parents.

I had a lovely time showing Margie how to care for an infant. As I expected, she was an amazing mother: practical, loving, and relaxed. She even stopped smoking and started eating, except on Wednesdays.

She kept her beautiful figure too, which she attributed to drinking two quarts a day of blue Crystal Light.

With the confidence gained from wedding catering, Sam prepared baby food for Margie's new baby, making wholesome pulverized concoctions, all based on applesauce.

Darcy paid scant attention to the tiny boy after painting his toenails fire engine red.

Margie's son had long baby-boy lashes that curled back from glittery round eyes. Whenever music came on the radio, his chubby arms and legs pumped wildly.

LeeLee was often pictured on the *Clarion* social page with her new husband, but we never saw her in person.

Sid visited once, bringing a soft blanket appliquéd with blue elephants. He seemed happy to see the baby, and happier still to leave.

ONKWEDO

I may never feel completely at home in Onkwedo. My people may always be gathered in heaven or a big city, but I am beginning to belong to Onkwedo. People nod to me in greeting, and I have grown to like that, an acknowledgment that we share the world in that moment.

In the aftermath of the cathouse, I think there is a change in Onkwedo. The women in town look slightly smug. They are dressing better and there has been a surge in gym memberships. The YMCA had to add two sections to the belly dance class and four new Pilates machines. Sometimes I think I can see the after-effects of the lodge: women walking around Onkwedo a little dreamy, their mouths lifted at the corners, their usually careful hair messy and a little wild. I see them in the supermarket, standing too long in the produce aisle, choosing just the right cucumber. I notice them sniffing things. The roses are in bloom now, pink and lush, and wherever I go, I see women bending over to smell them. It's a particularly good season for roses. And the bending over is a particular kind of bending over, an offering, like something good might come along at any moment from any direction.

There are nearly perfect times every day. One is the half hour before sleep when we three sit in my big bed, leaning against the same wall where Vera and Vladimir rested their heads. Sometimes Greg is in the kitchen, rustling the pages of the *Onkwedo Clarion* or washing the pasta starch from the blue pot. I read aloud from some book I have found that bridges Sam's and Darcy's different interests, something not too scary, something without cruelty, a story with which to let go of the day.

Another perfect time happens in the mornings when they awaken. Sam sleeps under the poster of a famous chef. When his eyes first open, he wraps a sleepy arm around my neck. "Mom," he says, like the night was a necessary separation, now resolved. And from her pillow, Darcy looks at me as if to say, *Who in hell are you? You weren't in my dream.* And then I make them breakfast and help them find their way. It will take me a lifetime to be their North Star, the way my father was for me, but a lifetime is what I have.

Cleaning Nabokov's House

The last straw was the dishwasher. After a decade of marriage, Barbara walks out on her husband, John, while he instructs her on the proper method of loading cups and bowls. A newcomer to John's sleepy hometown in upstate New York, and now a divorcée, Barb feels out of place. John wins custody of their children (the judge is his friend), and Barb gets just one weekend a month of visitation (the social worker is John's new girlfriend). Lonely, depressed, and down to her last pair of pants, Barb spends her savings on a house—one where Vladimir Nabokov once lived and wrote. When Barb discovers an abandoned manuscript there, her life takes on new purpose. Opening a cathouse that serves passion-starved local women is Barb's remarkable first step to respectability. Client by client and word by word, Barb reclaims her life and prepares for the chance to regain the custody of her children.

FOR DISCUSSION

1. The opening sentences of the book describe the path Barb will take to reinvent herself. Why do you think the author used that technique? What are some other books with first lines that reflect on the whole book?

2. Discuss Barb's career path. How does each of her past jobs— *Psychology Now* fact-checker, Old Daitch Dairy correspondence manager, cathouse madam, *Babe Ruth* ghostwriter help her in her new incarnation as a romance writer?

3. Discuss the two characters who mean the most to Barb: Sam and Darcy. What are some signs that her children are having difficulty following their parents' divorce? What do their collections—Sam's cookbooks and Darcy's purses—reveal about their personalities?

4. According to Barb, "Presentation was my worst talent. After marriage" (page 92). Track Barb's success in life according to her wardrobe. When do the Pants get her through some tough times? Do you think the people Barb meets in Onkwedo and New York City judge her outfits as much as she fears? Why or why not?

5. Barb imagines Nabokov's manuscript as an ark: "Maybe *Babe Ruth* was the way out: money, legitimacy even, and a boat to float me out of this hideous custody mess, away from Onkwedo altogether" (page 106). In the end, does *Babe Ruth* help Barb solve her life problems? Why or why not? How does it help her sail farther into Onkwedo, rather than out of town?

6. What kind of first impression does Margie, Barb's literary

agent, make on the telephone? Does Margie meet or defy Barb's expectations when the two women meet in person? Explain.

7. Compare the two men in Barb's life: her experson John and her new love interest Greg. How are John and Greg similar, and how are they different? What are some early signs that Greg is a better choice for Barb? What redeeming qualities does John have, and what might be some of Greg's faults?

8. Compare two interview scenes in *Cleaning Nabokov's House*: when Barb is interviewed to evaluate her "TVQ," when she learns that she's not fit for her fifteen minutes of televised fame, and her selecting the athletes to staff her cathouse. How does Barb fare on each side of the interview table? Which scene do you find more comical, and why?

9. One of the main themes of the book is loss and loneliness. Barb is grieving for two family members, her father and her cousin. What kind of example did each of these men set? What inspiration is she able to draw from her memories of them?

10. As Barb opens the cathouse, she thinks, "I decided I was not selling sex; I was selling a fifty-minute full-control vacation from your life as you knew it" (page 163). How far-fetched is the idea of a cathouse for women? Is Barb offering women an escape, an empowering alternative to their unsatisfying lives, or is she turning the tables on men, objectifying them the way women are objectified?

11. Cooking plays a large role in Barb's life. What do we learn about Barb's character through her cooking and eating habits? Which

of her many breakfast identities do you think suits her personality best?

12. On her fortieth birthday Barb resolves, "I might not have a plan, but I had to act fast" (page 269). How does this birthday serve as a turning point for Barb? What finally inspires Barb to act: to spend her earnings, furnish her kids' rooms, hire a lawyer, and return to court?

13. Vladimir and Vera Nabokov are long gone when Barb moves into their house. How does their imagined presence in the house affect her? What does Barb discover about life and writing through her exploration of Nabokov's work?

A CONVERSATION WITH
LESLIE DANIELS

Cleaning Nabokov's House mixes uproarious humor with the poignant heartbreak of a mother fighting for her children. How did you handle this balance between laughter and tears?

I don't think that laughter and tears are about balance. Life can break your heart and be hilarious at the same time. If you were a psychotherapist, you might say that humor is my defensive strategy. If you were a *nice* psychotherapist, you might say that it is part of my adaptive coping strength. I was lucky to have an extremely funny father. We had a great time, joking and bantering. After he died, I found myself writing toward the place from where he used to answer, a kind of calling out. It struck me then that humor is a kind of duty: if you can be funny you should, because life can be so deadly earnest. The opposite of humor is boredom, not sadness. Laughter and tears dance the tango.

Like your character Barb, you also live in Vladimir Nabokov's house—though without finding a long-lost manuscript! What is it like to live in Nabokov's house? How did the house inspire you?

All older houses are a bit like ghost stories, with secrets to tell. What intrigued me was the fact of an absolute genius having lived in this same simple space, same wide views and unfussy geometry, juxtaposed with the fact that no trace of him existed. I looked for Nabokov in that house. I can find evidence of the architect, the original owner, but Nabokov exists only in the copies of his books on my shelves.

Since you've worked with writers as well as being a writer yourself, how much of your industry savvy went into creating the character Margie, who convinces Barb to become a writer? Do you give similar advice when you encourage fellow writers?

Margie is (to me) the fictional idea of a writer's agent, and a bit absurd as well, telling her client Barb what to wear. But the reality is that writing *is* intimate. I encourage writers to trust themselves, to find areas of freedom and excitement, and to forge ahead.

Darcy and Sam are such quirky and realistic kids. How did you create such authentic young voices?

My mother is a brilliant observer of children, I have learned a bit from her. Children haven't yet figured out how to manipulate their image to blend in, so their actions are wonderfully overt. As for the authenticity, I have a background in acting, and accessing authentic emotion is part of my training. The feelings are real; the characters and situation are invented.

Barb realizes that she is "too rebellious a cook" to take a cooking class in Onkwedo, as she ponders ways to make friends in town (page 96). Are you also a rebellious cook? Why is cooking so important to your heroine?

My ideal cooking is with people I love, collaborating in the kitchen, making it up as we go along. That way it becomes a marriage of personalities and tastes, and the results are always a feast. I also like to cook alone and feed people I care about—that's another kind of communion. Cooking to me is a lot like writing: you take things that you like and believe in and put them together in a way that is enjoyable for other people. Some cooks treat recipes as if they were laws. I treat them as suggestions.

Psychology, both real and invented, is sprinkled throughout the novel, particularly as Barb realizes that her customers really want to be listened to and understood. You grew up in a family of psychologists and have a degree, too. Did you draw upon your own family and research while you were writing?

I come from a family that had great respect for individuality and imagination. As I child I listened to my parents talk about their work and it fascinated me. That was our family culture. Psychology and fiction writing are very close together in that you are always dealing with how people behave, what motivates them, how others perceive them, and how they think about themselves. My sister works at a large mental hospital, and her every workday is like an extraordinary anthology of short fiction, by turns heartbreaking, fierce, hilarious, tender, bizarre. I listen to her talk about her day with awe and fascination and a feeling of great humility that human beings like her have the courage and imagination to reach out to others who are in such extreme places in their psyche and their lives.

In the novel Barb muses, "It probably doesn't matter where a writer writes, since his is living mostly inside his own head" (page 30). As a writer—and as someone who has worked with many other writers—do you think it matters where a writer writes?

I think there is often a restlessness in a writer that has to do with creating one landscape in your head while existing in another. And writers are just as superstitious as anyone else. If you think you need red walls and a fine-point pen, sweatpants, and a latte to get going, by all means line that up. But don't spend your life looking for the perfect red paint or lurking at the café. Those rules all seem untrue when you think of the adaptations that human beings are capable of making. And interruptions abound. My own preference is to work in solitude. And I don't mean "a room of one's own," I prefer an entire floor and, if it is available, an unshared building!

An actual unfinished Nabokov manuscript, *The Original of Laura*, was published in 2009, after you wrote *Cleaning Nabokov's House*. What do you think about *Laura*?

This was uncanny because I had finished a first or very early draft of my book and had sent it to my agent two months before the real Nabokov manuscript was mentioned in the press. We were both flabbergasted. I'd even named the girl in it various things beginning with *L*. I felt the fear that dogs me as a writer: that people wouldn't believe I had made it up, only that I was aping someone else. When I had a copy of *The Original of Laura* in my hand, I felt the humility we all feel before the forces of life and death. Nabokov died before he finished the work; it is an artifact, not a novel.

Please tell us about your next project. Will you write another book about books?

I am not writing about books. Love, yes. Families, yes. Art, I think so. Maybe some food as well.

ENHANCE YOUR BOOK CLUB

1. The breed Bull Dane is fictional. If you were going to describe yourself in canine (or feline) terms, what combination of breeds would best describe you? Barb has her first intraspecies connection with Matilda. Do you have an animal bonding story?

2. One of Barb's puzzlements about her new location is what do people eat there. She finds the local butter an early point of connection with Onkwedo. Have a local foods night at your group, where the snacks are all grown or produced within a hundred miles of where you live.

3. Turn your book club meeting into Nabokov night and screen Stanley Kubrick's 1962 adaptation of Nabokov's *Lolita* or the more recent version with Jeremy Irons.

4. Barb notices a lot of things about other people. Think of someone you saw today that you don't know. It could be a clerk at a store or someone sitting in a car at a traffic light. Make a guess about his or her life. Does he live alone? Does she have a hobby? If they could have exactly the life they wanted, what would it be?

5. If you were going to organize an afternoon of pleasure and relaxation for the group, what would it look like? Having a massage? Hiking in the woods? Going to a sauna? Taking in a baseball game? Visiting an art museum and lunching at a café? Watching a Roller Derby match? Having a spa day? Now . . . do it!